River Deep

PRISCILLA MASTERS

This edition first published in Great Britain in 2005 by
Allison & Busby Limited
Bon Marché Centre
241-251 Ferndale Road
London SW9 8BJ
http://www.allisonandbusby.com

A catalogue record for this book is available from the British Library.

10 9 8 7 6 5 4 3 2

ISBN 0 7490 8342 5

Printed and bound in Great Britain by
Bookmarque Ltd, Croydon, Surrey

PRISCILLA MASTERS was born in Halifax and is one of seven adopted children. The family moved to South Wales where she lived until she was sixteen when she went to Birmingham to work and then to train as a nurse. She is married to a GP and now lives in Shropshire. She works part-time as a nurse.

Also by this author

In the Joanna Piercy series

Winding Up the Serpent
Catch the Fallen Sparrow
A Wreath For My Sister
And None Shall Sleep
Scaring Crows
Embroidering Shrouds
Endangering Innocents

Medical Mysteries

Night Visit
A Fatal Cut
Disturbing Ground

For Children

Mr Bateman's Garden

"The intention of the coroner's enquiry is to establish who died, how, where and when that person died and the cause of death."

This is not always as simple as it sounds. . .

"Who saw him die?"
"I," said the fly
"With my little eye,
I saw him die."

Anon. "*Who Killed Cock Robin*?"

1

Monday 11th February. 4pm.

Nature is a free spirit. It has no master or mistress. Rain falling on hills will trickle down to the river and a thousand trickles turn a meandering body of water, usually obedient to its constrictive banks, into a wild and destructive torrent. Water will find its own level, ignoring homes and businesses, restaurants and even temporary graveyards. Instead of protecting a town it can threaten it. Embrace it as a python encircles its victim.

You cannot tame nature.

Even on such a wet day it is a pretty fisherman's cottage, seventh in a row aptly named Marine Terrace, its blue-painted windows staring out over the rebellious river whose level creeps slowly up its brick walls, unable to defend itself as the river rises, almost invisibly, sneaking first to the top of its banks, moving towards it with stealth, as though if seen the town will somehow defend itself. But the town has no defences–except vigilance and sandbags, and sandbags do not hold back a torrent.

You cannot contain nature. Rivers will go where they will. Corpses and the living, treasured possessions, crimes and the innocent. All can be drowned in the rampant waters of the Severn.

The cellar below number seven, Marine Terrace, is not quite so pretty as its exterior. Small, square and dark, the only light a watery grey streaming in through a tiny, dirty, nine-paned window. Rain batters the glass seeking an entry but the putty stays firm. There is no leak. It is watertight.

Although it is only mid-February the cellar is warm, insulated from the weather. Warmer than the 12° centigrade the bluebottle (Calliphora) requires to lay her eggs, more than one thousand of them. She has been attracted by a scent irresistible to her but disgusting to anyone else. *Putrefaction*.

Calliphora has been lured down to the cellar by the rising river which carries a cocktail of aromas, but this particular scent is the most alluring of them all. She has followed her instinct and now she fulfils her life's function to reproduce. She has found the source, moist and warm, temptingly rich and has gained access through the large, old-fashioned keyhole, drawn by the smell as a man is to a woman's perfume. And she has been rewarded with an ideal breeding ground. An open wound in a slowly decaying body.

While the body decays the river still rises. Nature progresses inexorably.

The river licks the panes of the window and whispers, "*Let me in. Let me in.*"

She *will* have her way. She creeps up the glass, one millimetre at a time.

Though the cellar is still dry, rats are sensitive to the rising water level. One scurries along the back wall, its whiskers tickling in alarm. If not for the threat of the water he might have been tempted by the food source. But survival is more important than food. He runs past. And looks up. The only exit from the cellar is a climb of irregular stone steps, at the top a door. The rain is growing ever more fierce. More insistent. It spits beneath the front door, rat-tats against the outside walls, splashes onto the walkway outside and forms puddles which spread by the minute. Like moving inkblots. Expanding. Joining. Irregular shapes which keep growing.

Outside in the cooling evening air a man stands halfway across the English Bridge, his head turned towards Marine Terrace. He is both fascinated and appalled by the power and the will of the river. He stares into the water and studies the antique lamp-posts crazily reflected in the moving black waters, saplings and debris bouncing along in the flow.

And now he turns from the river and accepts the invitation of the town.

In the cellar Calliphora has finished laying her eggs. She buzzes around the room searching for an exit but no scent guides her back to the surface so she settles on the cellar wall and awaits her chance to escape.

A lone hitchiker stands on the Copthorne road, thumb out, hoping for a lift to Oswestry. Aware that the rain is simultaneously both friend and foe. It makes the hiker less visible to the traffic but those who do spot the unfortunate are more likely to stop – out of sympathy.

A lorry driver pities the drenched figure, slews and stops, making the hitchhiker run eighty or so yards. A door is flung open. Words are exchanged. Fate is sealed.

He will be a useful witness.

During the night the inkblots join to form a huge black pool which spreads across the walkway in a swift movement, pauses for a moment at the front doorstep of number seven, Marine Terrace, before inching up the steps and pouring beneath the door.

Once inside she joyfully heaves the cellar door open, descends the steps in a gleeful waterfall and fills the cellar.

Water will find its own level.

Safely above the water Calliphora flies up the stairs to the ground floor room. There is only one – apart from the kitchen – and that is clean. Nothing to tempt her in there. The rats in the cellar squeak and scream. Some of them will drown.

But rivers have no conscience. Only determination.

In the corner Calliphora's eggs are growing fat, well-fed on flesh and blood.

Their food source lifts and bobs a little, an apathetic swimmer in a waterlogged suit, air in his clothes creating a buoyancy aid.

Tuesday 12th February 2002. 7am

A grey, misty dawn.

The man wakes to silence, crosses the room and draws back the curtains. There is no traffic. So the silence is explained – yet unexplained.

The scent and sound of sizzling bacon drifts up the stairway and distracts him. But in spite of the mouth-watering aroma of his breakfast this morning he is less comfortable than the night before. Stale cigarette smoke fugs the windows; the atmosphere is sour. The man feels unaccountably nauseous. He descends and stands in the kitchen doorway.

She turns to greet him from the stove. "Well," she says, frying pan in her hand. "The river's beat us all."

The man starts.

"Rose higher in the night. They've closed both bridges. I hope your car . . ."

"Sorry?"

She slews round. "Haven't you *noticed* how quiet it is?"

The man listens. A pulse of silence pounds away in his ear.

"No traffic." She tips the bacon and a slimy egg onto the plate, shovels a tomato to join it. Turns to hand it to him.

The man is gone.

She spoke the truth. The decision *has* been made to close

the bridge. Both bridges. Welsh and English simultaneously. Frankwell is flooded, Abbey Foregate under water, Mardol drowning. The river is winning her battle. *She* is the tyrant now. So Shrewsbury is sealed off to traffic, to become, once again, a moated medieval island town, safe, isolated and unwilling as a virgin within the embracing waters of the River Severn. Those outside must stay. Those inside are trapped.

He is inside.

He is walking down Wyle Cop, approaching the English bridge from the safe height of the town, panicked by the blue strobes of the emergency services. He is ordered back by a firm but friendly Police Constable new to the job, PC Gethin Roberts, a Welshman. It is his first crisis and he feels proud and important to play his part. He puts the man's anxiety down to the fact that properties nearby are filling with water. Maybe . . . His eyes drift towards Marine Terrace. "Not your house, I hope, Sir." He speaks in a pleasant, Shropshire burr.

The man says nothing.

"We've had to shut the bridge to all traffic. Too dangerous, you see. The flooding's terrible round the Abbey." They both glance at the tall, red castellations of the site of Brother Cadfael's adventures surrounded now by duckboards and oily waters. A few brave shoppers, determined not to be beaten by nature step gingerly over the slippery planks. A cyclist swishes through, creating a wash behind him. "We're sending crews in to make sure nobody is left inside."

The man starts. "No body, Constable?"

Gethin Roberts pulls his yellow waterproof tightly around his shoulders. Glances up at the darkening sky. "Will it ever stop raining, do you think?"

No one answers. The man has gone. Vanished again into

the rain. Afterwards the constable will scold himself for not taking down details. A description. A name. Something to identify the man by other than his strangeness. For the rest of his career in the police force PC Gethin Roberts will regret not having fingered a hot suspect when he had the chance. But like most significant moments in a life, he did not know it was a chance. And now he is distracted by a van driver approaching the bridge from the other side, anxious to make a delivery. "Sorry, mate," he says chummily. "Can't go across there. River's still risin'. You'll just get stuck." The van driver tugs a mobile phone from his jeans pocket and starts shouting into it, waving his free hand. The constable watches the driver execute a clumsy three-pointed, one-handed turn and vanish into the grey back towards the Abbey.

A grey Hyundai van sits, abandoned, in the car park behind the *Lion & Pheasant.*

Inside the empty house the body floats towards the top of the stairs, bumping against the half-open door. Calliphora sticks to the wall. Biding her time.

The waters continue to rise until eleven o'clock in the morning, the weather dry now but the mountain streams still draining from up river. The town suffers with quiet dignity as she has done ever since the Saxons named it *Scrobbesbyrig* in times approaching prehistory. Far downstream the sea tide turns and the water level rises suddenly, its escape route cut off. It spills into meadows, floods the football ground, seeps into homes, bumps the kegs in the cellars of the Abbey Inn. The pressure of river-water heaves against the front door of the house in Marine Terrace. An open invitation to the four policemen and two firemen who have been detailed to make a final search of riverside properties.

Inside the cellar of number seven, Marine Terrace, the

river has reached the top of the cellar window, now a porthole which peers into subaqua scenes of greeny brown, indistinguishable shapes of debris. Tins? Bottles? A shoe? A plank of wood? A duck's feet?

At the top of the steps the cellar door creaks like an ancient galleon and moves with the will of the wash. It is a sea battle between wood and water; the floating corpse an inert witness.

Still standing on the middle of the English bridge PC Gethin Roberts continues, bossily, to dissuade people from walking into the town.

So the day passes.

The hitchhiker has reached a destination.

At four o'clock in the afternoon, wearing fisherman's waders PC Gary Coleman tries the door of number seven, Marine Terrace. Calliphora escapes and joyfully buzzes along the waters. Freer than the people of Shrewsbury town who cannot fly.

The sudden gush of water hits the far wall of the room and creates a wave which surges towards the cellar door. Coleman flashes a beam strong enough to penetrate the gloom. And picks up the flaccid swimmer. For a second he is too stunned to say or do anything but stands with the water swishing around his ankles. Then he fumbles in his belt for his two-way radio. "Ten nine. Ten nine," he manages.

The code for a police officer in need of urgent assistance.

2

It always begins in the same way – with a telephone call invariably reaching her at a time and place which is inconvenient. And it is always the same person who initially rings her, Jericho, her assistant, as stolid as a Shropshire potato and with as sharp a pair of eyes.

He had caught her in a packed Tesco's this time, and she with a basket of perishables. Agnetha's day off, nothing for tea and hungry mouths to fill at home. Hence the trip to Tesco's. So, recognising the number, she was wary with her, "Hello."

"I thought you'd want to know about this one, Ma'am. Straight away."

She nestled against the corner of the deep freeze. "Carry on, Jerry," she said. "I'm all ears."

"Washed up by the floodin' river," he said in his deep Shropshire burr, the word *floodin'* as powerful as a profanity. "John Doe. Unidentified male." He allowed himself a slice of poetic licence. "Nearly knocked Police Constable Coleman off his feet. He was checking the properties flooded by the river and this guy swims towards him."

Martha rolled her eyes across the packets of oven chips. "If he was dead, Jerry," she pointed out needlessly, "he wasn't able to swim, was he?"

"Well – " He was miffed. "In a manner of speakin'. What I mean is he floated towards him. It was a terrible shock. Knocked into 'im." There was a certain amount of malicious pleasure in his voice.

"I'll be home in half an hour, Jericho," she said decisively. "Get the Senior Investigating Officer and the police surgeon to ring me then, will you?" Mentally she substituted *steak au poivre* for frozen pizza and chips for tea. The facts, she already anticipated, would be unsuitable for twelve-year-olds' ears. And she would need the privacy of her study to absorb them. She glanced around her. Not the public arena of Tesco's Superstore.

She queued for her turn at the checkout and wondered why she ever gave Agnetha a day off. Particularly on a Tuesday. It was practically bound to attract an urgent case referral.

Her curiosity was awakened as she covered the few miles home, the roads jammed with traffic turned away from the town centre. Shrewsbury was sealed off by the 'floodin' river', yet again.

She swept into the drive that led to the white-washed house and parked around the back. Easier to unload the shopping. She opened the front door cautiously. Bobby, her Welsh Border collie, was ballistic to see her. He hurled himself at her legs, barking his urgent demand for a walk. But Sam would have to walk him tonight. She would be occupied.

There were eight messages flashing on the answer-phone. She worked her way through them. Her mother, wondering how she was as she hadn't been in touch for a day or two and was she eating properly? Martin's mother, wondering how she was as she hadn't been in touch for a day or two and was everything all right? Miranda, wondering whether she fancied going to see a new film at the pictures and was everything all right? Click. No one, wondering nothing. A friend of Sam's suggesting they play football tonight, two for Sukey; one a pipe-voiced girl and the other a half-broken-voiced male and finally, click. No one again. She wished people would at least inform her who they were before they turned tail in front of the answer-phone.

The front door burst open at precisely half past four and, not for the first time, she reflected how very unlike two twelve-year-olds could be. Sam, with his lop-sided grin, dropping his sports bag on the kitchen floor (without investigating she knew it would contain the filthiest washing) and opening the fridge. When he spoke his mouth was already full of a peanut butter doorstep.

" 'Llo, Mum."

Sukey, on the other hand, delicate disco queen, minced in on the highest heels she was allowed, and gave her a sideways look. "Hi, Mum," she said warily.

Martha smiled back at her son and daughter. "Nice day at . . .?"

"Don't even ask", Sukey practically spat, cat-like. "I lost my hair elastic. The one with the gold fish on. And that awful Robin Pearson. . . " She wrinkled her face. "I think I hate him, Mum."

Martha opened her mouth but Sam got in there first. "He isn't awful." Spraying bread and peanut butter across the kitchen.

"Pig." Sukey made a face as some landed on her maroon school sweatshirt. "And he *is* awful." Trying to pick the sodden crumb off the sweatshirt. "He grabbed hold of me. . . "

"Well – don't hang on to the football when it lands your way then. Women," Sam finished disgustedly.

Sukey wasn't even listening. She was rinsing the speck of half-chewed peanut butter from her sweatshirt. Martha wondered whether they would ever stop quarrelling.

"There are some telephone messages for you both. I've written them on the pad and left them on memory. And . . . ," she hesitated, "I'm going to have to take a couple of calls before tea. And possibly go out later."

Immediately they both shot the same swift, guarded

glance at her. It took her aback. She knew they knew a little about her work but she wasn't always quite so aware of its effect on them. It wasn't something you readily shared with a pair of twelve-year-olds.

"I'll take the calls in the study."

"What's for tea?" Sam again, ever conscious of his stomach. He'd finished his peanut butter doorstep.

"Pizza." She felt apologetic.

As she closed her study door behind her she heard them whispering to each other, their differences forgotten. She hated it when they whispered. She felt so excluded – so lonely – so aware that they were twins and had each other whereas she had no one. When Martin had been alive it had not mattered. She had him – they had each other. Nicely paired. But since he had died she was very aware that they had shared her womb for nine long months. They were bonded. She was alone. The outsider. And her job isolated her even more. She'd had to tell them so much when they had been so young. That anything they heard in connection with her work was secret. That they were never to talk about it outside this house. That on the other side of the whispered conversations and scribbled names on the telephone pad was often suffering and grief, bewilderment and loss. Sometimes terrible violence and dark secrets. Headlines too. Whatever they overheard – through half-open doors, or extension phones accidentally picked up, or the answering machine, or on stray papers – they must stay silent. They had known this for all their conscious lives. She closed the door behind her.

The study had been Martin's. Nine years ago it had been unmistakably a masculine retreat. But she had changed it, with plainer, lighter paper, a few good paintings battled over at Halls, the local auction house, different curtains with an abstract design and bold soft furnishings. She had deliberately opted for feminine design yet somehow, subtly, the room still reminded her of him so when she entered it she sometimes wondered, *if Martin returned from the dead how much would he recognise?*

It was not simply the furnishings of the study which reminded her of him. It was in the proportions, the structure. She crossed to the french windows, mentally sweeping aside the curtains and seeing the lawn stretching towards the apple tree like a carpet of the brightest green. Of the room? He would know it. The house? He would recognise *most* of it. There had been only cosmetic changes. Superficial titivation. Nothing structural. Of her? She was different. Older. Thinner, more careworn. Quieter. More subdued.

Sam and Sukey? In nine years they had completely metamorphosed from plump toddlers to skinny children and now were on the verge of another huge change – becoming adults. Surely he would not know them. Or would he? They were flesh of his flesh, blood of his blood. Genetically linked. Does one recognise the gene?

She closed the tiny gap in the curtains, sat down at the desk, switched on the reading light, stared at the wedding photograph and waited for the inevitable phone calls.

There were three things she appreciated about the Police Force. The first was their punctuality – their very adhesion to the clock. It made life so organised. If rigid. The second was their ability to relate salient facts concisely. And the third was their seductive politeness. Particularly in the case of Detective Inspector Alex Randall who would almost certainly be the Senior Investigating Officer.

Bearing out her thoughts the phone rang at exactly five o'clock, the telephone bell and the chiming of the hour from the clock on the mantelpiece indistinguishable. Knowing who it was she murmured a soft hello and her name.

"Evening, Mrs Gunn. Detective Inspector Randall here." He was invariably formal. Initially. Later on formalities may well be dropped as they worked more closely.

"Alex," she responded warmly. "Thank you for ringing."

"That's all right."

"I hear you have a bit of a problem."

"To say the least. And on such a night. The river's the highest it's been since the millennium floods. We never thought we'd get it so bad again so soon. And we've got enough to do without this."

"Oh yes. Jericho said something about . . .?"

"Well, I'm not sure what he's told you but it looks like a homicide. The strangest incident of my career." He chuckled. "Poor old Coleman had been detailed to check out Marine Terrace and make sure no one was in the properties. He opens the door, flashes his torch around and spies a body floating face down in the corner. Gave him the shock of his life it did."

"I'll bet."

"We got the police surgeon to certify death at the scene. According to him he was long since dead."

"Drowned?"

"She didn't think so. There was no sign of it. Besides – she thought he'd probably died before the water had flooded the house. She decided it would be a good idea to have Doctor Sullivan take a look at him at the scene and then talk to you before we move him to the mortuary." It was standard procedure in a case of suspicious death.

"Did Delyth Fontaine have any idea of cause of death?"

"Nope. And she didn't want to disturb the body too much."

"And Doctor Sullivan?"

"He's just there now. He'll be speaking to you as soon

as he's come to some conclusion."

"Any idea who the dead man is?"

"No identification on him."

"He was clothed?"

"Yes – in a suit."

"But nothing in the pockets?"

"No." And that suggested something. He continued, "We've got a few lines of enquiry to follow up."

Knowing how they worked she could anticipate them. "The property?"

"That and others."

"Perhaps the water washed his wallet out of his pocket."

"Maybe." It was in the policeman's character to always sound dubious. "We're making a thorough search of the whole house – including the cellar."

"Is it safe?"

"The water level's receding at the moment. It's halfway up the cellar walls but expected to surge again at around midnight. I expect Doctor Sullivan will give you a call when he's examined the body."

"OK, Alex. I'll maybe see you later. I'll wait for Doctor Sullivan's call." He rang off.

So not even frozen pizzas tonight then but a trip to a flooded house with a corpse floating inside it. What a job. She leaned back in the chair. What on earth had possessed her to be a coroner, this job which sewed up so neatly the questions of how, when and where a person had died? Even going so far as to pose these questions in her own court.

A feeling of finality. Skilled as a doctor, married to a lawyer, she had always felt that death was the final untidiness of life. And for many people that untidiness scarred the bereaved. Like the policeman she was anxious for the cause of death to be ascertained as soon as possible. For the man, dead as he was, to be restored to his family and to be given a decent, dignified burial.

But . . . Given the dramatic emergence of the unidentified man's body it would not take long for the Press to get hold of the story and put it through a mincing machine. The sooner they could give out factual statements the better. Two things were urgent. Identification and cause of death. Who was he? How had he died and when?

She spoke to the police surgeon next, an elderly GP called Delyth Fontaine who had been in the job long enough to know it inside out, almost instinctively. She rapped out the details, that she could not give a cause of death, that it was almost certainly suspicious, that the man had been dead, in her opinion, for more than twenty-four hours. That in spite of the circumstances she did not think he had drowned. Martha thanked her. It was enough to ensure a post mortem was unavoidable. They needed a skilled pathologist to begin to unravel the mystery.

Doctor Mark Sullivan must have been waiting for her phone to be free. As soon as she replaced the handset it rang again. In an echo of Randall and Delyth Fontaine he was concise, professional and factual. Well used to dealing with both the law and the medics. Only someone who knew him very well would occasionally sense the slight slurring of a few of his consonants, a momentary hesitation while he chose appropriate words, a silence when he should have spoken. Martha knew him very well. She had known him in the years before she had become coroner. Before he had started drinking.

"We have a muscular, well-nourished man – in his early forties, I should think." A pause. "I've left his clothes on so haven't picked up on any obvious cause of death. He could have fallen down the cellar steps, maybe drunk, banged his head, either simply died of a head injury or drowned when the water filled the cellar. There are plenty of possibilities and I'm not going to be sure until I've done a post mortem. There's a slash in the left side of his jacket, over the heart so my guess is there's a wound there." Another pause. "He died at least twenty-four hours before we found him. Rigor mortis is wearing off. From what Delyth and the policeman said I think his body might have lain in the cellar and floated up the stairs. Unfortunately or fortunately the River Severn decided to play gutter Press and expose the evidence." In spite of the witticism he sounded tired. His speech was getting slower.

"What's your gut feeling? Are we looking at a natural death, simple concealment or something more, Mark?"

"Don't know, Martha. I really . . . don't . . . know. Probably a homicide."

"Have you picked up any superficial injuries?"

"A bit of bruising on the hands and face which could be ante, peri or postmortem."

"I see."

He gave one of his sudden warm, soft chuckles. "You know me, Martha, I like to wait until after the PM. Keep my cards close to my chest. I've watched far too many pathologists make monkeys of themselves playing the guessing game." There was something infectious about his chuckle. She laughed too.

"Martha – I was wondering if . . ."

"I would come and view the body in situ? Yes – it seems a good idea. Give me half an hour."

"Good." He sounded relieved. "And wear galoshes."

There were always a multitude of domestic arrangements to tend to before she was free. Having cajoled Agnetha into leaving her bedroom door ajar and turning her CD player down, put a pizza and oven chips into the oven, thrown salad into a bowl and drenched it in bottled

French dressing she bribed the twins into loading the dishwasher after tea and doing all their homework before changing into some trousers and a mac. She tried to ignore the fact that the twins were whispering again as she came downstairs. Twenty minutes later she was back in her car, wellies loaded into the boot and heading back down the drive, towards the town.

The roads were wet and shiny black, lit by orange lamp-posts and eerily quiet. Folk were staying at home, intimidated by the river, guarding their property and impotently watching. She parked on some elevated ground near the Abbey and squleched her way over the duckboards to cross the English Bridge.

No one could doubt that something was going on here tonight. The scene was lit with swiping blue strobes; floodlights beamed on Marine Terrace.

Two policemen stepped forward, recognised her and waved her through. The sky was thunderous with sudden flashes of forked lightning. The entire scene looked as threatening as a Boris Karloff movie. She dropped down the steps towards the river and walked along the path, feeling the water licking at her wellies as it dribbled again towards the properties. She was glad to reach number seven.

The front door was wide open, the scene well illuminated. A sodden room which stunk of the river-bed, three people inside. The fourth no more than a pile of soaking clothes. Randall was the first to spot her. He gave her a wide grin which she knew was relief. Once she had viewed the body it could be removed to the mortuary. Concealed from prying eyes and the first step taken in the investigation.

Mark Sullivan was standing in the corner, his back to her, the body at his feet. The atmosphere was dank and dirty and smelt like the grave. It was the river water combining with early putrefaction, mixed in with the contents of flooded sewers. She looked around her. It probably had been a comfortable – if small – home. Light wallpaper, stained furniture which had bumped against the walls. Her wellies stuck to the carpet and her steps squelched each time she lifted her foot.

"We found him here." Sullivan indicated a door, swinging slightly. "It leads to a cellar."

She peered round. Alex flashed his torch down the stairs. River-water lay halfway up the cellar walls. Lime washed. It looked empty. No racks of wine here. She moved back to study the door. There was a stout bolt at the top. Shot back. She knew both the policeman and the pathologist would have noted all these details. She turned her attention to the body, rivulets of water still streaming from his clothes. Short brown hair, a half-open fish mouth. Pale skin which she knew would be cold to touch. Randall was right. It would be impossible to examine him properly here. She smiled at one, small detail. Randall had already bagged off the hands. She spoke to both of them. "Look – I don't see what we can achieve here. Let's get him down to the mortuary. And we'll hold the PM tomorrow? In the morning."

She walked slowly across the bridge, glancing back at the melodrama. Underneath the river was roaring like an unleashed animal. She was glad to leave it behind and reach her car.

3

The following morning brought no relief from the town's problems. The ring road was jammed with traffic denied access to the town. BBC Radio Shropshire announced every hour that both the Welsh and English bridges were still closed and likely to remain so. The announcer further informed its listeners that the river Severn was expected to peak sometime on Thursday.

Martha fingered her steering wheel knowing that the inhabitants of Shrewsbury would be justifiably apprehensive. They were all affected whether or not they lived in the potential wash of the river, and the truth was bleak. The TV might be flashing out pictures reminiscent of the Blitz, portraying great camaraderie, togetherness and team spirit, dinghies, canoes, going to work in fisherman's waders and so on but the reality was sick, gnawing worry. A fear that the insurance would not cover the real cost of the damage. Loss of business. Burglary of empty property, relatives suddenly foisted on families with no notion when they would leave. All this added to the stress of being invaded by contaminated river water. And now – on top of all those problems in the town – an unidentified body had turned up. For the already overstretched police force it must have seemed like the last straw – a crime scene difficult to investigate and seal off, possibly even a murder investigation. Martha smiled and channel-hopped between the local radio station and Classic FM. She wouldn't swap places with a police officer planning an imminent holiday! She inched her way forward in the traffic queue and finally arrived at the mortuary at ten minutes to nine, parking next to the Panda car.

They were waiting for her, Alex Randall, Mark Sullivan,

four other officers – one of whom was introduced as PC Gary Coleman, finder of the body – the mortuary assistant, a pathology student from Stoke and the inevitable SOCOs with their array of specimen bags. They were all gowned up, gloves on. The body lay in the centre, still dressed, on the post mortem table. The lights were white-bright and tilted full on him. There would be no more secrets and no privacy.

Their greetings were cursory and formal. They had a job to do. Alex Randall touched her arm and started speaking from behind her. "We may have an ID," he said quietly.

"Oh?" She turned around.

As a woman it was hard not to respond to Alex Randall. He epitomised the traditional police officer. Tall, dark-haired, with serious hazel eyes, craggy, irregular, almost ugly features and a deeply buried sense of humour which he hid effectively behind formality. She had known him for a couple of years without ever seeing his face crack into a smile.

Then one day he had been explaining a case to her where a woman had fallen, drunk, with her face down a lavatory. Her friends had subsequently pulled her out, cleaned her up and dumped her on the steps of Monkmoor police station. And quite suddenly, as he had described the state of the woman's clothes, her hair and her mortification, his face had cracked and, instead of the ugliness, she had glimpsed a man full of life and humour – away from the job. Sometimes she idly wondered about him and waited, as for the sun to explode from behind a cloud, for that smile that wrought such a transformation. But it was rare. As rare and welcome as sunshine in an English summer. Of his personal life she still knew nothing. It was a closed book. And she had picked up no gossip about him. Even from Jericho. Which made her curious because Jericho gossiped about everyone.

Randall carried on talking softly into her ear. She caught a waft of his sharp, strange after-shave overlying the pervading stink of mortuary-formalin which always reminded her of long ago pathology lectures in the medical school.

"The house this guy was washed out of was rented to a James Humphreys, a businessman from Slough, who moved up here a couple of months ago when he got a job managing the Jaguar garage. He fits the description. Right build, right age and we've picked up a Jaguar in a pub car park which belongs to him. He used to leave it there overnight. According to the estate agent who rented him the property, Humphreys was waiting to see how the job panned out before bringing his wife over to Shrewsbury – which is why he'd rented Marine Terrace. He was last at work on Sunday, left round about four in the afternoon. Since then there's been no word from him."

She put her hand out as though to pause the proceedings. "Have you made contact with his wife?"

"There's been a bit of a problem. She isn't at home. The local force are doing all they can but I thought in view of the circumstances you'd want Mark to proceed with the initial examination?"

She nodded. Peter, the mortician, was well able to tidy corpses up to completely conceal the signs of a post mortem.

So one of the policemen tied her into a cotton gown. She slipped her feet into a pair of theatre clogs, pulled a paper hat over her hair so a stray strand could not contaminate trace evidence and they were ready to start. She didn't need gloves. She was here as an observer only. She knew better than to touch anything.

The police photographer took some flash pictures and Martha watched the river-water trickling slowly into the grooves on the post mortem table and pooling in the sink. One of the SOCOs filled a small specimen bottle with it. They would analyse it for diatoms and make sure it really was river-water which dripped from the dead man's clothes.

They moved in closer. A ring of curious spectators.

In one way all corpses share a common appearance. Young or old, male or female, black or white. They do not look alive. In fact it is hard to imagine them ever having been alive. This makes the pathologist's job easier. It detaches him from thinking too hard about the living, breathing person and from the circumstances which led to this.

Mark Sullivan broke the silence. "Better get on with it, I suppose." His voice, echoing around the room, bouncing off the white tiles and clinical floor, was directed at the mortician.

Two of the police officers cut the suit very carefully into halves, slicing along the seams under the arms and at the side. They did the same with the shirt, the tie, the socks, the underpants. All were placed on a table nearby ready for examination. Now the body lay naked and exposed.

Mark Sullivan's description earlier had been accurate. Humphreys was well-nourished and muscular, dark-haired and about forty. In good shape. It wasn't hard to surmise that he had probably been physically attractive – alive. Adding to the fact that the suit had looked expensive, Martha's mind wandered. She was surprised he had not kept more regular contact with his wife. They were assuming he had died sometime Sunday night or in the early hours of Monday morning. Yet his wife was "missing", "uncontactable". She wondered whether Mrs Humphreys was, perhaps, away on holiday. It was a nice time to go. But in these days of ready communication she was curious to know where Mrs Humphreys was.

This was something else that intrigued her. No ID in his pockets? No mobile phone? She leaned across to speak to Randall. "Did you find his wallet?"

He shook his head.

"A mobile phone?"

Again he shook his head. She met his eyes and read his concern there too. "He could have been robbed," he said, but without conviction.

She turned her attention back to the post mortem. Mark Sullivan's eyes had fixed on a small elliptical wound a little below the dead man's left nipple. Right over the heart. And from the set of the pathologist's face she knew he was already querying this as the cause of death. But it looked such a small, almost insignificant injury to fell this man. Sullivan would have to delve deeper to find out the truth, expose skin, bone, finally the very chambers of the heart. However he actually said nothing, but stood motionless, his hands clasped together, as the mortuary assistant performed the preliminaries, measuring the height from crown to heels, and checking the weight.

She knew that Mark Sullivan was waiting for her to make some comment. She contrasted him to the policeman. Shorter, early forties, cropped brown hair and tired but shrewd blue eyes. He invariably looked as though he'd passed a rough night. He gave her a tentative grin.

Before even making the first cut he was busily making his observations into the tape recorder. While Martha looked on. She was not meant to be an active participator but an impartial observer – the conductor of the orchestra whose role was to make sense from the various discordances between the law and medicine. So as Sullivan penetrated the skull and brain of the dead man she observed that James Humpreys, presumptive, had been in good health and shape – right up to the moment of his death.

At first there was little to see. Some marks on the shoulders and torso which they all knew could have been caused by a fall down the steps or being bumped around in the cellar by the rising tide of flood water. As Sullivan worked on the head she turned her attention to the chest. There was inevitable discoloration of the skin, a pale, dead fish appearance and to the right of it a puzzling mark. Small, perfectly round, pinkish bruising. She wondered what he would make of this. Sullivan worked steadily, his hands seeming to grow steadier and more confident the longer he worked. His face gradually looked less lined, less tired, more relaxed as he became increasingly absorbed. Martha watched him work, seeing the man he should be and wondering why he invariably did look so strained. As he finished with the head and turned his attention back to the chest area she was even more aware of his competence. He stood back and looked first, his latexed fingers touching the small, round contusion in the centre of the chest that she had noticed. "I wonder what caused this," he mused.

Randall leaned forward. "I don't know. We couldn't see anything in the house that would have caused it."

"Well – whatever it was – there's very little bruising. It was inflicted within a very short time of his death."

"Is there nothing in the cellar that could have caused this wound?" Martha looked at them both.

Randall answered. "Not that I've seen."

"I'll need to study the underlying tissues. It looks superficial but inflicted with some force. Now – let's look at this."

Sullivan's index finger stroked the injury in the chest now, which gaped and smiled like a baby's mouth. Gently he brought the edges back together. Peter handed him a ruler and he measured the wound very carefully. *Two cen-*

timetres. They all marked the number and knew its significance. *The width of the blade of the causative instrument cannot be larger than the size of the wound. But because a man may move either to defend himself or to try and escape when he feels the first prick of the knife a small knife may make a big wound.*

Sullivan frowned and pointed out more detail. The wound was asymmetric, tapering thinly at one end, blunt at the other. "Fish-tailing," he murmured then smiled at the policeman and Martha knew he relished this Sherlock Holmes touch.

"So, Alex," Sullivan said. "You're looking for a single-edged instrument, with a blade narrower than two centimetres."

"Well we haven't found it yet," Alex answered grumpily, as though he imagined the pathologist thought he was handing him a solution on a plate. "But we'll get a team to search the area – as well as we can," he said. "The cellar's still half underwater." His eyes clouded. They all fell silent and Martha knew what they were thinking. The Severn, snaking round the town, no more than four steps from the front door of Marine Terrace. Expected to peak some time on Thursday and they would all have to wait.

"We may never find it," the policeman finished. *It could be washing along the bottom of the river. Embedding in the mud or shifting with the ebb and flow of the water.*

But at least they had a description of a knife and the width of a blade. Which led to the next question: how long was that blade? Knife wounds could be surprisingly deceptive. On the surface there might be little to see. But even a wound of two centimetres wide could be lethal. If it had penetrated a vital part of a vital organ. Such as one of the two ventricles of the heart.

Now they were all curious to know what else Sullivan

would discover. But he was acting cautious and slow, still studying the skin. Once he had investigated the wound he would have destroyed this untouched witness. Again the police photographer flashed some close-ups.

"There's no damage on the skin," he mused. "No marks of a hilt – which makes me think it didn't go all the way in. Although the clothes would have protected it to some extent."

Already Martha was hearing a defence. *Accident. Fell against the knife. No clear intent*. From her point of view this was still not a clear case of homicide. It was *possible* that Humphreys had *fallen* down the cellar steps, a knife in his hand. Nothing but an unfortunate and terrible accident. The lights had been off because of the flooding. There had been intermittent interruption of the supply for some of Sunday and most of Monday before it had been completely switched off on Tuesday as the water level had risen. Humphreys was in a strange house – not his own. He may well have been drinking. Sullivan would certainly be sending serum samples for blood alcohol as well as other mind-altering substances. If such a knife was found in the cellar accidental death was still a possible verdict.

Sullivan gently threaded a blunt-ended probe into the wound and when it met resistance he read the mark. "And the blade was round about fourteen centimetres long." His eyes found those of Randall. He knew how important all these details were to the policeman. "Give or take," he said. "I'd be inclined to look for a slightly longer blade. Two or three centimetres longer." A pause. "I'd like to look at his clothes again."

He crossed the mortuary floor and stood, staring at the suit, then at the shirt, his gloved fingers quickly finding the slash wound in the jacket which corresponded to Humphreys' injury. When he studied the shirt they could all see a small amount of bloodstaining.

"I thought there would have been more blood." Martha spoke for all of them.

Sullivan's lips tightened. "Not if my suspicion proves correct."

She did not question him. When he was ready he would tell her. But, like most pathologists she had worked with, he liked to distil the facts before suggesting a theory.

Alex Randall was still looking at the suit. "Nice," he said.

One of the SOCOs spoke up. "People who flog Jags for a living tend to know their suits, Sir."

"Is it English or foreign?" She didn't even know why she asked the question.

PC Coleman answered, his face pinking up a bit. "Italian by the labels. But you can probably buy them over here. In London. Or Slough. For a price." He cast a critical eye over the fabric. "Not a good fit though. Trousers a bit loose and long." He shrugged. "Maybe he'd lost weight. Or maybe the material lost its shape in the water." Who could know except the missing wife?

They laid the suit to one side. It had told them what they had already known. Humphreys breathed money.

And now Mark Sullivan moved on to perform the vital part of the operation – the delicate investigation of the fatal wound. And although the subject was gruesome, Martha enjoyed watching the pathologist work.

The more absorbed Mark Sullivan became in his work the more she forgot what he looked like and saw only a sober, methodical, professional man. She had heard whispers, mainly from Jericho, of marital disharmony, of alcohol abuse, of domestic violence and police involvement, of nights spent at the mortuary because he could not or would not go home. Jericho could be quite a malicious gossip. But when she had faced her assistant with the indisputable fact that unhappy couples could easily separate he had had no answer to give. So Mark Sullivan remained an enigma and she was left with her curiosity. Every time she looked at him she wondered.

His fingers probed beneath the skin and fished out some white eggs, something like cod roe, from the mouth of the wound. "Calliphora," he announced, as though introducing a friend.

"I'm sorry?"

"Bluebottle eggs." He decanted a couple into a white-topped specimen pot. "I said the fly. With my little eye. Can't be too careful. We'll get an entymologist to positively identify but it may help with the time of death."

She raised her eyebrows and Sullivan continued explaining.

"If I am right and this really is Calliphora they like their corpses fresh. The open wound in the chest plus the fact that the temperatures have been high for the time of year proved too tempting for a marauding bluebottle."

It was hard not to feel repulsed.

He continued his scrutiny of the chest, standing back for the police photographer to record the proceedings before sawing through the sternum with a wire, examining some notches on the ribs then carefully probing further. Martha peered over his shoulder but did not interrupt him. He was absorbed, muttering to himself, using his gloved index finger delicately to explore the penetration of the weapon. She knew exactly what he was doing. Once, in an unguarded moment, he had confessed to her that while investigating cases like this he built up an almost fey picture of intent, assault, events. He was doing this now and she did not want to break the spell so stood still, making observations of her own. His face was composed. He glanced up and she flushed. He knew she'd been watching him.

He had reached the heart now, pushing aside the major vessels and immediately the explanation for Humphreys' death was apparent, also the reason for the lack of blood-staining on the shirt and other clothes. The organ lay in a sack of blood which had leaked from a small puncture wound. The tip of the knife had reached the left ventricle and blood must have spurted out yet been contained in the pericardial sac. Sullivan made a guttural noise, almost feral. He had found what he had searched for. The cause of death. He looked up and there was the gleam of discovery on his face. Of knowledge. For him the picture was complete. But turning around to look at Randall she could see he did not understand. And Martha knew better than to quiz.

Almost losing interest, Sullivan turned his attention across to the lungs and found some blood-stained frothing in the larger tubes – the bronchi. And all the time Martha could tell his interest was waning because he had found what he was looking for. "No sign of disease," he muttered into the tape recorder. . . "Healthy and muscular. Really good strong heart. No sign of atheroma." He looked up at the rim of faces. "My guess is he was quite an athlete."

She nodded her agreement.

His examination of the abdomen and lower limbs was much more cursory. The stomach was empty, all other organs healthy and intact. He filled a couple of bottles with blood samples. They would be sent for toxicology and alcohol and drugs levels. Some would be merely saved. In case . . . Finally he swabbed the sex organs for semen, but she could tell his interest had gone. The puzzle was solved. She waited until he was sewing up the thorax with big, untidy stitches before speaking. "So?"

"Someone stuck a knife through his heart."

"Yet there was little blood on his clothes?"

Sullivan agreed. "Very little blood loss at all."

"Strange." She was fishing for information.

"What did you think of the lungs?"

"He didn't drown. Some frothing blood in the trachea. He aspirated."

"So the cause of death was . . .?"

"Pericardial tamponade. Quite rare. Invariably fatal."

Sullivan began to wash his hands.

Randall cleared his throat. "Is it a homicide?"

"Ninety-nine per cent yes. *If* you'd found the knife still in the wound I'd say it was a very unusual way to commit suicide or a very unlucky accident. If the knife isn't in the cellar." He turned from the sink. "What am I saying?" He grinned. "I'm being overcautious. Of course it's a homicide. Quick and professional. He was a strong man. His killer must have been even stronger. Or lucky. Just the one stab wound. But what a hit. The knife had a single-edged blade of a maximum of two centimetres wide and a minimum of fourteen centimetres long give or take a centimetre. Long and slim like a carving knife. Not serrated. No untidiness. It was sharp. The wound is clean and not ragged. If you forced me to make a comment on this I would suggest that he was very shocked by what happened. The knife penetrated the left ventricle and was driven right in. There is some compression of the material around the jacket pocket which corresponds with the wound on Humphreys' body."

"Would that have taken a lot of force?"

Mark Sullivan gave her a strange, sad smile as though he had woken from a dream. "You're expecting me to say something about 'extreme force' or someone with 'arms like a chimpanzee', Martha. But the truth is once you've penetrated the skin the rest is a piece of cake. It's even possible a woman could have done this – if she was reasonably fit and was in a position to assault Humphreys without him first being able to fend her off."

A vision of a woman? A lover? Someone near but not to be trusted? Humphreys' wife?

"Could it have been an accident?"

"I'd take an awful lot of convincing but the usual defence is that the deceased 'fell' against the knife thus causing his own injury."

"It's possible?"

"Like I said, I'd take an awful lot of convincing. If he hadn't taken a while to die."

She stared at him.

"Think of it, Martha," he urged. "The blood doesn't gush out but leaks slowly into a bag to leave the circulation. The pericardial sac acts as a staunch."

"How long?"

"That no one knows." He grinned. "It's something pathologists like to argue about over their late-night drinks at medical conferences. Who knows? Now I might be able to join them. The truth is it depends on how fast the blood leaked out. The wound was only small. The tip penetrated – not the full two centimetres maximum width of the knife blade. Possibly 500 mls. loss would be sufficient to cause death when combined with a penetrating wound to the heart. There is even some argument that the wound itself is enough to put the ventricle into fatal arrhythmia but generally the accepted estimates are between ten or so minutes and an hour or two."

"Would he have been conscious?"

"We don't know. At least we can't say with certainty."

The police officers were standing back, unfamiliar with

medical terminology. Alex Randall spoke for all of them. "So – for the benefit of the uninitiated, in words of less than ten syllables – can you explain, doctor?"

Mark gave him one of his lop-sided smiles. "Yes. Sure. Sorry, Alex – and the rest of you. The knife entered the heart, in this case the left ventricle. There was a lot of bleeding into the pericardial sac – the bag the heart lives in. This caused a lethal condition known as cardiac tamponade when, because of the increased pressure and loss of blood, the cardiac output falls – eventually causing death." He put a friendly hand on Randall's shoulder. "You don't need to know all the details, Alex," he said, "except that the stab wound was the direct cause of this man's death."

The officers were silent. Martha could almost see the cogs of Alex Randall's mind start to turn, almost hear the metallic grind. A stab wound to a police officer's mind is homicide. This would spark off a major police investigation. And discount the theory that Humphreys had caused the wound himself.

Mark gave a short laugh. "I think I'd like two questions answered at this stage," he said. "The first is – why no ID?"

Coleman was the one to answer. "He might have been one of these guys who empties their suit pockets," he said. "Keeps their shape."

"So did you find his wallet, cheque book, credit cards and mobile phone anywhere in the house?"

Coleman shook his head.

"Or in the car?"

"No."

"And the second question?" Martha asked.

"What made that round mark on his chest? It was done shortly before death and was quite a hefty whack. It probably had nothing to do with his death. I'm simply curious.

I can't work out what did it." He untied his long, rubber apron and spoke to the mortuary assistant. "Better tidy him up," he said.

Martha moved away while Peter did his job. Mr James Humphreys had been a well-dressed man who had died a violent death. Why?

Shrewsbury was not a violent town. Its ancient buildings, unchanged for centuries, reflected a safe town whose inhabitants were largely peaceable. It stood on a hill, safe from marauders, encircled by the protective River Severn except for a narrow strip in the North East. And that was watched over by the Castle which nowadays houses the Regimental Museum. So in the streets people walked in security. It was as though the embrace of the river, combined with the geographical fortification of the town, made them feel insulated against the twenty-first century. Salopians still lived in a gentler, earlier era. Here there were no marauding gangs of vicious villains, little crime or drug dealing. No prostitution – unlike a century ago when areas like Mardol had been the haunt of drunken seamen, prostitutes and pick-pockets. Grope Lane had not found its name by chance! Neither had Butcher's Row or Fish Street. People walked on history in this town. And yet there was enough blood in its past. There had been a bloody battle of Shrewsbury six hundred years ago and centuries before that Dafydd ap Griffith had been hanged, drawn and quartered at the spot now marked by the High Cross.

And now there was another savage murder to add to its archives. How long would Humphreys have lain in the cellar of Marine Terrace if the River Severn had not flushed him out? The crime would have remained concealed for longer. For how much longer? And why had no one come forward to claim him yet?

"Alex," she said impulsively, "I'd like to visit Marine Terrace again. Can that be arranged? Maybe tomorrow?"

He nodded gloomily, still tussling with the prospect of a major investigation on top of the problem of the floods. "Provided the river's gone down and we get no more rain. The property's been under feet of water. The cellars are still partially flooded. It's a right mess. We've sent frogmen in. There doesn't appear to be anything more down there except a few drowned rats but it's a difficult crime scene to search completely. And potentially dangerous too. We're really going to have to wait for the Severn to recede all the way back before we can be absolutely sure we're not missing anything. And that could take a week."

He was distracted by his mobile phone. He frowned, spoke into it for a moment or two, flicked the off button, his face taut to make a significant announcement. "Well, we may have something like an answer soon. Mrs Humphreys has been located and picked up. She's in a Squad car, on the M54 – less than half an hour away. We'd better get her husband cleaned up and ready for viewing." The mortuary assistant busied about his work and the police officers clustered in the corner, talking.

"Martha." Alex's eyes were on her. "I don't suppose… It might be an idea…"

She put the words into his mouth. "You want me to stay?"

"You're going to have to make contact with the family at some point."

She nodded. "OK."

It was less than half an hour later when they heard a car pull on to the mortuary car park. Minutes ticked by before the bell was rung and they heard voices. One loud, female, the other Peter, the mortuary attendant.

They let Alex Randall deal with Mrs Humphreys. As the

Senior Investigating Officer it would be part of his job to liaise with the family of the murder victim so it was helpful if he made early contact. And it didn't seem quite right for the pathologist who had just carved up her loved one to have too much to do with grieving relatives. They heard her step, the clack clack of high heeled shoes, before they caught sight of her passing the window. A tall, well-built peroxide blonde, in her thirties. Alex led her into the viewing room. They could make out his shadow behind the curtain, head bent, hands lifting the sheet while she bent forward. Then suddenly everything changed. There was a shriek. The woman jerked back. Randall stiffened. Martha stood up. Mark Sullivan looked up from his notes. "What's going on?"

Alex told them what had happened. He had drawn the cloth away from the face. Mrs Humpheys had drawn in a deep breath, stared, then gasped and looked up, confused. "I'm sorry," she'd said, "I'm so awfully sorry. But this man is not my husband."

Alex had tried to persuade her that she was shocked, asked her to look again, to make absolutely sure. Was there any possibility that she could be mistaken. But Mrs Humphreys, whose name, they learned later, was Cressida, was adamant. The dead man was not her husband. He was not James Humphreys.

So who was he?

4

They had a brief, whispered discussion in Sullivan's office while Mrs Humphreys was given a cup of tea by Peter.

"He fitted the description," Randall said defensively. "And he was found in the house Humphreys was renting. It seemed so obvious."

"Humphreys could be our killer," Martha suggested. "Or alternatively it might have been a case of mistaken identity. Someone thought he was Humphreys." The two men looked at her. "In which case where is Humphreys now?"

Blank faces stared back at her. This had been an unexpected turn of events.

Alex opened the door to leave. "We'd better take Mrs Humphreys round to the garage and see if we can shed any light on her husband's whereabouts." But he halted in the doorway, his face still displaying incredulity. "I just couldn't believe it when she said it wasn't him. I kept saying, You're sure? You're sure? She got quite cross in the end. 'I know my bloody husband', she said. Then she kept asking us where he was. We could hardly excuse ourselves by saying that we *thought* we'd had him here – on the slab. Now we could have a missing man on the books as well as an unidentified murder victim. All we could tell her with confidence was that the properties had been finally evacuated on Monday evening when we'd known the river was going to burst its banks. None of the officers on duty remembers seeing anyone in number seven. Humphreys could have gone off to stay with a friend – although when we asked around the garage no one volunteered any information. I got the feeling they hadn't got to know him that well. It makes it more difficult that she doesn't know any of her husband's colleagues at the new job. We're taking her up to the Jaguar garage now."

When he'd gone Martha was thoughtful about the phrase Randall had quoted, "*I know my bloody husband.*" A certain amount of venom seemed attached to Cressida Humphreys' words. Admittedly she had had a shock. But surely *relief* that it was not her husband's corpse she was looking at would have been her primary emotion? Not, "I know my bloody husband." But in mitigation her husband was still missing. Perhaps it was a little premature to expect her to feel relief.

Mark Sullivan was watching her.

"This is an intriguing little problem," she commented.

"Yeah. Glad it's not mine."

She left then, followed the squad car out of the car park and turned south. She had a full day's work ahead of her.

Thursday 14th February – St Valentine's Day

Martha awoke at seven to the sounds of *Dancing Queen.*

She'd known she was asking for trouble to hire an Abba lookalike, soundalike Swedish au pair. But unfortunately Sukey had spotted Agnetha over the banisters when she had come for interview, shrieked at her name and silky blonde hair, slipped her hand into hers and insisted the post had been filled. The subsequent interview had been a bit of a farce, the outcome a foregone conclusion. The two had bonded and were usually to be seen sporting flares, crocheted hats and tacky, shiny party dresses. Added to that the house permanently reverberated to the sound of Abba hits while they became spiritual sisters with only a few years between them.

Poor old Sam was thoroughly left out. But between football practice, rugby practice, cross country, hockey and American football practice he lay on his bed, read magazines about acquiring fitness, strength and muscles, took the occasional shower and fell asleep, usually with a plate of crisps balanced on his bed. When he wasn't doing this he was walking the dog or riding his bike.

In contrast Sukey was all party energy. Martha often watched her and wondered where her blonde mane had come from. Not from her. Her hair was thick, dark and unruly "with a touch of the red". Must be her mother's Irish blood. While Martin's hair had been – well – even putting it kindly – wispy and mousy. Not his best feature. That had been his eyes. Warm and brown as Thornton's toffee. Cream – not the black treacle variety. And his teeth had been like Sam's, crooked, irregular, very unique. She had sometimes mused that had Martin committed a crime and left a bitten apple core at the scene he could have been identified by his bite as precisely as through a DNA trace.

Martha rolled over in bed and realised the phone was ringing. She sat up. Jerked out of her reverie. Maybe it was Alex. The shockwaves caused by yesterday's statement from Mrs Humphreys had taken them all by surprise. And left them with a pile of unanswered questions. She was curious to know what had happened next. It could be one of the frustrations of her job that while she was informed at the discovery of a corpse she was not always kept up to date as the police investigations proceeded. This left her with burning unsatiated curiosity.

An unidentified murder victim lay in the mortuary and the rule was: no identity, no inquest. For the identity of the victim was just as significant as the pathologist's evidence. Unsatisfactory it might be but there had been occasions when this rule had dragged a case out for years. The police were not bound to keep her informed how their investigations were faring.

But from about a year ago Alex Randall had fallen into

the habit of keeping her up to date with his progress and this in turn had made her intrigued by their investigations and bold enough even to make some suggestions of her own. She was fast learning how the police worked. How they thought. The first case in which she had played this more active role had been old bones discovered in the Abbey which had proved to date from the eighteenth century. It had been the first time she and Alex had developed anything more than a very brushing acquaintance and she grew to welcome his clipped, informative phone calls. Since then they had been involved in a few more cases. Like any old, small town Shrewsbury had its secrets. So she picked up the phone with a recognised frisson of excitement. Maybe he had tracked down the real Mr Humphreys. But she was in for a disappointment. An irritating click returned her greeting. It was a bad start to a strange day.

"My last summer . . ." The two "sisters" were warbling together in the kitchen. She could hear Sam's heavy footsteps clomping wearily down the stairs. She wrapped her maroon satin dressing gown around her, tucked her feet into a pair of M&S black mules and made her way downstairs.

The two girls were swaying in time to the music, pieces of toast in their hands smothered in Vegemite. Agnetha swore by the stuff. And the scent permeated the entire kitchen – always. It turned Martha's stomach. Sam was shovelling a bucketful of crispy nut cornflakes dampened with milk into his mouth, intermittently swigging orange juice from a pint glass at his side. He had a thing about vitamins and hydration. His sports bag lay bulging at his feet.

She greeted them all with a blanket, "Morning," and plugged the kettle in, wiping her hair out of her eyes in a thick handful. She needed a coffee fix. Quickly.

"Good morning, Mrs Gunn." Agnetha's smile was wide, welcoming, difficult to fault. Sukey ignored her mother by pretending to be too absorbed in the music to respond to anything that wasn't Swedish. Sam carried on munching doggedly as though in danger of missing out on a calorie or two. Only Bobby's ears pricked up. He sensed he was due a walk and she would oblige as soon as the twins had left for school. Agnetha and Sukey finished their toast and their song and stacked the plates in the dishwasher, all done gracefully in time to the music. Sam simply abandoned the battle scene, leaving his dishes still on the table.

By eight-fifteen the house was eerily quiet, Abba blissfully silenced for the day. Martha threw on a pair of jeans and an anorak and unhooked Bobby's lead from the back of the door. He shrieked out a couple of ear-piercing barks and leapt high enough to bump her hip. Pointless ordering him to calm down. She opened the back door and Bobby whisked out of sight while she fumbled her feet into a pair of wellingtons.

At the back of house was an area of protected forest, largely spruces and pines, criss-crossed with a myriad of soft, sandy paths, populated by rabbits and a delight to Bobby who found much to sniff at and chase. It was one of the reasons why she had bought this house, a fake Georgian mock-up which had begun life as a farmworkers' cottage, been extended, whitewashed and pretentiously called The White House. In fact the name would have been fine had it not shared it with the official residence of the President of the United States. But when she and Martin had first viewed the house she had fallen in love with the woods behind and relished the space in which to exercise one of the world's friskiest dogs. Bobby was his successor but just as frisky. Mongrels, in her experience, usually were. Also the seclusion of the property had seduced her. Neither she nor Martin could ever imagine chatting over the garden fence to their neighbours. She shoved her hands deep down in the oilskin pockets and pondered. The trouble was that elected seclusion when you were half of a couple could feel dangerously like isolation when you were alone.

She stepped quickly through the woods, her eyes focused on some far off point ahead. It was a great time to think. The dew dripped off the branches and there was a fresh, crisp feel to the day.

Her mind flicked back to the anonymous corpse. There were several interesting points to mull over. Whoever the man was, he had been found in the house James Humphreys was currently renting. And James Humphreys had disappeared. She picked up a twig, absently chucked it into the undergrowth, sending Bobby scuttling after it and bringing back a quite different twig a few seconds later, while she wondered whether the real James Humphreys had turned up yet – dead or alive. By now Alex might have tracked him down. At work even. The Jaguar garage was outside the town so not threatened by the floods. There was no reason to stop business continuing as usual. Humphreys' colleagues might even have been able to shed some light on the dead man's identity. She picked up another stick and threw it in response to Bobby's eager, lolling tongue. Maybe Humphreys had not been the sheep but the wolf in this case. Not victim but villain. She was suddenly very curious to know how far DI Randall had progressed in his investigations.

She sensed the regret in the dog when she turned around at the top of the hill, but she had a full day ahead of her with many cases to sift through. Her area of jurisdiction extended far beyond merely Shrewsbury to include

Church Stretton and Oswestry, Market Drayton and Whitchurch and all the little villages within these points. And winter was a time of a surging death rate which supplied her with plenty of work. She paused for a moment, savouring the whipping breeze, hoping it did not carry more rain to add to the town's sufferings and looked back at the house. It hit her then quite suddenly what an isolated place it was, half a mile from the nearest road, reached only by a potholed track, surrounded by unpopulated farmland and backed by trees. Her nearest neighbour was nearly a mile away.

From the top of the hill she watched the red Post Office van wind up the track and minutes later when she was almost back she saw it thread its way just as gingerly back down towards the main road. As she rounded the back of the house she recognised a second car approaching. This time an elderly Ford. It was Vera's day to give the house a clean up.

She greeted her cleaning woman guiltily, ignored her despairing look at the pile of washing dumped by the machine, had a brief chat about what wanted doing in the house and ran upstairs to shower. Half an hour later she was driving her Mercedes towards her office, in Bayston Hill, an area to the south of Shrewsbury, down the A49, the road that finally led to South Wales. And her parents' house in Cardiff.

Her offices were in a large Victorian house, invisible from the road, up a secluded drive lined with rhododendrons and dark firs. She pulled up at the front and ran up the steps. Jericho was waiting for her with his catalogue of things to be dealt with: telephone calls to doctors and the police, correspondence, a sheaf of new guidelines for coroners she needed to browse through, appointments in the diary to speak with relatives. She worked her way through steadily until three, her lunch a sandwich and coffee on her desk taken between telephone calls. She always vowed she would emulate the Continentals, meet a friend, have a *proper* lunch, but somehow she never did. It always was a sandwich grabbed between phone calls, a quick swallow when the phone on the other end was picked up. Continental lunches were like the extravagant suppers she always *meant* to cook the children. The menu invariably had to be changed to something easy and quick at the last minute. She never had *enough* time. Not simply *quality* time. *Any* time. But the job was demanding, the responsibility enormous. She loved the work. She also loved her children. She chewed her ham salad sandwich thoughtfully. Relationships, she thought, making the same, tired old excuse. No time. But even forming the thought made her feel empty.

She was halfway through an after dinner coffee when at three-fifteen a call was put through from Alex Randall.

"Believe it or not the rain's stopped, the river's receding and the sun's out," he said, almost jauntily. "Marine Terrace is safe to visit. The water level in the cellar's down. We've made some headway into the case. I wondered if you would like to revisit the scene, Martha. It might inspire you." The briefest of pauses. "I know what a hands-on coroner you are." He was reading her mind.

For the first time that day she did look out of the window. Bayston Hill was, as the name implied, on an elevated site. Her window faced back towards Shrewsbury. She had a prime view of the spires of St Chad's and St Mary's, the green fields of the tennis club, the enveloping river, spilling across the fields. Alex Randall was right. The sun was beaming down, golden, on the world as though apologising for the few days' foul weather which had caused so much mayhem. She needed no persuading.

"Fine," she said, hearing the lift in her own voice. "Lovely. I'll see you in ten minutes? On the English Bridge?" She lifted her handbag from the hook on the back of the door, slipped her jacket on and made her excuses to Jericho.

He arrived in a marked car which surprised her. She always imagined detectives preferred to work incognito. But the Panda car had the advantage of a driver who dropped him off right in the middle of the English Bridge whereas she had had to park in Gay Meadows, the Shrewsbury Town football ground, and walk. She crossed the English Bridge, now open to traffic and met him in the centre. They both looked down at the swirling waters, mud-stained but quieter. "It's a relief to see the waters recede," she said.

"Even if it's only so we can gain access to the crime scene."

"Quite. Did you find the knife?"

"Not yet."

They walked. "So have you found the real Mr Humphreys?"

He nodded. "I suppose that's the main headway."

"How did you track him down?"

"Surprisingly easy, really. We took Cressida round to the garage and there was a touching reunion."

"Where had he been?"

"Says he'd caught the flu and was bedridden for a couple of days."

"Where? He certainly wasn't at Marine Terrace."

Randall's eyes sparkled. "Apparently staying with a friend."

"So why didn't he ring his wife?"

"Said he didn't think she'd worry, that he'd felt too rotten and, besides, that she'd told him she was going away for the weekend and probably would have her mobile switched off for most of the time."

"And was she away?"

Randall nodded.

"He didn't even ring work?"

"No. Said he felt too ill."

"What's he like?" she asked curiously.

"Just what you'd expect. Slightly paunchy, well-dressed, plausible."

"And can he shed any light on our dead man?"

"Nope."

They descended the steps, still gritty with river-debris, and though she had been told there was no longer any danger, and that the waters were receding, Martha still felt apprehensive as they paddled along the narrow pathway to the row of cottages. Unidentified objects swept past them in the river, impossible to identify. The flow was too fast and in the dwindling light they looked like brown icebergs, indistinct, while the water was murky and mudstained. The town was still quiet, even the traffic somehow subdued. No one was driving fast. And as they crossed the bridge motorists were glancing down at the river as though they still didn't trust it. They reached number seven.

Apart from the police tape threaded through spikes around the front door, rattling in the wind, Marine Terrace looked innocent, nothing like a murder scene, masquerading again as a pretty, seaside cottage. But from the moment Alex Randall pushed the front door open the illusion was gone and she breathed in the murky scent of a river bed and its foul secrets. Which, had it not been for the invasion of the River Severn, might have been preserved a little longer.

So she pushed aside the image of seaside towns, Whitby or Tenby, Lyme Regis, Scarborough or Skegness, and instead toyed again with the thought: When *would* Humphreys have discovered his visitor?

When the scent became too strong? When Calliphora's thousand and one eggs hatched, filling the cottage with blue-bottles?

What was down there to draw him down into the cellar? A bottle of wine? A fuse box? Nothing? Or had it been a place to hide the victim of *his* crime? Would *anyone* be so crass as to hide a body in their own cellar?

Randall flashed a torch around the room. And this afternoon, more powerfully than before, in the cold and the wet, she was even more conscious of flood damage. She put her hand over her nose and mouth to try and block the stench but she could still taste it through her fingers. Something dead, something rotting. From beneath the ground. This must be the scent of a grave. She felt bound say something. "Unpleasant, isn't it?" He agreed with a nod, reluctant to open his mouth and taste what he too could smell.

There is a false image conjured up by the word 'flood', of sparkling, clean blue river-water rinsing out one's home. Reality is quite different. The wall was marked two feet up – inside as well as out. The carpet squelched underneath their feet, making a sucking noise and sticking to their feet as they walked through sludge. It reminded her of Irish bogs her mother had told her folk tales about, featuring will-o'-the-wisps and leprechauns, pixies and fairies who lured small girls into the sucking, drowning mud. But while her father had told her mother off for telling such stories he had had tales of his own, of Druids and Bards, of babies who were left on mountains to die and wolves who lived in the forests and preyed on the unwary and weak, the children and old people, dragging their bones to their lairs. Martha shook herself. But the air still stroked her face with ice-fingers and she felt an echo of a little girl's fear – of the cold, the dark, the unknown. It was a terror adults rarely experience.

Even the windows were coated in green slime, as were the few items of furniture, the three piece suite, a small coffee table. The atmosphere was as fetid as a river bed. "What a shame," she murmured. "What a terrible shame. Who would have thought it would be so very awful? And these are such pretty cottages in the summer."

Not only the summer. She had walked this way late one Christmas Eve, seen holly wreaths dangling from the door, spied into a cosy, Dickensian interior, with an oak dresser hung with gaudy Welsh mugs, a log fire, chintz sofa, Christmas tree spangling in the corner. It had been the last Christmas she had shared with Martin and she had known it would be. Maybe it was that that had seared the Greetings Card picture into her brain. A lost idealism. A tragedy about to happen. Giving warning.

Closing her eyes for no more than a fraction of a second, only a long blink, she recaptured the terrible longing of that moment, that Martin would somehow, miraculously, not die.

"What a difference a couple of feet of water makes," Alex said, smashing into her thoughts with an observation. "And we don't even know when it'll be safe for the inhabitants to return." He sighed. "Despite today's sunshine more rain is threatened – particularly over the Welsh hills. And we all know where that ends up."

Martha cleared her throat. "So where exactly was the body lying when Coleman first saw it?"

He covered the space to a door in the corner in three giant steps and pulled it open. Instantly the dank smell rolled up like a London smog. "These steps lead to the cellar," he said, flashing his torch downwards. "The body had been dumped down there. It moved up when the waters rose and pushed the door open. The door opens inwards. Poor Coleman. He won't recover from that in a hurry."

"I'll bet."

How quickly normality descends.

She was at the top of the cellar steps now, peering down. "So what was in there?"

"Nothing. We've scoured it. No knife. No wallet. No mobile phone."

"No wine, no fuse box?"

He flashed the torch on her face.

"There would have been no reason for Humphreys to go down there," she explained. "Did he even know there *was* a cellar?"

"Yes. He admitted it."

"Hmm. And was there anything else to find?"

"Nothing down here."

"And in the rest of the house?" She was anxious to leave the cellar, close the door.

"Various belongings. A smart suit laid out on the upstairs bed, as though Mr Humphreys was planning on going somewhere.

"Or had just arrived in from work and got changed."

Randall agreed.

"And I suppose he wouldn't have realised the implication of the river rising."

"Possibly not, not being a native of Shrewsbury."

"Have you any idea who the dead man is yet?"

"Not a clue. No one else has been missing from the garage. We even took Humphreys down to the morgue to view the body but he couldn't enlighten us." A brief pause. "Or at least that's what he *said*."

"Oh? Should I be reading something more into this?"

Alex half turned back towards the light. New lines were

engraved between nose and mouth. Joined by recent frown lines. "You know me, Martha. Everyone lies."

Maybe it was a hint towards his personal life. But if it was she could not interpret it.

Tacitly moving together they emerged outside, in the fresh, chilled air. Alex locked the door behind him.

"And where is Mrs Humphreys now?"

"They're booked in to the Prince Rupert. It's not really anything to do with us after that. A domestic."

"What do you mean?"

Randall laughed – almost coyly – and she caught sight of very white, very healthy teeth. "The friend he's been staying with is a female, a receptionist from the garage."

Martha felt her eyebrows lift. "And what exactly was his story?" They were walking through the gloom, up the steps, back towards the orange lights of the lamp-posts which lined the English Bridge.

"He said he'd been advised to leave Marine Terrace on Sunday – about five in the evening – by our boys who were putting out the warning that the river was rising. Interestingly this is exactly true. We were warning people then. Marine Terrace is one of the first places to get flooded. However the two officers in charge of the area near the English Bridge -"

"Roberts and Coleman."

"Exactly. They don't remember anyone being in number seven. According to them they banged and banged on the door but no one answered. They assumed it was empty."

"How does he explain that?"

"First of all he said he'd answered the door to them. When I confronted him with the fact that the officers had not seen him he changed his story, said he was upstairs, changing, and just heard them." He gave her a sharp look. "It didn't exactly inspire confidence."

"Had he been at work on Sunday?"

"Until four. It's a busy day for the garage."

"Sunday night was the extreme earliest time our corpse could have met with his death, according to Doctor Sullivan," she mused. They leaned over the parapet. The river was difficult to ignore.

"And Humphreys was with his friend from late Sunday afternoon because of the floods. So he says."

She turned to face him, square on. "Are all policemen so cynical, Alex?"

Deep in his eyes she caught a flicker of hurt, a wounding that she had not meant. It caught her off-balance so that she wished she could have pulled the words back. But they had been said. And could not now be unsaid.

"Umm." His voice was hesitant. "After a couple of years on the job." He cleared his throat noisily. "We start off – I started off – idealistic." He gave a vague grin. "I think I probably started off even more idealistic than most."

It was hard to imagine. It must have been a long time ago. How old was he now? Forties? So – a rookie cop with an Adam's apple and a skinny neck?

"Things happen." His eyes flickered away, back towards the threatening river. "It changes you. Forever. Once you've lost it, the idealism I mean. Once it's gone you can't recapture it. It goes for ever. Sometimes I think . . . "

She waited, wondering whether now he had begun to talk, he might continue.

"I believe. . ." He cleared his throat again, rasping and dry. "It's what marks the young from the old, Martha." A hint of a smile, "Cynicism engraves lines of doubt and disbelief on our faces. Lines that mean we will never take people at face value ever again."

She was sure there was some personal deep suffering behind the words. But just as instinctively she also knew that the time for exploration had passed over. His controlled, regular face was back again, the one she recognised. The shutters had dropped and erased the character lines.

She smiled a vague response, which he returned in the form of a tight grin. "The alibi we finally squeezed out of him is that this woman who is a part-time receptionist at the garage offered him a place to stay because of the floods. Her husband is conveniently away from home four nights a week, driving lorries up to Scotland for a road haulier's. Seems like Humphreys availed himself of her hospitality. She says he was with her from about five o'clock on Sunday evening. She said he seemed unwell on Monday and Tuesday and stayed with her on the other side of the town – right up until this morning when he went back to work."

"How truthful is she?"

Alex shrugged, heaved a deep sigh and shifted his weight to the other leg. His profile, in silhouette, picked out by the orange light, looked sharp and grim. "Difficult to say. I mean she strikes me as a bit of a liar. Sheelagh, her name is. S-H-E-E-L-A-G-H." He spelled it out. "Sheelagh Mandershall. Peroxide blonde. Apparently she and Humphreys 'hit if off straight away', wouldn't you know? When she heard about the flooding of the properties she offered him a bed straight away." A sudden, mischievous smile. "And who knows what else."

She mirrored his smile. He suddenly reminded her of Sam, catching her eyes after a particularly spectacular tackle. Muddy and triumphant. Bloody but unbowed. And somehow thoroughly masculine.

"So what explanation does Mr Humphreys have for a dead man being found in his house?"

"None. In fact he did look thoroughly shocked. Unless

he's a consummate actor. He says he left the place empty around five o'clock Sunday evening, coincidentally less than an hour after Sheelagh's husband had departed for Glasgow, and locked the door behind him. He wasn't expecting anyone to call. He doesn't know anyone of that description. And he hadn't anticipated the river flooding the property. Not really – not like that. He thought it was all dramatic talk and that it wouldn't happen. And before you ask, Mr. Mandershall's tachometer proves he was well away by five and we have a petrol receipt for the Lake District at a little after seven. He's in the clear."

"Was the door locked or unlocked when Coleman tried it?"

"Unlocked. In fact – ajar."

She dipped her head. "So who else has keys to the house?"

"According to the estate agent, only himself. Humphreys had two."

"Are they both in his possession?"

He put a hand on her arm. "Hey, Martha," he said, grinning. "Who's the detective?"

"Sorry," she said, embarrassed. "I can't help it. I always want to ask questions. Female nosiness?"

"Well – as it happens Humphreys does appear to have mislaid one of his keys." He moved away from the parapet. "And now that's an end to it."

"OK."

"Just one more thing, Alex, is your gut feeling that your man was killed in error, the killer thinking it was Humphreys?"

"I don't think so but I don't really have much of a gut feeling at all yet. Nor will I until I know who he is. Then maybe I can understand what he was doing there in the first place. Then, again maybe, I can begin to work on who killed him. Identity is everything, Martha. I don't need to point that out – especially not to you."

"Is there anything more?"

"Just police stuff, really."

"What?"

"The door was secured by a Yale. No deadlock. Easy to get in. Trouble is folks in Shrewsbury feel safe. They don't expect to have their homes broken into so they don't generally bother with unnecessary expense like burglar alarms or complicated locks. This town still lives in the idyllic sixties. Peace and freedom." He held up two fingers in a forward-facing, sixties peace and love 'V' sign. "It's a backwater, Martha, and I think many people in the UK would give their eye teeth to live in a similar backwater. Quite honestly a nicked credit card could have slipped back the Yale and got you into Marine Terrace."

She nodded. "Did you point out to Humphreys that the dead man could have been mistaken for him?"

"We did."

She waited. "With no particular response?"

"Not a thing. Not a flicker of an eyelid. As I said. He either knows absolutely nothing about this business and it's pure coincidence that the dead man turned up in his cellar or he's an accomplished actor."

"You must have plenty of lines of enquiry. Witnesses? Someone must have seen the man arrive there on Sunday. There were plenty of people around. Your police officers for a start."

"They had enough to do."

"But police officers are trained to observe, aren't they? Have you put out appeals on the radio and television? Our 'John Doe' is someone's husband, brother, son, father. Surely he is missed?"

Randall gave her an amused smile. "Doctor Gunn," he

said formally. "We're doing all we can. As you say there are plenty of lines of enquiry. And. . . ." He'd been stung into revealing more than he'd intended. "We do have a car."

"A what?"

"Well – a Hyundai van, to be precise. Grey, two years old, left at the Friars Lane car park since Monday. Ticket issued Monday morning, ten am, valid for eight hours. The Traffic Department alerted us this afternoon."

"But I don't see the connection. Our man died on Sunday night."

"I know but it's something – maybe a lead."

"And the trace?"

"It belongs to a Mr Haddonfield, from Oswestry."

He was smiling, mocking her interest. Waiting for her to prompt him.

She couldn't resist. "So?"

"Mr Haddonfield of Oswestry has, it seems, disappeared." He was still mocking her.

"You have a description?"

Randall nodded. "Early forties, five-eleven, dark-haired."

"So?"

"It doesn't look as if he's our guy either. For one thing the timing's all wrong and for another a man answering that description and giving that name was picked up hitch-hiking along the A5 towards Oswestry on Monday night. The story he gave to the truck driver was that his van had been trapped by the floods and that he would pick it up when they had receded. In the meantime, he said, he would use his wife's car."

"He gave the truck driver his name?"

"Yes."

"So where did the truck driver drop him off?"

"On the outskirts of Oswestry. He had a mobile phone

and had rung his wife up to meet him at the dropdown point."

"So?" Her curiosity was killing her. "What does Mrs Haddonfield say?"

"That she never heard from her husband after Monday lunchtime. That it wasn't her he rang. That she was working, anyway, he'd known that, and that she wouldn't have been able to get away. In fact she was working so late she'd stayed overnight on Sunday at the hotel where she works – particularly as the weather was so foul and she had an early start on the Monday morning."

"But the truck driver . . .?"

"Confirms that Haddonfield telephoned his wife and asked her to pick him up."

"What does Mr Haddonfield's phone supplier say?"

"That his line was unused from midday Monday."

"So was it Haddonfield?"

"The truck driver says so and we have the Hyundai van at the police compound."

"I don't understand what connection this can possibly have with our case," she said slowly. "The timing's all wrong. Everything's all wrong."

"I know that," he said. "But you know it's very hard for pathologists to be precise about time of death."

"I think within twelve hours on a relatively fresh corpse is not exactly precise," she objected.

He seemed annoyed. "Well – whatever – we've invited Mrs Haddonfield up to the mortuary for a viewing. Just in case."

"I'll be very interested to know what happens."

Randall nodded and strode towards the waiting Panda car.

It was four-thirty. Too late to return to the office but she didn't want to go home either.

Towards the town, lights were being switched on. Life was returning to normal now the waters were receding. The night would be cold. Already one or two stars were visible in the sky, over a pale, full moon. *There would be no rain tonight*. She headed towards the town.

5

It looked inviting with its bright lights and intriguing shops. She never had enjoyed shopping until she had moved to Shrewsbury. Randall was right. Here the illusion was of old-fashioned England. The town centre had its shopping malls, Pride Hill and the Darwin Centre (named after the great evolutionist) but it also had quirky, individual shops which sold jewellery from Cuba, food from the Mediterranean, wines from all over the world. There were old family businesses which had moved from generation to generation, hardly changing – except for computerising their sales. She felt a strange sense of security when she shopped here. It reminded her of going to Dublin or Belfast, Cardiff or Swansea with her parents when she had been small. Today she wanted to buy some ham, cheese and olives from Appleyards and a bottle of wine from Tanners so she wandered into Wyle Cop.

She was thinking as she walked. Now it was Haddonfield who could be either victim or villain. How quickly a sheep can turn into a wolf. And if he was the dead man a wolf becomes a sheep again. *It is only a matter of wearing the fleece.*

To her left the shops had obviously suffered from the river's invasion. Already signs were up offering reductions on flood-damaged goods. But it was as she progressed towards the town that her eye was caught by a sign fixed crookedly to one window. "Drowned Stock". Martha gave a little chuckle. Someone, it seemed, had a sense of humour. She had discovered the shop six months ago when it had first opened. Called merely Finton's it was an antiques shop and the window had held one piece of furniture, a small, unpromising country-made oak dresser with a couple of Toby jugs on top, a disappointment when her passion was for paintings. She had peered through the window and seen more pieces of antique furniture and a few curios. Even so she had been tempted inside. The back of the shop was filled with the most eclectic collection of goods she had ever seen: copper warming pans, horse brasses, candlesticks, fire buckets, plenty of odds and ends with amongst them scattered genuine antiques. But it had not been the stock but its owner who had drawn her eye.

A genuine gypsy. Complete with long, wild hair, hooped earrings, a gold stud in his nose, dark, dark eyes with a fearsome expression, a tie-dyed red sweatshirt and grubby black jeans. He had looked villainous yet intriguing. She had not spoken to him then but had suspected he had a sense of humour. The Drowned Stock notice was proof of this. As she pushed open the door she felt forced to admire his attempt at humour. The floods must have caused him quite a headache – particularly now – only a few months after he had opened his doors.

So she walked in and squelched across a seagrass floor, avoiding the two huge dryers which blasted boiling air into the room. He was arguing with a short, plump, bespectacled man holding a clipboard. Neither took any notice of her browsing.

"Look – you can see for yourself, you toad. The whole lot wants replacing."

The little man murmured something which the shop owner obviously didn't appreciate. He eyeballed him back. Martha would have backed down at such strong opposition but the presumed insurance investigator must have met this degree of threat before.

"I'm sorry, Mr Cley. But company policy says. . . "

"You can stick your company policy right up your . . . "

"I have explained." The insurance investigator picked up his bag and dropped the clipboard inside. He made one last ditch attempt at reason, conciliation. "It doesn't help, you know, Mr Cley, being aggressive."

Finton took one step forward. "Oh? Look – I don't care what you say. I've paid my premiums and I specifically checked that I was covered for *full flood damage*."

More murmurings from the suited man.

It only earned him Finton's eyeballs again. "Arse around with me, mate, and you'll have your head stuck up your own. You can check with your company if you like but I warn you I'll be exposing you to the *Shropshire Star* if I don't get the answer I want within twenty-four hours. You and your company'll be splashed right across the front page. No one – not even genuinely safe house owners – will touch you with a very long barge pole. You'll be dead. Worse. You'll be out of a job. Like I will be," he added quietly, almost an aside. The suited man moved away, produced a camera and a tape measure and went about his business. Then the shop owner acknowledged her presence. "Hello again." He gave a disarming grin. Beautiful teeth. "I have seen you before, haven't I? I don't forget faces. At least, not ones I don't want to forget."

He had a beautiful voice too. But he was scruffy. Tall and thin, aged about thirty, with unruly hair and a silver ring on his finger. He was attractive enough to have landed a part in any film, but only as a gypsy, a pirate, or some other villain. He should have looked a complete ruffian. But the teeth and his voice saved him and identified him at the same time. Public schoolboy, masquerading as a villain. She smiled at him and he smiled back and held out his hand. "Finton," he said. "Finton Cley. Owner of this establishment."

Martha felt herself blush. "Martha Gunn," she said.

"You are joking?"

It was not the response she'd expected. "No. It really is my name."

"And you don't . . .?"

Now he was being rude. This was beyond the pale. "I don't anything," she said coldly. "I called in on the off-chance that . . ."

"Not to gloat, I hope. You look too nice for that." He tossed a scowl over into the corner. The insurance man didn't appear to notice. "Help pick over the drowning pieces?" he said hopefully, "Give me a hand salvaging my future?"

"I don't know if there's anything . . ."

"Do you want to browse?" His eyes were flickering across to the insurance investigator's scrutiny of fungus growing in the corner. Even to her untrained eye it looked more than a week old. "Yes," he called across. That's what happens when the flood waters recede and the weather's warm. All this seagrass'll have to be torn up."

The insurance investigator murmured something unintelligible and Finton turned his attention back to her. "So what is it? Browse or the personal attention?"

Her eyes picked out a dark painting dangling from one of the beams. He followed her gaze. "Yes – nice, isn't it?"

She laughed, putting the faux pas behind her. "Antique shop owners always say that – praise the would-be purchaser's taste."

This time he blushed. "Well," he said gruffly. "What else would we say? Laugh because you homed in on the worst object in the entire place?"

"Is it?"

"Certainly not."

"Look – I don't really see anything."

He lost interest in her. "OK. Fine. Do call again. Goodbye."

As the door pinged behind her she wondered whether Alex Randall and his team had called into Finton's Antiques as part of their investigation.

She continued up the hill towards the town, passing the *Lion & Pheasant*. Part pub, part small, cosy, private hotel, her mind flicked back to the puzzle of who lay on Mark Sullivan's mortuary slab. There seemed no way it could be Haddonfield but if he wasn't dead where was he? And if the body was Haddonfield's how on earth had he magicked himself from Oswestry back to Shrewsbury, a distance of thirteen miles. Too far to walk. If he had returned why had he pursued the double journey? Had he forgotten something? Important? How had he returned? To his death? And what about the anomaly over the phone calls? And the timing? Martha shook her head. She didn't envy Alex Randall unravelling this one.

She reached the top of the steep hill, continued along the High Street and made her purchases in Appleyards, breathing in the scent of freshly milled coffee as she chose ham, olives, French cheese and sun-dried tomatoes. She called into Tanners wine shop on the way back down the hill and dawdled over the selection, finally picking a New Zealand Shiraz from the bin. She loved the place and its atmosphere of Georgian elegance. The best wine shop she'd ever been to. And that included London and the famed Fortnum & Mason's. She felt released, free as she walked back down the hill, but as she reached the English Bridge her mobile phone rang. It was Mark Sullivan. She could barely hear him over the roar of the water still threatening. She was vaguely surprised to hear his voice. He didn't usually approach her direct but dealt with

Jericho who then passed details on to her. Besides – she had not been aware that Mark Sullivan knew her mobile phone number.

"Where are you?"

"Believe it or not, on the English Bridge. I can just make out Marine Terrace."

Sullivan gave a huge chuckle. "Not turning private investigator, are you, Martha?"

"Absolutely not." She defended herself, "I was calling in at the deli and couldn't resist a rummage through Tanners' wine bins."

"Don't make me thirsty."

"Did you want something?"

"It'll keep."

"Why don't you pop over later, Mark," she said impulsively. "I've bags of food and some very interesting wine."

"How interesting?"

"New Zealand Shiraz."

"All right. Nine?"

"Fine."

It was only after she had pressed the End Call button that she realised she hadn't told him where she lived.

The house was quiet and dark when she returned. Sam was at rugby practice and Sukey and Agnetha were huddled together on the sofa watching *Abba the Movie*. Even Bobby barely raised his head from his paws as she walked in. By the light of the TV she could see that Sukey was sucking her thumb. She left them together and started preparing an evening meal.

When Martin had been alive she had begun this formality of eating well and together in the evening. The twins had been small then but they had still sat around, like a family should.

Now the twins were bigger – and particularly with Sam's

necessary calorific intake – she had continued with the tradition. She and Agnetha often shared a bottle of wine and the meal usually stretched into the evening.

It was an oasis of contentment.

6

At tea the talk was all of Sam's football, and Martha forgot about the complications of work. Life seemed so much more important than death. Sam's face was still flushed with effort and pleasure as he tried to affect modesty, failing miserably when he described how he'd scored the winning goal and was the hero of the entire school. Martha felt a warm glow from a secret, maternal source. By eight o'clock she'd heard a breakdown of the entire match four times over from starter's whistle to triumphant, shoulders-high march back from the playing fields. The hero was flopped on his bed, worn out with being the Beckham of Shrewsbury School. Sukey had retired to Agnetha's room, doubtless to try on clothes, shampoo their hair in Borne Blonde shampoo, play records and swap Scandinavian pop star stories. Martha had time to herself to shower and change into black snug-fitting trousers and a cream sweater.

At nine Mark Sullivan arrived, fidgety on the doorstep, wearing horn-rimmed glasses, holding out a bottle of wine loosely wrapped in pink tissue paper and looking uncomfortable. She tried to put him at his ease by greeting him warmly. "Hello. Come in." As she closed the door behind him she commented, "I didn't know you wore glasses."

He tapped them. "Contact lenses, usually, but after wearing them all day my eyes get tired."

She led him into the kitchen. There was the wine to open, the Tanner's New Zealand bottle winning over Sullivan's claret. He watched her remove the cork without offering to help and they walked into the sitting room, he carrying the tray holding the cheeseboard and olives, she bearing the opened wine and two glasses. He glanced around the room with frank curiosity but without comment, waiting for her to sit down first. They sipped their drinks slowly and made small-talk about the town and the floods. A couple of times he pulled his glasses off and rubbed his eyes as though he really was tired. He waited until they had both eaten, she perched on the big, soft sofa with her feet tucked underneath her, and he on the adjacent chair, before he moved the conversation back to the case. "I didn't really come down here to talk about the town and the floods. I promised Alex I'd let you know we still haven't identified John Doe," he said.

"I did wonder." She wriggled her feet around. "Just that Haddonfield was seen on Monday whereas you seemed pretty sure our man died on Sunday?"

"Our man had died about thirty-six hours before we saw him," he said. "Rigor mortis had almost completely worn off and besides – there was the evidence of our good friend, Calliphora. Her maggots were well-fattened."

"Ugh." She wrinkled her nose.

"So has Haddonfield turned up, then?"

"Couldn't tell you, Martha." He stretched out, relaxed, his arms folded behind his head, the glasses off and his eyes half closed. She could almost have thought he was about to drop off to sleep. He looked longer, younger, different. "Once Mrs Haddonfield had taken a peep at our corpse and said it wasn't her husband she was whisked away by the efficient Detective Inspector Randall." He smiled lazily. "And my brief acquaintance with the lady was at an end. I've never known a case like it. To believe, twice, that you have the right man only to have the wife swear otherwise. Two women in the mortuary in as many days. Not good for a poor old pathologist like myself." Whatever he said, he didn't look too troubled.

She drank her wine thoughtfully and set it down on a cork coaster on the coffee table. "So Alex still has a missing person as well as an unidentified corpse."

Mark savoured his mouthful of wine then smirked. "As well as a case of assault."

"What?"

"I heard through one of the junior officers on the case that Mrs Humphreys broke her husband's nose right outside Monkmoor cop shop while he was placed nicely in front of the CCTV camera. It was almost rehearsed."

She threw her head back and laughed. "I don't believe it. And is the errant husband going to press charges?"

"Well," Sullivan said with a sharp twinkle in his eye. "I don't think he would have done but in spite of all the first aid the officers could administer, the offending protuberance swelled up considerably and his looks were apparently much diminished. I don't rate his chances with Sheelagh any more."

"What you mean is," she said wickedly, "that Sheelagh the Sheila didn't find him quite so attractive."

"Quite," Sullivan said. "What a very adventurous life some men lead. Makes me feel quite . . ." And suddenly the tired look was back, haunting him. He fell silent. Deeply silent and she watched him thoughtfully as the torpor sunk his eyes. He set his glass down on the other side of the table as though he was too tired even to hold it.

"Mark," she began tentatively. "You do understand, don't you. We can't hold an inquest until I know who he is."

"I think I'd come round to that conclusion myself." He was sitting and staring at the ruby wine glass. She'd switched on the standard lamps around the room so the light was soft and flattering. But it made his face look even more hollow.

"What I find hard to believe is that no one's come forward to identify our John Doe. He didn't look the sort of man who would not be missed. He was well-dressed and relatively young. He didn't look like a down-and-out but someone with a job – with a family. People like that don't just drop through the black holes of society. Men like that simply don't just go missing, Mark. And yet. His pockets were empty. There was nothing to tell who he was. No ID. No mobile phone. No wallet. The police have scoured the house for anything that might tell them who he is. I know forensic evidence will have been lost in the floods but this is bizarre. What was he *doing* there? Where's the murder weapon?" She wriggled her feet again. "It's as though part of the puzzle is not knowing who our corpse is. Once we know his name we'll know his killer's name." She drank some more of the wine. "Or am I being fanciful?"

He grinned back at her. "Just a bit."

"Oh – it's such a tantalising puzzle."

Mark was eyeing her very carefully, glasses back on. "If you're so curious to know where the investigation's got to now you'll have to talk back to Alex Randall. I've no idea how his case is progressing. Maybe he's found out something more."

"Right."

They chatted idly like old friends until a little past eleven. Both being doctors they found plenty of subjects they were both interested in and more besides. But of his family Mark Sullivan remained silent and she did not probe. Neither did he mention Martin or her children even though the strains of Abba could be heard bouncing down from the top floor and Sam's heavy footprints went twice up and down the stairs. For food, she guessed.

Something else registered too. Neither of her children

popped their heads round the door to wish her goodnight. It was as though neither Mark nor her offspring had any desire to acknowledge the other's presence. It didn't really matter. Sullivan was no more than an occasional work colleague. An acquaintance. But one day someone might enter all their lives. This fact sat at the back of her mind heavily, like a piece of uncooked dough.

He gave her a quick peck on the cheek on the front doorstep as he left but didn't offer the usual platitude of "seeing her soon". He simply left. Had she been a teenager she would have read much into this omission but as it was she simply sighed and closed the door behind him without waiting for his car to manoeuvre around in the drive. Then she took a small nightcap of brandy up to bed with her.

She did not read but lay in the light of the Tiffany lamp, staring up at the ceiling, sipping the brandy and wondering at her life – so far. Her job she loved. Such an involvement in death might, to many, seem morbid. But it gave her an opportunity to be of real worth to people at a low point in their lives. Martin's legacy, her two children, filled the other parts of her life.

In many ways she was blessed. She knew that. She had had a brief but happy marriage, had been left with two fulfilling children and a career she loved. She was financially solvent and had a home. So . . . She fell asleep still listing her blessings. She had a career, a home, children and a dog.

Alex called into her office early the next morning.

"Haddonfield's been officially listed as a missing person," he said, standing with his back to the window, arms folded. "There's no sign of him. Since the lorry driver set him down on the outskirts of Oswestry he's vanished. And there's something else odd that I can't explain. The dead man was wearing one of Humphreys' suits."

"What?"

"Yes. Humphreys' suit. Do you remember Coleman saying it wasn't a very good fit? It wasn't because of the water stretching it. It was because it never was his suit. On an off-chance we showed it to Humphreys and he identified it. Shirt too. So it's no use describing our corpse's clothes. They weren't his."

This lobbed the ball right into another court. "So all our assumptions about a well-dressed man etcetera etcetera are meaningless? He wasn't well-dressed at all but wearing borrowed clothes."

"Exactly. We don't know what he was wearing. In fact we don't know anything about him. No ID. No clothes either."

"So were his own clothes at Marine Terrace?"

"No. Humphreys has identified all the clothes as belonging to him."

"Underwear too?"

Randall's eyes gleamed. He'd always loved the way her mind worked. Logical, tenacious. She would have made a good policewoman. But she had chosen medicine and then made a strange sideswipe of a career move. Coroner of this quiet corner of Shropshire. He wondered what had lured her here. She was not a local woman. She had told him her parents lived in Wales. Her husband, he understood, had originated from Birmingham. So why had she decided to do such a job? One that dealt solely with death and its detritus. Grief. Relatives. The law. All the messy side of the healing profession.

Maybe it was that – the formality of the law after the chaos of medicine. Making some logical sense of events after nature – or man – had inflicted her worst. He remembered now that her husband had been a solicitor. Maybe he had influenced her choice.

Anyway. He sat down.

"Our corpse wore Calvin Klein boxer shorts which Humphreys insists are not his." Randall couldn't resist one of his swift, elusive, mischievous smiles. "Although if you ask me, one pair of Calvin Kleins looks very much like another and Humphreys does have a drawerful of the things."

"How do you know?"

He winked. "The search, Doctor Gunn. And the socks our corpse wore were English, Marks and Spencers, plain black wool mix. Humphreys has said it's impossible for him to be sure whether they're his or not. And it was the only time during the entire interview I was absolutely certain that this statement was the truth."

"You don't like Humphreys much, do you?"

"Aa-ah." Randall shook his head decisively. "I – do – not. He's a cheat. What's worse is that because he's got away with cheating he keeps doing it and getting more and more conceited and sure he won't get found out."

"Hasn't the broken nose sobered him up a bit?"

"Not enough for my liking. I'd have made an even flatter job of it."

Martha laughed out loud. "Oh, Alex," she said. "You are funny. I'm not sure you should be making an expression of intention of police brutality to me, the coroner. If someday I'm investigating a death in custody you might just find my hand on your collar."

"I sincerely hope not," he said.

"You're sure about the clothes?"

"The shirt, tie and suit *were* all Humphreys' – and he's telling the truth. The collar size was wrong for our corpse and he's even produced a photograph where he's wearing the tie – an electric blue silk affair. Very flash." She remembered it. Not for being flash but for being cut from around a dead man's neck.

Martha was thinking about the slash through the jacket and shirt which corresponded with the fatal wound. "And our dead man was wearing Humphreys' clothes when he was killed. So was he maybe a thief? Was he looting the property as it was empty?" Even more vividly it conjured up a vision of Humphreys, returning to the flooding cottage, finding someone who had borrowed his clothes and in a fury . . . killing him? Knowing Alex Randall he would already have considered this option.

But.

"Alex," she said slowly, "Your 'John Doe' didn't go to Marine Terrace naked except for boxer shorts and maybe black M&S socks. But you said . . . ?"

"Exactly. Everything else in the entire place belonged to Humphreys."

"Well – if James Humphreys is telling the truth, and presuming your man didn't go there naked, either the murderer took away our man's clothes, having persuaded him to put them on before sticking a knife into him or our man came to Humphreys' house already in Humphreys' suit. Masquerading as him. Why would he do that?"

"Maybe his own clothes were wet," Randall suggested.

"But you don't do things like that, break into a house, steal a man's suit. Oh – none of it makes sense."

"That about sums it up, Martha," Randall said jauntily.

"And you've found no one who saw him arrive?"

Randall shook his head. "We've put signs up on the English Bridge and a couple through the town using artist's impressions. No response."

His face changed and he chewed his lip. "Martha," he said. "I hope you don't mind my discussing the case with you? After all, it's a bit out of your remit."

"Not at all," she said, folding her arms and moving away

from her desk. "I find it interesting – if a little frustrating. Just to be handed the bald facts at the end of a protracted investigation will seem a little tame in future, Alex. You must have to explore many blind alleys in an investigation like this. I don't mind you sharing them with me. Better that than being kept in the dark."

He sighed, suddenly despondent. "If only you knew how dark, how many blind alleys; how many missing persons. You wouldn't believe how many men in this age group who loosely fit the description have vanished. It's quite depressing. And what with the floods and a still anonymous body, I was glad to hand Mr and Mrs Haddonfield back to the Oswestry force."

"Really?"

"Well, Haddonfield seems to have disappeared from there and officially Oswestry is outside my jurisdiction."

"But not outside mine."

"That's true," he admitted.

"Anyway, if I can help . . . "

"Thank you. I'd better get back. I did want to keep you up to date."

They both knew a phone call would have sufficed.

Martha stopped him with a hand on his arm. "Alex," she said thoughtfully. "I know I'm a suspicious creature and I really don't want to give you more work."

"But?"

"Two things. When your police officers went to the Jaguar garage on Tuesday why didn't Sheelagh Mandershall say that Humphreys was staying with her?"

"Simple. She wasn't at work that day. In actual fact a friend did tell her someone had been asking about him but Sheelagh assumed it was something to do with either the floods or his wife chasing him up. By the time she knew otherwise Cressida Humphreys really was on the scene."

He smiled. "And your second question?"

"How did the lorry driver know it really was Haddonfield?"

"He told him."

"What if it wasn't? I mean, Haddonfield hasn't been seen by anyone who can positively identify him. What was he doing in Shrewsbury anyway?"

"Shopping. He's a window cleaner and no one wants their windows cleaned when it's pouring with rain. The only connection with us appears to be that his van was left here because of the floods. As I said, it's up to the Oswestry police to investigate that side of things. I'm convinced he left our patch on Monday night. His wife spoke to him by telephone on Monday and she's confirmed that our man is definitely not her husband which is good enough for me. The timing's all wrong, anyway. Haddonfield was still alive on Monday night whereas our man died on Sunday. It must surely be coincidence."

"Hmm."

"Mrs Haddonfield arrived home at about nine pm on Monday to an empty house. And that, it seems, is that."

"Did she go out later?"

"We don't know."

"So what's happened to nosy neighbours?"

"It was a filthy night. The nosy neighbours had their curtains tightly shut and were glued to the soaps. No one saw or heard anything. She says she was at home all evening, didn't budge and didn't hear the phone go. And try shifting that as an alibi. Not that she needs one."

7

Martha heard nothing from Alex Randall for a few days. She was busy anyway. There was plenty to distract her from the puzzle of the unidentified man and she knew the police, under his direction, would be doggedly pursuing their investigations. But while she didn't exactly forget about the case it did sit at the back of her mind, pricking her curiosity at times. So she scoured the *Shropshire Star* for detail but there was none. It didn't even get a mention. Besides – at a guess – if Alex had really broken ground he would have let her know. So she sat back and waited, reflecting that whatever the sayings, no news was exactly that – no news – neither good nor bad.

The citizens of Shrewsbury, in the meantime, had their own threats to think about. The river still swirled across the fields and intermittently inched its way across the Frankwell car park. Vulnerable inhabitants watched every drop of rain falling from the sky with dread and clung to the elevated ring road, looking down on the flooded meadows. Shopkeepers in the town were busily refurbishing their premises, one eye cocked over their shoulder so they would not miss another stealthy invasion of the river. There was a tangible sense of apprehension overlaid with anger at the delay in the installation of flood defences. The twenty-first century bleat was printed in the newspapers. Somebody should be doing something. Somebody should pay. As though man held the answers to this problem. They were misguided. Not man. Nature. The Salopians were not understanding. Nature has us in her grip. Not vice versa. And try suing Nature or applying for compensation.

Martha did wonder how Finton Cley had fared at the

hands of the insurance investigators but she hadn't walked past his shop or called in. She had spoken to Mark Sullivan a few times on the phone about other subjects. They were in constant touch through the very nature of his job but they had not discussed the case of the unidentified man and as far as she knew he remained that – unidentified. Anonymous. It was as though both of them knew they must wait for the ponderous steps of the Shropshire police force. There was no point speculating. It was a waste of energy. Evidence and proof would be gathered eventually and only that would reduce broad speculation to narrow fact.

Mark didn't sound well. His speech was slower, hesitant and occasionally very slightly slurred. If she had not observed him so clear-headed at her house that night she might have thought it was the way he always spoke. But it wasn't. She suspected he was drinking, but friend-like, felt compelled to excuse him – even to herself. If he was drinking it was for a reason. She didn't know anything about his personal life but she could hazard guesses. Possibly something was very wrong at Mark Sullivan's home but it wasn't her business. She might suspect he had marital problems but she didn't really want to know so she deliberately didn't raise the subject with Jericho. Of course, as she hadn't actually seen Mark since the night at her house when he had so obviously been fine, her observations were purely made over the phone. She might have been wrong but she didn't think so.

Sukey and Agnetha had discovered the Abba website and a chatroom linked to one of the stars. According to Sukey, who treated her obsession like a religion, they linked partly in Swedish and partly in English and he (it was one of the boy members) was really "cool". Martha knew the word had nothing to do with temperature and everything to do with acceptability but she had no objection anyway. It kept them occupied for hours.

Sam was, according to the school, getting seriously sporty. One Wednesday afternoon, a fortnight after the body had been discovered in Marine Terrace, the PE master rang her at work and asked her to call in on the following afternoon.

Intrigued, she arrived at the school promptly at three and made her way to the gym. It wasn't difficult to find the sports master. She could hear him before she saw anyone.

"Come on, you boys. You aren't trying. Take the ball and RUN. That's better. No . . . Backwards. Backwards, boy."

He was a small, wiry man with curling, black hair, wearing jogging pants and a sleeveless white T-shirt that showed off a pair of impressive, weight-lifter's arms. He was marooned in a sea of scarlet T-shirts, black shorts and trainers. They were practising rugby skills, passing the ball to each other. The scent of sweat and feet was overpowering. She took a step back. The master spotted her and trotted towards her.

"Carry on, boys," he shouted back over his shoulder. Then he grinned again. "Mrs Gunn? I think we'd better go in my office."

She followed him into a shoebox of a room, its walls plastered with photographs of triumph. Teams, cups held aloft, winners' ribbons. This was a school that appreciated success. Not for them the stigma of winning. Pride beamed at her as did the man across the desk.

"Do sit down."

She sat, for some unknown reason, glad she had worn trousers today, well-fitting, dark blue, with a white sweater. He leaned forward, eyes pinning hers. "I think we should have a bit of a word about your Sam." He leaned across the desk again, this time to shake her hand. "Paul Grant, by the way." He had a pleasant North Eastern accent and smelt faintly of grass. There was a smear of mud on the right knee of his jogging pants.

She returned the smile. "Martha . . . Gunn."

He launched straight in. "You see the lad's got a rare talent."

She nodded dubiously.

"No. I mean it. I've watched him. And I've seen a few eager young players in my time. It takes more than that. Nature's got to give you the right build. You've got to have single-minded devotion and a certain strength. Not just in your legs. In your character. I can't put it any clearer than that. There's a certain magic about really good footballers that makes your toes curl."

He must have got the impression she wasn't taking this seriously enough because he fixed her with a stare again.

"Mrs Gunn, he could get a place at a football training school. Young Newcastle or somewhere. Maybe Liverpool. A club from the Premier Division would be glad to take him on."

She stared at Paul Grant. And understood that to this man there was no higher calling in life. He would not understand why she was not jumping up, screaming with joy, tears rolling down her cheeks at the thought of her boy. Her boy being potentially one of the chosen few. Again he leaned back across the desk, speaking urgently, his eyes boring into hers but with less certainty now. "If I make that phone call they'll come down and scout him." He waited for her to absorb this statement. "I didn't want to do it without you and Sam's dad's say so."

She gaped at the man. Didn't he know? Had *no one* thought to tell him? "Sam's father is dead, Mr Grant."

The PE master looked as though he'd been struck down. "His dad is dead, is he? I imagined . . ."

She knew what he'd imagined. "That his father stood in goals and had a knockabout on the lawn? If anyone did, Mr Grant, I did. His father died when Sam was just three years old. He's never really had a dad."

The statement felt disloyal so she felt she must replace it with another.

"Not that he remembers."

"Well I take me hat off to you, Mrs Gunn. The lad's a rare footballer. I'm surprised he started playing with a w . . ."

She wondered whether he had been about to say "woman" or "wench" and gave him a suddenly saucy grin. "It's the awful mix in me," she said wickedly. "Welsh father, Irish mother. Lethal combination. Quite wild. Now what's the education like in these 'football schools'?"

"Not up to here," he admitted.

"Then I need to talk to Sam and to his other masters."

Paul Grant raised a hand in objection. "You know what schools like this are like. Private schools. Sam's an all-rounder. They'll all say he should be concentrating more on their subject." A touch of humour. "Whatever it is." *They both thought Latin*.

"As you are on yours, Mr Grant," she rejoined.

He gave a frank, likeable grin. "No. It's more than that, Mrs Gunn. He really is good. Talented. It's a pleasure to watch him. The teams *need* lads like him. He could be coached to something very interesting. Special-like."

"I'll think about it, Mr Grant."

The PE master put his hand out to shake hers with a faint touch of respect that had been absent from his greeting. "If he's going to make a career in football this is the way he'll have to go, Mrs Gunn. And he doesn't have much time," he warned. "They pick 'em young these days."

She left the school, perturbed and preoccupied. As she unlocked her car door and fastened her seat belt she reflected. There had been a few times since Martin had died when she would have given anything – anything – to be able to consult him. *To be able to ask him just one question. Just one. What shall I do next?*

She dropped her head onto the steering wheel. This was one of those dreadful occasions when she was reminded afresh of the big hole created by his absence. In some ways she wasn't so alone. Both sets of grandparents were still living but even without consulting them she knew they would advise according to their class and generation. Education, education, education. Football was merely "kicking a ball around". *Education* was what counted. But today's world was different. Her children had not turned out how she and Martin had imagined they would. She blinked away the vision of her holding one twin, Martin the other, swapping to burp, swapping to feed, swapping to change their nappies. Martin who was somehow fading as each year closed behind him. She couldn't picture him reaching forty years old. And she had never seen him touch a computer because nine years ago many people didn't, whereas nowadays few people were without some QWERTY skills. She sighed and drove slowly towards the town. But the difficulties of the day were not over yet.

Still agitated and a bit depressed, she parked the car in the Gay Meadows football ground and wandered into Wyle Cop, stopping halfway across the English Bridge to read the police appeal on its yellow sandwich board. She wondered whether the police had had any response. She stopped walking and peered down at the swollen river, recalling the newsflash that it was due to peak again at roughly nine o'clock tonight. It was a strange fact about the Severn that because it meandered lazily cross country its worst levels could often be predicted hours, even days ahead. But the flooding was nothing new. An elderly inhabitant of the lower reaches of the town had once told her that years ago, as the river rose, vulnerable homeowners simply abandoned their cellars – then their ground floors. Something which would not be tolerated now. "But," the elderly inhabitant had argued, "Shrewsbury has *always* flooded."

Always has, always will, she thought and read the flood height level gauge: 5.25 metres on November 1st 2000, 4.86 metres in 1998, 5.16 in December 1960 and the highest, 5.37, in 1946, flooding a beleaguered town still recovering from World War Two, although only two bombs had actually been dropped on Shrewsbury. One which caused little damage and the other destroying a cottage on the Ellesmere Road and killing its occupants, a mother and two children. The real fear for the town had been not the war nor the floods but the influx of American servicemen and concern about the morals of the local girls.

Glancing across at Marine Terrace she knew her old, pretty memory would be now always superimposed by the other, the floating corpse. It never would look wholly peaceful, innocent or idyllic again even though the police tape had now been removed, and with that, the one external sign that anything untoward had happened here. Then, quite suddenly, as she turned away from the house, she felt acutely uneasy. Frightened. As though something dreadful was about to happen.

The light was fading across a radiant red sky. *Shepherds Delight. In her mother's voice. Calliphora buzzed across an empty sky.*

Blood red, the setting sun sparking across heavy waters.

Shooting gold. A man was walking towards her. In a smart suit, briefcase swinging. As he drew level he put his hand up to the side of his head. Their eyes met. His mouth opened. And she knew who it was. Humphreys. She knew him because he looked a little like the dead man. Same height. Same build. Same clothes. And she knew him because he had a swollen, broken nose. He opened his mouth as though to. . . *Scream. . .*

They passed each other. Still shaking she clutched at the parapet and tried to convince herself that she had not had a vision. It had been – coincidence. She had . . . It was a man crossing a bridge, at sunset, talking into a mobile phone clamped to his ear. *It did not convince her. It was Munch's The Scream.*

She continued along Wyle Cop, heading for a friendly light. Rejecting the black and white half-timbered casement windows of the closing shops. She reached Finton's and was inside before she had consciously made any decision, the bell clanging noisily behind her.

He was smoking in the corner. And she could tell from the dried grass scent of the rollup that it was a joint. He glanced quickly down at it then obviously decided she was no threat or else that it was too good to stub out.

"Hello again." He took a glowing drag.

She knew that marijuana was illegal but she didn't really disapprove of the drug. While, in her role as coroner, she had frequently pronounced that alcohol had contributed significantly to a victim's death, whether through drink-driving, alcoholism, simple lack of judgement or an increase in aggression – and the same was true of cigarette smoking – she had never believed that marijuana was even a minor contributory cause of mortality. Therefore she held a tolerant attitude towards the drug. Besides, she was relieved to be inside. The scene behind her was so surreal.

So disturbing. So frightening.

He was staring at her. "You all right?"

She nodded. Not trusting her voice to sound normal.

"You look as though you've seen a ghost."

She managed a strained laugh. "Not a ghost. A tableau." Another nervous laugh to match a nervous voice. "Munch's *The Scream*, actually."

Finton took another deep, thoughtful drag and his eyes were far away. "One evening I was walking along a path with the city on one side. The fjord behind me. I was tired and ill; I stopped and looked out across the fjord – the sun was setting – the clouds were dyed red like blood. I felt a scream pass through nature." He scrutinised her. "Sounds like a hell of an evening out there. What exactly happened?"

"I saw only the picture," she said. "That awful, unbalanced terrible nightmarish picture."

"What precisely did you see?"

Before she'd said a word she knew how silly it sounded. "A man walking across the English Bridge – towards me."

He took another deep, thoughtful drag from his cigarette. "Why did it remind you of *The Scream*?"

She shook her head. She could not say. She tried to explain the inexplicable. Rationalise.

"It must have been the light effect. As he drew level he put his hand up like so." Her hand was shaking as she covered her ear, mimicking the action. "It was just a mobile phone. But it's a very bloody sunset out there." She wanted to use his name. "Mr Cley."

Finton gave a humorous stare at his joint. She knew had she been younger he would have teased her about her formality before offering her a drag. But even as he looked up he had already rejected the idea and said, quite seriously, "Finton's my name."

She acknowledged with a nod.

"And was he dressed in dark clothes?"

"A suit."

"Well – whoever he was – he's certainly got to you. You're as pale as a ghost."

Was that what she had seen? A ghost? Was it not James Humphreys but the corpse, searching for his identity? Was there then some significance, some warning, in the vision?

She tried to change the subject. "You're obviously familiar with the painting, and the painter."

"I took a degree in art," he explained. "Specialised in Symbolism. So, for fjord think River Severn?" He was still laughing at her. When she didn't reply anything he lapsed into reverie. "I always thought the tortured subject was Munch himself. It would have fitted into his life. Bit of a mess like plenty of artists."

His joint had gone out. He gazed at it with mild regret. "'Fraid I haven't any Munch to sell you, Martha Gunn." His eyes gleamed with a hidden joke. He was laughing at her. "But if you can wait a couple of days I'll see what I can knock up."

She allowed her eyes to drift down towards his empty fingers and she smiled at him.

"That's better," he said. "Come on. Have a brew. I can spare you one. I think you need one. Now tell me all about it."

She sat down nervously. The work of a coroner must of necessity take place behind closed doors. Newspaper headlines sit on the shoulders of violent, unexpected death, so coroners must be bound by the strictest rules of decency, privacy and confidentiality. She could not discuss any of it with this gypsy boy. Certainly not the reason behind the crazy, puzzling vision she had had on the bridge, not five hundred yards from this shop. Not any part of it. But as she accepted the mug of tea and wrapped her chilled fingers around to steal its warmth she wanted, with an ache, to confide in someone. And if not to him to someone, some human being with sympathetic ears and a response. This is what you lose when you lose a partner. Someone to share secrets with. Someone standing at your side on the touchline, both of you cheering your own son. She felt a sick wave of isolation.

Obviously impervious, Finton Clay grinned across. "Then tell me about yourself," he invited.

"Well, I work in Bayston Hill."

"A doctor," he pronounced.

It was true – in a way. "How did you know?" Not quite denial.

"Something about you. Something professional." He watched her critically. "Something guarded. Warm, caring, but in a very controlled sort of a way. Clinical."

She felt her eyebrows lift. "Oh?"

But she was reluctant to tell him more about herself and instead curled her fingers tighter around the coffee mug before turning the conversation neatly around to him. "So. Tell me about you."

It was a not unusual story. A father who had died (she picked up on something there), a mother who had "gone to pieces", a struggle through art school, a sister long-term depressive, dependant on alcohol and drugs for whom Finton – to his credit – felt partly responsible.

She stayed and drank two cups of coffee and found herself telling him about Sam's big chance. He gave the subject plenty of thought. "How old did you say he was?"

"Twelve."

"Why not give him the choice?"

"Because any boy of twelve would choose football,

Finton, without even considering his long-term future." She felt bound to add, "And you know footballers are more or less finished at thirty. And that's if they escape serious injury when they're younger."

"They're not finished at thirty. They just don't play competitive Premier League football. But they can survive much longer than thirty."

When she didn't respond he said, "What does your husband say?"

"He's not around to ask." She let him think she was divorced, that Sam's father was absent through choice. She didn't want to "do the widow thing". But it was twice in one day that she had had to explain.

"I see."

He was quiet for a minute or two, staring into the distance. Then he picked his head up. "Martha Gunn," he said, smiling, his hand on the move. For one awful moment she was sure he was going to cradle her own hand but it went no further than his lap. "There is no correct answer. Just two roads. Sam either takes the one or the other. Whichever road he chooses he will not know how his life might have turned out had he taken the other one."

They stared at one another. Maybe the dope had got to her too. The simple statement seemed like a deep, timeless philosophy.

When she left the shop she still felt nervous, her perceptions heightened. The gloom had spread; the air was damp and cold. But years ago, when Martin had first been diagnosed, she had learned there is only one way to deal with insubstantial funks. Turn around and face them. Say *Boo.* And because the town was silent, holding its breath, fearing the Severn might isolate it yet again, she started walking up the hill, making the excuse to herself of a visit to the Barclays cashpoint on Castle Street although really she relished the climb in the cold air. She would withdraw money and check on her balance. Striding out it would take her little more than fifteen minutes there and back and she needed to clear her head.

It was a mistake. Threading along Dogpole and St Mary's Street she found herself standing in front of the High Cross and, not for the first time, wishing she knew less about the town's violent history. When they had first arrived, she and Martin had taken one of the walking guides.

"On this very spot in 1283 Dafydd ap Griffith, brother of the last native-born Prince of Wales, was brought as a prisoner of Edward I and hanged, drawn and quartered." And he had not been the only one. In 1403 Harry Hotspur's remains were left to rot here as a warning to other rebels that the might of King Henry IV was absolute, his response to treason merciless.

The town was now dark, deserted and quiet. For the first time she would have welcomed Saturday crowds. Noisy families, sweethearts, shoppers. Buskers. *Big Issue* sellers. She hurried uphill to the corner, let herself into the Barclays foyer and heaved a deep breath. The thirteenth century receded. She was back on familiar ground. But the walk had cured her. She strode, with confidence, back across the English Bridge and did not stare at people walking the other way, wondering.

It was late by the time she arrived home. The English Bridge was closed to traffic again and there was gridlock round the Abbey. Turning out of the Gay Meadows took precious minutes. She was anxious to get home now. It was only when she was on the ring road, driving steadily, that she returned to the encounter on the bridge. Had it been Humphreys or had she been deluded? If it was him, what had he been doing there? "Silly," she said to herself.

"He practically *lives* there."

But he had been heading away from Marine Terrace. He could have been going anywhere. To the pub, to a shop. Anywhere. OK then. Who had he been talking to on the phone? She narrowed her eyes and gripped the steering wheel. She didn't even know that it was John Humphreys. It could have been anyone. But her mind was not listening to reason. It rippled on. What connection was there really between Humphreys and the dead man and Haddonfield, the window cleaner? Because she didn't buy the story that it was all pure chance.

As she covered the last few metres of the drive she could pick out lights on the top floor. A silhouette crossing in front of the window. Sam's curtains were closed and she could tell by the light from behind it that his television was on. But downstairs was in darkness. She pulled up outside the front door and switched her engine and headlights off. Something had caught her eye on the doorstep. Something red.

She locked the car and bent down. It was a wreath. Of red roses. She scooped them up, searched for a card and couldn't find one. She unlocked the front door and stepped inside, puzzling. If someone was leaving flowers why hadn't they rung the doorbell and delivered them properly? *Someone* would have been in for most of the day – Vera all morning, Agnetha throughout the afternoon, joined by the twins after four thirty. How long had the flowers lain on the step? Both Vera and Agnetha would have noticed them. They always used the front door. They had to enter and exit through the front door to set the burglar alarm. Why had they left them there? She would have thought that Agnetha would have taken the flowers inside. She loved flowers. She would have put them in the sink to keep them watered, preserved the card. Martha glanced upwards again. She should be running down the stairs to share the experience with her. Flowers delivered were not an everyday occurrence in the White House. They were special. She fingered the wire which bound the flowers to the circlet of moss. They must have arrived after four-thirty and Agnetha could not have heard the doorbell. But had no one been required to sign for them?

Once inside, in the light, she searched for the card and still couldn't find it. It must have fallen off, maybe on the step. So, still holding the flowers, she went back outside with the porch light full on. And still couldn't find it. She kicked the door closed behind her and carried the flowers into the kitchen. She put them on the draining board and splashed them with water. They still looked fresh. Agnetha and Sukey were running downstairs.

"The flowers, Agnetha," she said. "On the front doorstep. Why did you leave them there?"

The two Abba lookalikes stared at each other.

"I did not see any flowers when we came home, Mrs Gunn. Someone must have left them since we arrive back from the school. But why they did not ring the doorbell? Who are they from? Are they not . . .?" She glanced at Sukey, obviously puzzled.

Yes, Agnetha. Wreaths are sent in sympathy. After bereavement. Our customs are the same as yours.

"I don't know. I didn't see a card."

"But Mrs Gunn." Agnetha peeled back one of the roses. "It is here. Look."

The card was damp and as inappropriate as the flowers. *With Loving Sympathy,* and a flowered cross at its right upper border. The message inside was handwritten.

"Message for Martha."

There was no signature.

8

She fretted over the incident for days, feeling threatened by the mystery behind it. Someone must have driven up the track and left the flowers there. She had questioned Sukey, Sam and Agnetha but they had seen nothing. They could only reiterate that they had not been there when they had returned from school. They seemed unconcerned but Martha could not dismiss the gesture so lightly. She didn't know where the flowers had come from and she didn't understand the significance of the message. What message? At night she tossed and turned, asking herself the same question. What message? It felt more like a threat.

She took the wreath out of the laundry and dropped it in the wheelie bin, but the next time she put some rubbish in it, it was still there. The card she placed in a drawer where she saved old Christmas cards and other useless oddments. She locked and bolted the doors very firmly at night. There was not a lot else she could do. But like the unidentified body it was another story without an ending. *A message for Martha.*

Then Alex called in at the office one week later, on a fine, bright day in early March. The warming weather had exploded the town into sunshine daffodils. The town of flowers was living up to its name as spring finally came and the threat of floods diminished with the drier weather. People were scurrying around with renewed energy. It was the traditional time of new beginnings. Except that she made the mistake of blurting out her simple mystery.

"You have a secret admirer," he said smiling. "Most women would feel flattered."

"Maybe I would if it hadn't been for a wreath, the With

Sympathy card, the cryptic message. I don't feel flattered, Alex. I feel . . . exposed. Is that silly?"

"No. Not considering the high-profile work you do combined with the fact that you live in a remote area and alone. Well, I mean alone with the children."

"And Agnetha," she said, suddenly wishing the flowers had been from an admirer, meant for the au pair. But the message had been addressed to her, personally.

At last Alex took her seriously. "You could always have brought the card, flowers and their packaging in to us," he offered. "We could have fingerprinted it."

"Oh," she protested. "I'd feel silly. I'm sure you're right. It's nothing."

He nodded dubiously. "Well, I don't know. If you read the gift as a threat . . . And none of them saw a car arrive."

"No."

"Or heard the doorbell?"

"No."

Now she felt it was he who was making a fuss and shrugged. "Forget it."

"Well," he said finally, "you know where we are."

"Yes." It was time to change the subject. "I think I saw Humphreys," she said slowly. "About a week ago, crossing the English Bridge."

"Very possibly. He's still around. Back in Marine Terrace, in fact. His wife's gone back to Slough."

Her eyes gleamed. "And Sheelagh?"

"I don't know," he said. "She isn't really part of the investigation – apart from giving Humphreys an alibi." He was chewing his lip. A sure sign that he wasn't quite happy with that last statement.

Martha waited but he wasn't going to enlarge. "So how is the case going?"

"We think we have an ID for John Doe."

"Really? You should have said. Who is he?"

"We haven't actually got a positive ID yet which is why I haven't let myself get too excited."

"OK – who do you think he is?"

"I'm saying nothing," he said. "After two false alarms I hardly dare hope." He was teasing her.

"Alex . . . "

"We *believe* his name is Gerald Bosworth."

"And how did you get on to him?"

"His wife saw the pictures flashed on the TV and rang her local force."

"Which is?"

"Chester. They've faxed up some photographs and it does look like our man. However his wife said he was supposed to be on a business trip to Hamburg so if it *is* him goodness knows what he was doing in Shrewsbury. There's Humphreys not at home when he should have been. Haddonfield vanishing into thin air. And now a guy turns up murdered in Shrewsbury when he should have been out of the country."

"I just hope you have the right man this time," she warned. "When are you bringing her up to view the body?"

"Later on today. The trouble is our John Doe has now been dead for more than a month and he's had a post mortem. It could be a bit of a shock."

"You could use dental records."

"She wants to see him. I think something in her simply doesn't believe any of it."

"I can understand that – particularly as he wasn't even supposed to be in the country." She frowned. "What on earth was he doing *here*?"

Alex shrugged. "Who knows? I don't suppose you'd like to be around when she comes, would you?"

"I should if there's a likelihood it really is this Gerald Bosworth." She smiled. "He sounds awfully upper class."

"Well the wife doesn't."

"So when . . .?"

"In the morning? Ten?"

"I'll get Jericho to look at my diary."

The morning bloomed, bright, clear and cold. Frost had visited again. She could tell that before opening her eyes. The bedroom seemed unnaturally light and chilly – even with the central heating on. She threw back the duvet and crossed the bedroom to open the curtains. The sky was a clear, Wedgwood blue, the fingered branches of the trees thrown into silhouette against such brilliance. Her bedroom was at the back of the house, overlooking the woods. In summer this brought hoards of flies who buzzed around the sap-scented trees. But in winter the view was even more special, a far panorama back towards the town, the spires of which peeped over the top of the branches: St Mary's, St Alkmunds and St Chads. RSPB enthusiasts had nailed bird boxes to the trunks, large and small, so owls had made their homes there and swooped and hunted through the clear winter's nights, and blue tits fussed around the feeders full of nuts. In spring the woods were as overcrowded as a council estate with every nesting box noisily taken. And, in autumn, sometimes when she drew back the curtains her breath was taken away by the vivid colours of the dying leaves. Another few weeks and the trees would be wearing their spring best.

She had awoken early for some reason. Maybe because the sunlight had penetrated her curtains and acted as nature's alarm clock or maybe it had been the cold or perhaps because the thought of an unseen watcher who lay flowers at her doorstep still disturbed her. Tantalised her with a phrase.

What message? She had even questioned Agnetha again and had a vehement denial. "There is no one, Mrs Gunn. I have a perfectly nice boyfriend back home in Sweden. I do not want to meet a man here, in England. The flowers – they must have been for you. It was your name written. The Sympathy card . . . well." Martha guessed the phrase had a different meaning in Sweden than here.

She threw back the duvet and crossed the bedroom. The house was still peaceful. In minutes the day would begin with footsteps, music and voices. But for now she treasured the silence. Even Bobby hadn't started scratching at the door of the laundry where he slept. A blackbird, perched on the forsythia bush outside, was singing. It was a moment of rare peace.

Then abruptly the day began. Somewhere, probably in Sukey's room, the music started playing. There was the heavy thump of Sam clomping to the toilet, Agnetha's light step tripping down the stairs. Running water. The spell was broken. Martha was under the shower in a moment and wrapping a towel round her by the time Agnetha knocked with some welcome morning coffee. Agnetha would take the children to school while she took Bobby out for a walk.

She left through the back door and started walking briskly, at first, only aware of the cold. The morning was more comfortable from the inside. The air vaporised her breath. She thrust her hands deep into her pockets, ignoring the nip around her ears, and planned to wear the dark wool suit with a cream blouse. One of the worst aspects of being a coroner was that more days than not she felt obliged to wear funereal clothing when her favourite colour was red and her special outfit a very snug pair of jeans which fitted her with a pull yet felt comfortable.

Bobby scampered on ahead, his nose pressed into the

ground, his breath noisy in puffing, steamy pants. She felt overwhelmed with affection for the furry black hound and walked quickly to catch up with him. The woods were almost always empty at this time of the morning, the branches hoary with frost. Her feet crunched across frozen clay. She could almost convince herself that this was her own private forest. She rarely saw anyone else using the footpaths. The RSPB volunteers threw out dark hints about coppicing and thinning, of woodland management and control but she loved to think of them as wild.

Today was one of the dog's naughty days. He scampered after rabbits and eventually she lost him. She didn't worry. He'd find his own way home. She stood at the highest point, turned and stared back at the house, suddenly registering how visible her bedroom window was from this point. She stared for a long, long time. Thinking. Anyone standing on this spot could see right into her bedroom. She shivered. It did not do to stand still and think. One must keep moving in such chilly weather. Particularly when she had unwelcome thoughts. But even striding back towards the house the image continued to disturb her. She pictured herself standing, as she had only minutes ago, at the window, staring out. Undressing without *quite* pulling the curtains together. And being at the back of the house she had never shrouded her windows in net or voile. She hated the stuff anyway. But it did leave the windows exposed.

With Deepest Sympathy? She practically ran all the way back to the house. Three-quarters of an hour later she was changed, made-up, her hair brushed and tidy. Temporarily. The fierce Irish inherited from her mother kept it wild. Like the woods. Bobby had turned up on the back doorstep not even looking penitent. Just panting and tired, his flanks rising and falling. She made a pretence of scolding him and he handed her his paw to shake. She put him in his basket in the laundry. Agnetha wasn't back yet from taking the children to school. She sometimes stopped off and browsed around the record shops and today was not Vera's day.

She set the burglar alarm and stepped back out through the front door, stooping. "Oh, Bobby," she scolded. He'd caught a mouse and, dog-like, had presented it as a peace offering on the front doorstep. He'd often done this before; he was only obeying his instinct. Scolding and smacking made no difference though Martha still felt she should show disapproval in some way. She threw the mouse into the bushes trying not to look at it. A little blood had been trickling from the corner of its mouth. Freshly killed. Poor little thing. A field mouse, tiny and inoffensive. Nature could be so cruel. She put the incident behind her.

It was nine-thirty. She wasn't due at the mortuary until ten so she had time to call in the office, collect some papers and have a swift word with Jericho. He stood in the doorway, a grizzle-haired clerk, watching, while she leafed through her letters. There was nothing too desperate. She told him where she'd be for the rest of the morning and arrived at the mortuary with a second to spare.

At the same time as a pink Porsche Boxster. A pair of long legs extended out, black skirt, split almost to a tiny rump and an impossibly small waist. Then a skin-tight red sweater encasing disproportionately large breasts. High-heeled boots completed the outfit. Obviously Mrs Bosworth, if this was who she was, did not share scruples about wearing suitably funereal clothes. Martha watched her with fascination. *A real live babe*. She walked behind her, invisibly observing and breathing in the scent of cigarettes and expensive perfume.

Mrs Bosworth bounced towards the door, rang the bell with a red-painted finger nail which Martha noted, again with glee, exactly matched her sweater. Wow. Martha noticed these things. They did not happen by chance but by womanly design. *She* may have planned her *outfit* but this woman had paid proper attention to *detail* – right down to the fingernails. And the scarlet boots with pointy toes and spiky heels.

Mark Sullivan opened the door himself. His eyes widened as he scanned the woman from head to toe before noticing Martha standing behind her. But it was Martha's hand that he grasped and she was glad of that. "Hello, Martha." Then he turned his attention to the woman. " And you are . . .?"

"Freddie Bosworth. Frederica really." Her thick lashes dropped slightly as she spoke. Martha assumed a suitably grave face and waited for Mark to perform the introductions.

He did it perfunctorily. "Martha Gunn, our local coroner. She'll be conducting the inquest."

The woman's eyes flickered across her with a tinge of disdain. (Martha may have approved of Frederica Bosworth but *she* hadn't passed the return test). However, tucked behind the female appraisal was a clear spark of worry.

The three of them stepped inside just as Alex Randall pulled onto the car park, tucking his tie inside his jacket as he climbed out of the fluorescent squad car.

"Hello . . . hello." He strode over. "Sorry I'm a bit late." His eyes rested on 'Freddie' with a faint air of confusion. Sullivan filled in the gaps. Alex introduced himself formally as the senior investigating officer and they all moved inside to the viewing room.

Freddie was digging the blood red finger-nails into her

palms as Mark Sullivan drew the sheet back. Her small shoulders twitched. She hardly looked at the face but stared, unfocused, around the room. She looked very shocked, her skin yellowy pale. "I'm sorry," she said. "I'm so sorry. I'd have said earlier . . ."

"Is it your husband?"

Martha could read the bones in the woman's hands, strong, practical hands, with dry skin and long nails. She peered closer. Intriguingly, the nails were stuck on. She studied the woman's face even closer and read habitual, old tension, a few smoker's lines sprouting around the mouth. Grief hadn't kicked in to join them yet. Her eyes met Freddie's wide blue ones as she nodded. "It is him," she said. "It's Gerald all right though none of it makes any sense at all." She frowned. "I don't understand. I didn't think . . ."

"Can I have a fag?" she said next. The three of them looked at each other. It was against all rules. But sometimes rules are meant to be broken. Alex led her into Mark's cluttered office and opened the window and they all watched her drag on a cigarette for a few minutes without interrupting. "I'm sorry," she said. "I thought he was in Germany." The puzzlement carved more lines into her face so she looked old. "He never went then? You said he's been dead a while. How long. What's a while?"

She looked so pale Martha fingered a chair. "Why don't you sit down, Mrs Bosworth?"

Frederica sank into it, looking around at all three of them. "It's been such a shock."

They believed her. She looked genuinely shaken. Her hands trembled so she was finding it hard to put the cigarette to her lips.

"What's he doin' *here*, do you think?"

They looked at each other.

"He doesn't even *know* anyone in Shrewsbury. I don't think we've ever been here. It isn't our neck of the woods. We go across to Manchester if we want to shop. How come he told me he was in Germany? What was he up to?" Her blue eyes were pitiful. She wasn't crying so much as shocked. They were staring wide open. "I don't understand any of it," she said again.

"I'm so sorry," Martha said. "It definitely *is* your husband?"

The blue eyes fixed on her. "No doubt about it, love."

She lit another cigarette from the butt of the first one. "So what did he die of? The local bobby just said he'd met with an accident? Was it his car?"

Both men looked at Martha for their cue. "Freddie," she said. "Mrs Bosworth. There isn't an easy way to say this. Your husband was murdered."

"What?"

"He died from a stab wound which entered his heart. There was a lot of bleeding."

"What? You mean all over his clothes?"

"No. Into the lining around the heart. There's a medical term. But it won't mean anything to you."

Freddie's hand shot out and clamped around her wrist. "What is it?" she asked. "I'm going to be hearing plenty about it. You may as well tell me."

"It's called a cardiac tamponade."

Freddie responded with a twitch of her shoulders. Alex drew in a long, deep breath. Martha could tell he was thinking up a list of questions.

"I'll be holding an inquest," she said, "but there are bound to be police investigations."

"A funeral . . .?" Freddie said weakly.

"There are a few formalities to be completed first," Martha said. She stole a swift glance at Alex Randall. "The police will want to question you." She turned her head around. "Alex, if you'd prefer to use my office . . ."

"It's up to you, Mrs Bosworth."

"I don't care where," she said. "But get me out of *here*."

Mentally Martha tacked on the phrase, "*away from him . . .*"

The fight had gone out of Freddie Bosworth. She looked frightened. She was gnawing her lip like a hungry rat. And yet there was still a steeliness behind it, as though she was bracing herself for some huge pressure. Martha contrasted the woman who had bounced into the mortuary to the one who was subsequently led out. Maybe it was the shock of seeing her husband dead. Maybe as she had walked in she had half-hoped that it was not him and her husband really was somewhere else – alive. Maybe in Germany. Martha could remember denying that Martin was dead. It is only when you look down on a cold, empty face that you begin to accept death.

The pink Boxster followed Alex Randall's Ford out of the car park slowly, Mark Sullivan watching through the window.

"Well," he said, "what do you make of that?"

"I don't know," Martha answered slowly. "I just don't know. But . . . Do you remember one of the old Agatha Christies?"

"Which one? There were quite a few as I remember."

"By the pricking of my thumbs."

"Oh, yeah," he said. "I know the one. Something wicked this way comes."

9

So now they knew who the man was. He had a name, Gerald Bosworth, a wife, an identity. And, from Martha's point of view, they could proceed with the inquest.

Alex Randall rang her that evening, a little before eight. "Well," he said. "That was a weird business."

"I thought from here it would all be plain sailing."

"So did I," he said. "Instead I think I've got a whole host of other questions. There's something very fishy going on here, Martha."

Her curiosity was kicking in again. "Would you like to come round?"

"Would you mind? It's unburdening myself really. It isn't part of your – "

"I'm not doing anything special."

"Well, in that case I'll be with you in ten minutes."

This is the nice thing about Shrewsbury. It masquerades as a big, important, town. But this is half a fallacy. Important it certainly is. And not only to the people who live here. No fan of medieval buildings or ancient towns would deny it is that. But big it isn't. Despite the burgeoning housing estates, Gains Park, and so on, it is a village with delusions. It may have its own football ground, its own prison, the best hospital for miles around but it really is still a village. Nowhere in the town can be farther away than ten minutes. Provided the bridges are open and the traffic allowed to run freely. So she set up a tray of coffee things with a few biscuits, confident that Alex would be with her while the coffee was still hot.

He was. A few minutes later she heard his car crunch over the gravel and opened the front door. He was dressed casually in dark jeans and a navy sweater and looked tense.

There was a tightness around his eyes and mouth, and his forehead was lined with underlying worry. She hadn't realised the investigation would weigh so heavy on him.

She led him into the study. This seemed the appropriate room for him. This was not a social call. She poured the coffee while he settled himself in the one upholstered leather chair. Martin's chair.

Alex accepted a couple of biscuits and leaned right back, sprawling his long legs out in front of him, as Martin had not done in his last few months of life. She had not realised she had missed such a small thing.

"It was a rum do, Martha," he said finally. "Our Mrs Bosworth is a nervous woman. Eyes darting everywhere all the time we were taking a statement. Nearly jumped out of her skin when PC Coleman knocked on the door. Skittish as a cat."

"Well, take into account she's just found out her husband's been murdered and she may just know a little bit more about it than she wants to let on."

"I know. I know." His hand moved in front of him as though broadly taking this into account. "I realise this must have been an unbearable trauma for her. But it isn't the first time I've interviewed family who've just been confronted with tragedy. Grief I anticipate. But so much of my job is interviewing people who are trying their hardest to pretend they're innocent when they're not. And she reminded me of them." He was silent for a moment, frowning, his eyes moving around the room. "There was something in her manner. Something furtive." He seemed to feel the need to defend himself. "You know me, Martha. I'm a practical man. I hate 'instincts' and 'feelings', 'tingling of the toes' and . . ."

She smiled. " . . . pricking of the thumbs."

He looked up. Their eyes met. "Exactly. That is *exactly*

what I mean. But Freddie Bosworth was terrified. Believe me. And she acted as though she had a part to play. More like an actress than a wife who's just found out her husband's been murdered. This was something more. I swear she was very frightened we wouldn't believe her." He thought for a moment. "And when Coleman walked in she looked as though she was seeing a ghost. I thought she was going to collapse."

Something wormed its way into the back of her mind. "Have I met Coleman?"

"He was at the PM." Randall was puzzled but polite.

"Which one was he?"

"Dark hair. About six feet tall."

"And well-built," she finished.

Suddenly she could picture the scene. Freddie Bosworth in the interview room, Coleman walking in. For one fragment of an instant of a second, shadowed against the door.

For that moment Freddie Bosworth had thought it was her husband. But her husband was dead. And she'd just identified his corpse.

"Don't despise your instincts, Alex," she said firmly.

His face relaxed. "My sentiments exactly." He drank his coffee. "Guilty conscience." He held the cup up. "Nice coffee." He set his cup back down on the tray with a surprisingly dainty gesture and leaned back again in the chair, legs splayed. "If I've learnt anything in this job it is to stop believing statements. She says her husband had no enemies. It's bloody obvious he did. A knife through your left ventricle is hardly the work of a best friend."

"Mmm." She had to agree.

"I'm sure she's going to be the key to this affair but finding a chink in her armour is going to be difficult."

"Mmm," she said again. "So tell me a bit more about this Gerald man who makes his wife nervous even after he's dead. What was he supposed to be going to Hamburg for?"

"She describes him as a businessman. He imported cars, mainly from Germany, Holland, Belgium and Spain, all models. The prices are significantly cheaper there than here. It's a nice little earner."

Martha nodded. "When did she last see him?"

"On the Friday before he died – the eighth. He said he'd be away for ten days or so but apparently he often extended his business trips, roamed around the continent, meeting manufacturers and striking deals with them so she wasn't worried when she couldn't contact him."

"On his mobile?"

"It was switched off, she says, which is unusual. He's got a dual band phone but there are blind spots all over the place. She left messages. She says she last spoke to him on the Saturday and he'd told her he was in Hamburg, meeting up with clients and suppliers. We've had a printout from the phone company and no calls were made after Sunday afternoon. As far as they can make out his phone was switched off – or ran out of batteries – then and, surprise surprise, he wasn't in Germany but somewhere in the Midlands. Between Telford and the Welsh border."

"The handset itself?"

"Has disappeared."

"Is there any record of him flying?"

"He was booked on a flight from Heathrow to Hamburg on Friday but never checked in."

"Where are his offices?"

"Saltney. It's a couple of miles outside Chester towards Wales."

"And what do his local force have to say about him?"

"They had their suspicions that he was involved in some sort of tax fraud. Probably VAT avoidance. He could have been involved in drug smuggling. He made lots of trips abroad. Was known as a "flash" guy. Lived in a house patrolled by guard dogs. But they had nothing on him. He was either perfectly clean or clever."

"Or lucky."

"Well if he was lucky it finally ran out."

Alex continued "They were called there once. A domestic. *She'd* been beaten up. But, as is usual with these sorts of cases, she refused medical treatment and when it came to it declined to make a statement or press charges. They never heard from her again."

"How long ago was this?"

"About a year."

"Alex." She hesitated. He was a DI – well-versed in his job. He didn't need *her* to teach him how to 'suck eggs'. She had her own role to be getting on with. To satisfy the law that surrounds death, the relatives and her own conscience when it came to the inquest.

"Humphreys was in the car business too, wasn't he? Is there any evidence the two men knew each other?"

"On the surface no but we're looking into it. Gerald Bosworth didn't import Jaguars. They're in short supply abroad so there are none for the export market. Besides – there's little difference in the price you pay for a Jaguar over here and the continental price. It isn't *worth* importing them. If we could find a connection between the men – Humphreys and Bosworth – we'd at least have a start. After all, Bosworth died in Humphreys' house."

"Have you asked Freddie whether . . .?"

Randall nodded. "She denies knowing him." He frowned. "And oddly enough I would say she seemed to be telling the truth when she said she didn't know him, that she'd never met him."

"Mmm." Martha was silent for a while. Something was

tugging away in her mind.

Something to do with the river flooding. It had *diverted* events somehow. But she didn't know how. All she knew was when the river had altered its course it had changed events.

She stared out of the window at the black night. Wrapped in the river, this town was clinging on to its secrets. The body had been stowed in the cellar of Marine Terrace without the killer knowing its occupant would not be at home and that the river would flush it out. "Have you spoken to Sheelagh Mandershall again?"

"We've interviewed her twice – yes."

"What's she like?"

"A peroxide blonde. Early 40s. Well-dressed. Just a little plump. Watchful sharp eyes."

"I take it she vouches for James Humphreys."

"Oh, yes. She vouches for him all right. Says her lines like an actress. If what she says is the truth Humphreys was only in Marine Terrace for a few minutes. He could have stabbed Bosworth then but, according to Mark, Bosworth took a while to die. The cellar door wasn't locked. He could have stumbled outside onto the walkway. There were plenty of people milling around. Humphreys couldn't take the chance. Sheelagh assures us he would have finished work after four and that well before five he was with her. Sheelagh lives on the other side of the town. Humphreys' Jag was parked behind the *Lion & Pheasant*. He would have had to have walked to her house, which even at a brisk trot, would have taken forty minutes. He can't have done it unless they were in it together and she's covering for him. And I don't think her devotion runs quite that deep. He's still with his wife, after all. No. She and Humphreys were having a flirtation – an affair. It wouldn't have been a strong enough bond for them to share the secret of a murder."

She poured him a second cup of coffee and they drank companionably, yet she was aware their conversation skirted around their personal lives like a black hole. As the thought formed she looked up to see Alex Randall watching her. "I've had a copy made of the tape of Humphreys' questioning," he said, hesitating. "I don't suppose . . .?"

"I'd be very interested."

He'd brought a small tape recorder. There was a moment while he set it up then they both listened. She couldn't resist a smile. Humphreys' voice was unmistakably nasal – probably a result of his wife's revenge for his infidelity. Alex Randall's voice was calm and controlled. Detached and unemotional. It was obvious he was reading from a written set of questions. This was not unusual. These days forensic psychiatrists frequently directed the questioning. It saved precious time, gave the investigating officers an idea how to structure their queries to gain the greatest quantity of information and saved them from repeating themselves. The PACE clock ticked away inexorably no matter how close you were to a confession. Rules were rules.

The questions began innocuously enough. Name, address, everyday circumstances.

"Why did you decide to move to Shrewsbury?"

Some shuffling in the chair might indicate unease. "The garage where I worked in Slough lost the Jaguar franchise. We weren't making the sales so they pulled out. I knew someone in Shrewsbury."

"Would that be . . ." A pause while Randall must have been checking his facts, ". . .Mrs Mandershall?"

"No. Someone else."

"Another woman, Sir?" Randall was finding it hard to keep mockery – contempt – out of his voice.

"Yes, for your information. She was a secretary I'd worked with in Slough. She'd moved away some time ago. Anyway, she heard about our garage losing the franchise and told me there would be a vacancy for a sales manager in Shrewsbury. I applied and got the job. I wasn't sure my wife would want to move." The emphasis he put on the word 'want' was interesting. Randall picked up on it too.

"Why wouldn't she . . . want to move down here?"

"We've got children. Two girls. They're in a local school. A good one. It's a big thing to uproot teenagers. They weren't going to be keen. I wanted to be sure."

"And were you?"

A pause. Humphreys must have caught the sarcasm in Randall's voice. His rejoinder was quieter, more humble. At last Randall was penetrating the armour and finding the real man. "As far as the town was concerned I love the place. As far as bringing the family up well – "

The silence was so long Martha glanced at the tape recorder. It was still running.

"How did you find the house in Marine Terrace?" Alex's voice again.

"Through an estate agent."

"Did he warn you it was prone to flooding?"

"Only the cellars."

Martha smiled. An estate agent was hardly going to advertise the fact that the property had a problem.

"You didn't mind about that?"

"It didn't seem a problem. I wasn't going to use the cellars." Some of Humphreys' confidence had leaked back into his voice. Martha knew he had *wanted* to answer this question.

There was another brief pause before Alex's voice broke in. "Tell me about the weekend of the 9th and 10th of February."

"All right." Said resignedly. "I was at work all day Saturday and Sunday. It's busy at the weekends. I finished after four. Takes a bit of time to lock up, set the alarms, put the cars away. You know. I got stuck in traffic. Couldn't get near my house. I could see the river was rising fast. Police around. I left my car at the local pub. I've got an agreement with the landlord. I went into the house just to change into something more casual, pick up a toothbrush and things and I walked straight round to Sheelagh's." There was a defensive note in his voice. Maybe he had anticipated the disapproval from the detective. Martha heard a little click of annoyance from Alex Randall and knew he was bored with domestics, with infidelity, with James Humphreys' sordid little story. It wasn't interesting to her either.

"I was in the house less than ten minutes. I didn't have time to murder anyone." *Mark Sullivan had said it had taken Bosworth some time to die.* There was desperation in Humphreys' voice. He was pleading to be believed.

"Did you notice whether the cellar door was open or closed?"

"Closed. I'm sure. I checked. There was a bloody big bluebottle buzzing around the place and I worried I was going to get infested with the things flying up from the cellars – what with all the flooding and that. So I particularly made sure. Thought I'd have to get some fly spray in. On Tuesday there was the floods and everything was chaos. And then you lot got hold of me." A pause before he added. "My wife. . . She imagined . . ." She imagined him, hand up to rub his nose.

"Did you know the dead man?"

"I don't know why you ask me the same question more than once." Truculence was edging into Humphreys' voice now. He had the upper hand. That meant none of the questions had grazed him. "The answer's the same however many times you try and shock me, ask me, question me, try to bully me."

Alex – patiently. "No one is trying to bully you, Mr Humphreys. We're just trying to encourage you to help us. A man was murdered in the house you rent and we're anxious to find out who killed him. That's all." Again Martha smiled to herself. She could picture Alex's deliberate, exaggerated, patronising calm. He switched the tape off and looked across at her.

"Well?"

"I have a picture of him. He doesn't *sound* guilty so much as bemused. As though he can't believe what's happening to him. Almost as though he really is an innocent victim."

"Well, in a way he was. If he's telling the truth, somebody must have killed Bosworth before or after he went home to change. And then of course," Alex couldn't resist a smirk, "there's the swipe taken by his wife at him."

"He earned that one. Nothing innocent about that."

"No – but if you saw him now."

The Scream *flashed through her mind*. "I have," she said shortly. "I have seen him. He walked across the bridge in the other direction to me." Randall was looking at her enquiringly. "It was silly," she said. "He spooked me. But I suppose you're right. He did look a victim." *As did the woman in* The Scream. *Overwhelmed by anxiety and tensions, neurotic, paranoid terror*. "You don't think he did it?" Randall shook his head. Regretfully. "And I don't suppose Haddonfield's turned up?" Another shake of his head. "I have a feeling we won't ever have an answer to that particular mystery.

She refilled his cup. "I suppose we'd better set a date to open the inquest on Mr Bosworth," she said. "I shall want to speak to Frederica. I'll get Jericho to contact her in the morning. She'll want to arrange the funeral." Alex nodded. He left at ten-thirty, still looking troubled.

10

The next morning she drew out the post mortem report on Gerald Bosworth and studied it in detail, hoping she could learn something new from Mark's information. Under the heading of Shrewsbury Central Pathology laboratory, the date and time, the first entry:

Autopsy on: unidentified male. Address, date of birth.

At the time of the PM all this had been left blank. It was only recently that Gerald Bosworth's details had been filled in. Martha cupped her chin in her hand and stared into space. Why had there been no ID on Bosworth? No wallet, credit cards, mobile phone, chequebook. In fact no documentation at all. *Why had he been dressed in Humphreys' suit and not his own clothes?*

She sipped her coffee, trying to answer her own questions. The identity of the victim often leads to the discovery of the killer but none of the usual steps had been taken to conceal it – apart from the empty pockets. The body hadn't been hidden, at least, not effectively. Although you could argue that it had only been found through the intervention of the river. Martha shook her head. That wouldn't really do. The cellar door hadn't been bolted or locked. Apart from the removal of personal effects and the switching of the clothes the killer hadn't tried to prevent identification by obliterating Bosworth's features or removing his fingerprints. There had been no attempt to destroy the body – even to weight it and dump it in the swollen river. She took another sip of coffee, thoughtfully, and tried to imagine herself in the part of the killer.

Perhaps he had been disturbed by the rising river before he had had time to complete his plans. Whatever they were. Perhaps he had considered sinking the body in the river, but had been prevented by the presence of the police and other emergency services. Depending on when he had committed the crime. Probably after Humphreys had called in after work and left. He had possibly seen Humphreys emerging from Marine Terrace and opportunistically used the empty property. After all, the police had said it would have been easy to gain entry.

She put the mug back on the desk, her mind still busy. She'd been a coroner for a number of years and she could never remember a mix-up like this where women had twice been summoned wrongly in the hope of identifying what had been assumed were their husbands. One mistake was very, very unusual in this age-group. Teenagers were more common. She had frequently dealt with the parents of runaways who had shaken their heads, partly in relief that this was not their errant offspring, and partly in puzzlement over their actual fate. But she had never before witnessed the fiasco of mistaken identity over a man of Bosworth's age. It was strange. More than strange. Almost a sick joke which had, in turn, led to a double farce. She recalled Alex's account of Cressida Humphreys' expression as she had denied that the corpse was her husband. And the fiasco had been repeated when Lindy Haddonfield had also shaken her head. The same emotions. Mirrored. And finally Freddie Bosworth had identified the man. Her eyes slipped out of focus. So many thoughts were racing round *her* mind:

How much of a part had the rising river played in the three-act-farce? Aid or hindrance or had it made no real difference? Had the killer *utilised* the property emptied by the flood or had the waters *foiled* his plans either by exposing the body early or bringing the property to the attention of the authorities? After all – it had been the police who had discovered Gerald Bosworth. Had

Coleman not pushed open the door of the property, Bosworth would have remained undiscovered for a while longer. What difference would there have been had the Severn not played Joker? What would have happened if Humphreys had been home? Would Bosworth *still* have died? What had he been doing there, anyway? Waiting for Humphreys?

Her mind fixed on just one of the facts. Bosworth's body had been hidden in the cellar. No one would leave a cellar door open to a living room in February. Particularly when the cellar was damp and beneath the level of a flooding river. So almost certainly the cellar door had been closed but not properly latched and the force of water had pushed it open. Otherwise Humphreys might not have discovered the body until the scent of putrefaction alerted him. Unless he had innocently had occasion to visit the cellar, which he denied. Then what? Well, surely he would have told the police. It was a blind ending.

So Martha's mind tracked along another path. Why had Bosworth come to Shrewsbury? To meet Humphreys? Had there been a connection between the two men? She finished her coffee and sat, motionless. Something was stirring.

She continued searching the PM report. If anyone should be capable of discerning evidence from this cold, clinical document, she should. After all – she read post mortem reports all the time. She was well-used to the jargon. If there was evidence to tease from the corpse Mark Sullivan would have done it. And she should be able to read it.

Appearance: Well-nourished, muscular male.
Apparent age: early forties
Body weight: 82 Kg Rigor Mortis partly dispersed
Apparent sex: Male. Crown-heel length: 6ft1inch.

Crown-rump length: Blank

Hypostasis: Dorsal, Purple.

External features:- Well-nourished middle-aged man with gaping 2 centimetres wound, one centimetre below left nipple. Evidence of post mortem wounds on face, lower limbs consistent with contact injury. One centimetre circular contusion over mid-line of sternum.

Consistent with Bosworth's body bumping on the cellar steps and against the cellar wall.

There was a lot of other detail in the report, largely irrelevant but legally required, relating to the state of Bosworth's general health – lymph nodes, muscles, skeleton, skull circumference and so on. Largely normal. Martha's eyes skipped to the words beneath the heading, heart. Penetrating knife wound to the left ventricle causing leakage of blood into the pericardium, causing cardiac tamponade.

At the bottom of the page: Cause of death.

In my opinion the cause of death was:

1. a) shock, due to
   b) loss of circulatory blood due to
   c) cardiac tamponade due to
   d) penetrating wound to the left ventricle.

She stopped reading. As far as forensic pathology was concerned it was a well-done, efficient post mortem report. But it was such an incomplete picture. The wound had been skilfully or luckily inflicted. She knew it was not up to the pathologist to make stabs at the facts, merely to report the clinical findings but, even so, she was disappointed. What was missing was how long had it taken Bosworth to die. The reason it was missing was because a pathologist could only guess at the answer. No one knew – except the killer.

So had this killer sat and calmly waited for Bosworth to

die from the fatal stab wound? Had his victim tried to call out? To summon help? How weakened had he been by the initial blow? For how long had he remained conscious? And where? The cellar or elsewhere in the house? How had his murderer prevented him from escaping? Forcefully?

Jericho had thoughtfully attached more details. Deceased identified on March 7th by his wife as Gerald Bosworth aged 42 of 16 Gawton's Way, Chester.

She sat and did nothing for a minute. Then she picked up the phone.

It was time to speak to Frederica Bosworth. A man answered with an ever-so-slight Liverpool accent. When she asked to speak to Mrs Bosworth he asked politely who was speaking. She explained and there was a brief pause. Then Freddie spoke with a tentative, "Yeah?".

Martha reintroduced herself, realising as she did so that Bosworth's widow had no recollection of her at all. "We'd like to set a date for the inquest on your husband's death," she began and went on to explain that it would be a formality, would be adjourned pending police enquiries, but would enable the funeral to go ahead. She would be able to release the body for burial.

"Oh."

There was an awkward pause so Martha continued. "I wondered if there were any questions you'd like to ask me."

Freddie's response was confused. "Like what?"

"Sometimes relatives want to try and understand the circumstances surrounding their loved one's death." She paused. "It can help them to grieve."

She waited for some response to give her a clue how to proceed.

"All I want," Freddie Bosworth said fiercely, "is for you

to catch the bastard what did it. He was a good bloke, my Gerald." The line went quiet. "Not perfect – I grant you. But he didn't deserve that."

Martha made an expression of sympathy.

"What's the purpose of the inquest?"

"Simply to state who has died, when, where and how."

"So what's the point of it then?" Truculent now. "It's bloody obvious who's died. I've identified him. We know when and where he died. And as for how. Someone stuck a knife into his heart. I take it you're not going to make any contribution to find out *who* stuck the knife in so I can't really see the point of your involvement. Thanks very much. But no thanks."

"The inquest is a formal, legal requirement," Martha said icily. "It is *not* a police enquiry. It *will* take place whether you can see the point or not, Mrs Bosworth. In fact, usually relatives welcome it."

"Oh." Freddie sounded mystified. "All right then."

"We'll keep you informed."

"Thanks." She could have been acknowledging a mail order delivery. "But that's just what the police say. Trouble is there's nothin' to really tell me, is there?"

Martha put the phone down in a fury. She would let Jericho liaise with the woman and the police to set a suitable date for the inquest. He could organise her diary.

Martha had a pile of work to do but she couldn't shift her mind back into gear. It was stuck in the Gerald Bosworth groove, spinning round and round like a broken record. She felt fidgety and restless. It felt like very unfinished business. She dialled Oswestry Police and asked to be connected with the Senior Officer investigating the disappearance of Clarke Haddonfield. After a lengthy pause she was put through to a woman. "Hello, I'm Detective Inspector Wendy Aitken. I understand you wish to talk to me about Clarke Haddonfield's disappearance." The voice was brisk and not inviting.

Martha introduced herself and began by asking how the investigation was going. Wendy Aitken's voice changed. "Not very well, I'm afraid, Coroner. We've spoken to the van driver on numerous occasions as he was apparently the last person to see Haddonfield alive. We've shown him photographs and so on but he couldn't positively identify Clarke. He hardly looked at the guy he picked up. It was dark and rainy. He needed to concentrate on the road. Added to that Haddonfield had his coat collar pulled right up around his face. Our driver had the radio on and Haddonfield didn't speak much apart from into the phone. Watkins, the van driver, claims he deliberately didn't listen in to the conversation because he assumed Haddonfield was speaking to his wife. We've put a board up on the A5 appealing for people with information to ring in but as yet we've got nothing. In fact we've drawn a complete blank. We've had the SOCOs clean the cab out for DNA, blood, hair – anything really – and drawn another blank. Looks like Watkins often picked up hitchhikers on their way through to Wales. There's an absolute wealth of forensic evidence but nothing that takes us straight to back to Clarke Haddonfield."

"I take it the van driver's clean."

"As a newborn baby. He hasn't even had a speeding ticket in the last fifteen years."

Martha was frowning into the phone. *When did innocence become suspicious?* "Haddonfield was dropped off by a service station. Didn't anyone there see anything?"

DI Wendy Aitken gave a loud, hopeless sigh. "It's as though the elements conspired against us. Everyone in the service station was busy doing their own thing. Reading the paper, buying sweets, paying for petrol. It was chucking it down with rain and, of course, very dark. The cashier *thinks* she *might* have seen a lorry drop someone off but she isn't sure. She half remembers someone sheltering under the tree but didn't take much notice and she couldn't tell us anything other than that if she *was* right and there was someone sheltering underneath the tree he *must* have been picked up later because she didn't notice anyone there at nine o'clock when she finished her duty. And of course to add to everything traffic was heavy that night."

"What was the van like?"

"Big, white, eighteen hundredweight, long wheel base."

"Any markings on the side?"

"No," DI Aitken said crisply. "Original white van man with no distinguishing features."

"What was in it?"

"Car spares."

"Taking them to where?"

"Watkins Garage. Great big place on the A5. Family business – does MOTs, services, tyres, silencers. All perfectly above-board. My granny's got more to hide than they have. It was the Watkins' son, Evan, who picked up our hitchhiker and dropped him off. He says he did offer to take the man all the way home as the weather was so foul but he was refused. Apparently Haddonfield assured him his wife would be along in a matter of minutes. The last he saw of him he was sheltering underneath a tree. Watkins drove off and never saw him again."

"A public-spirited guy," Martha commented. "I don't suppose for a second that Watkins knew Haddonfield already, did he?"

"No. They weren't acquainted. I'm convinced he's speaking the truth."

"You've interviewed *Mrs* Haddonfield again?"

"Lindy – yes – again and again. She sticks to her story

that her husband did not ring her after lunchtime on Monday. Neither did he arrive home on Monday night. She claims she didn't get a phone call to go and pick him up. What's more, I believe her. I don't think a call was put through to her. The whole business is extraordinary and a bit of a brainteaser. I don't know where he's gone. I mean – the obvious answer is some sort of parallel life. Not a wife but a mistress whom he phoned and picked him up." She gave a short, huffy laugh. "And window cleaners do have a bit of a reputation."

"So?"

"I haven't unearthed anything like that. He was a bit of a jack of all trades. Lots of fingers in lots of little pies – and from his bank statements I don't think any of them made any money but there's nothing sinister there. Just poor judgement."

"His mobile phone printout?"

"According to our records he didn't have one. We think it was a pay-as-you-go and not registered in his name."

"So what's your impression?"

"Nothing concrete, I'm afraid, Coroner. Only very vague ideas. But I do get the impression that Lindy Haddonfield isn't *too* worried about her husband's disappearance. In fact she seems quite relaxed about the whole affair."

"Do they have children?"

"No." DI Aitken laughed. "Lindy's a bit of a glamourpuss. A beautician at a big hotel not far from her home. Not exactly the earth mother type."

"Isn't she?" Martha toyed with the idea for a minute or two, teasing it as a cat does a ball of wool. There seemed to be plenty of glamorous women hovering on the edge of the lives of three men. Gerald Bosworth's wife was a babe who drove a flashy sports car. She wondered what

Cressida Humphreys was like.

"Have you considered trying to take the van driver back both physically and mentally?"

"Well, we've driven him on the road between Shrewsbury and Oswestry more than once, getting him to pick out various landmarks. As for mentally. You mean hypnosis?"

"Yes. I just wonder if under relaxation Watkins might be encouraged to recall the Monday night, driving out of Shrewsbury on the bypass. When he decided to pick Haddonfield up he must have seen him quite clearly in his headlights. It's that image that will have imprinted."

"Mmm?" DI Aitken sounded sceptical.

"If you do happen to consider that line and record any conversation I'd be very interested to listen to what Watkins has to say."

"All right."

"Is that a yes?"

Wendy Aitken laughed. She had a nice laugh, high-pitched and cheerful. "More of a maybe. *Maybe* it is worth a try. We have been liaising with the Shrewsbury force to try and stage a reconstruction but we've shelved the idea for the moment. We consider the information appeal boards are probably more appropriate and may well be more productive."

"Fine. I wish you luck in your search."

"It won't be luck that solves this case," Wendy Aitken said soberly. "It's going to be good, old-fashioned policing." There was a brief pause during which Martha had the impression Wendy Aitken was gathering a question. "Do you mind me asking, Coroner, what is your interest in this?" Her laugh was embarrassed. "I mean, Haddonfield isn't dead. He's just missing. It's a puzzle but there aren't any disturbing features. He isn't old or vulnerable. He's just gone walkabout. I know you probably have heightened concerns because in Shrewsbury you've had a murder. But Haddonfield's disappearance is unconnected. I'm sure."

Martha wished she could agree with her. "To be honest, Detective Inspector, I don't know whether the two events are separate or connected. Put my interest down to feminine curiosity and a long nose. Haddonfield disappeared from the same town the very night after Bosworth was murdered and that seems a hefty coincidence."

"Which you don't believe in."

Martha squirmed. "Put it like this," she said, "I have yet to be convinced."

"I see."

"There is just one last thing. How did the van driver know it was Haddonfield?"

"He introduced himself. They shook hands." *And that, in itself, seemed strange. Or else it was her heightened sensitivity that made ordinary events seem odd. Like a man walking across a bridge, speaking into a mobile phone. How much less suspicious can normal behaviour appear?*

Martha put the phone down, still dissatisfied. Haddonfield had had his collar pulled up around his face. Why? He had been in the warmth and comfort of a van by then with no need to wrap his face up, other than to conceal his features and maybe muffle his telephone conversation.

Why had he refused the offer of being dropped off at his own home? The van driver had been obliging. It had been a filthy night. It would have saved Lindy from being dragged out into the rain. It would be more normal to have accepted Watkins' offer of a lift to the door. *Unless, as Wendy Aitken had suggested, he wasn't intending to go home.*

Why had he waited underneath a tree instead of inside the service station? His wife could have picked him up just as easily from inside the shop. It would have been warm and dry in there. She wondered whether they would ever know the whole truth.

In her mind she was asking the real question. Did Haddonfield have any connection with the murder at Marine Terrace? Or was it pure coincidence that he had vanished so soon after the murder? Was he simply a man who had not wished to go home to his wife? *Why get dropped off in his home town then?*

Or was he a killer?

The telephone broke into her thoughts, Jericho's pedestrian voice asking her if she would mind speaking again to Frederica Bosworth.

"Put her through."

She glanced around her office at the huge photograph of the twins, laughing into the camera. They had been three years old, even then as dissimilar as it was possible for twins to be. Martin was between them – looking tired and ill. It had been the era of tests which had all proved the same thing. The time had been one of desperate hope, weeks before the final, terrible realisation that these two beautiful children would never know their father. You could see the pain in Martin's eyes, the tight, bony fingers clinging to the son and daughter they had named with such fun, optimism and joy, Sukey and Sam Gunn.

Frederica's harsh twang interrupted her thoughts. "I'm awful sorry to bother you like this. Specially when we've already spoke like."

"That's all right, Mrs Bosworth. It's what I'm here for."

There was the sound of a dry sniff into a handkerchief. "Only I want to get on with the funeral and the police said

I would have to talk to you. Gerald was anxious to be cremated, you see. He was frightened of bein' buried alive. Had quite a phobia about it, actually, so I promised him. When you go, I said, I'll make sure you're roasted. It was a sort of pact. If it was me went first – although I knew that was unlikely, me bein' younger and all that. Anyway if it had of been me first he would have had me roasted. Know what I mean?"

"I do," Martha said quietly, "but there's a problem." The line went quiet. Martha almost wondered whether Frederica was still there.

"What do you mean there's a problem?" Her voice was shrill now.

"In cases of violent death we don't allow cremation."

"Why not? What do you mean, don't allow?"

Martha always hated having to explain this one. "Because," she began reluctantly, "sometimes there is doubt – challenge through the courts – and we need to review the forensic evidence."

"Dig 'im up?" Freddie shrieked. "I can't allow that."

"Mrs Bosworth – I'm sorry. I'm really, truly sorry but you don't have the right to refuse."

"I don't believe this." Her voice was almost screaming. "Me own husband? I'm takin' this to my MP. To the European Courts of Human Rights. The papers. See if I don't."

"Mrs Bosworth, it won't do you any good. It's the law."

"I don't believe you."

"If you'd like to come in and discuss it. . ."

"Not with you I won't. Bloody ghoul." She slammed the phone down.

Martha stared into space. This was an interesting turn of events. The question was – was Freddie Bosworth speaking the truth when she said her husband had expressed a wish to be cremated? Or did she have some other reason for wanting his remains so totally and completely destroyed. Leaving no DNA trace. No dental records. No final evidence or proof of identity at all?

11

Martha scanned the papers over the next few days half expecting Freddie Bosworth to have fuelled some tabloid sensation –

Ghoulish coroner threatens to exhume body – before it's even buried!

Or

Martha Gunn, Resurrection Woman, refuses right to cremation.

And all the time she was wondering about Haddonfield too and searched the pages for reference to him, wondering if his body had been found or if he had been spotted living it up with a blonde in the south of Spain, or even that he had been found suffering from amnesia in the general ward of a hospital. Anything other than this strange silence. It confused her.

She half expected another contact from Frederica Bosworth about the release of her husband's body for burial or querying some detail about his death but again the wires stayed silent. So she continued with her job and set the date of the inquest, Wednesday March 13th.

She waited a whole week before contacting Alex Randall to ask him how the investigation was progressing. It wasn't part of her duties to sit on the shoulders of the Senior Investigating Officers and the last thing she wanted to do was to inhibit him. But finally she caved in to her curiosity and dialled Monkmoor Police Station. She was soon put through and could sense, within seconds, that the case was no nearer solution now than it had been when Bosworth's body had surprised PC Coleman. She told him the date of the inquest, knowing that Jericho would already have informed him. "I'm trying to ascertain the answers to some basic questions."

"Such as?" She could hear the depression in his voice. And could sympathise. It must be a fearful thought, that you might fail to discover who had committed this worst of crimes.

"Well – for a start – was he killed in Marine Terrace?"

"We *think* so."

Sometimes the easiest of questions proved almost unanswerable. Who, when, how and where.

Randall continued. "I've spent a lot of time discussing the case with Sullivan. He's of the opinion that once the fatal wound had been inflicted it wouldn't have been possible to move Bosworth far. Certainly it would have caused attention had he been outside the cottage. Staggering. Of the appearance of having been assaulted. And remember the emergency services were hovering around from Sunday afternoon. Plenty of people were watching the river."

"So it's more likely that the fatal wound was inflicted when Bosworth was in the sitting room?"

"Again, Coroner, we think so. It seems unlikely that he would have allowed himself to be lured to the cellar."

Except, perhaps, on the grounds of watching the flood waters rise through the porthole window?

"Was there no sign of a struggle in the room?" She pictured the small, square room, tiny nine-paned windows, sparsely furnished. Coffee table. Dead centre. Two armchairs. Television set. There had hardly been space to stumble and fall.

"No."

"Have you found any connection between Bosworth and James Humphreys?"

"Again no."

"And Haddonfield? Has he turned up?"

"No sign of him according to Oswestry police."

She thanked him, asked that he keep her informed of any developments and rang Mark Sullivan, hearing the same tiredness echoing in his voice although his greeting was polite and formal.

"I just wanted to clarify in my mind some details as to Bosworth's injuries."

"Anything in particular."

"Yes – the bruises to his legs."

"Ah." *It was as though she had homed in on something he had been chewing over himself.*

"In your opinion were they the result of the body being bumped down the steps or of the water shifting him around?"

"Almost certainly they're the result of the body being bumped down the steps. He was quite a big man, remember. Even for another relatively well built man his would have been a dead weight to move." *It was an unfortunate phrase.*

"Would you mind just taking me through the reasoning behind this conclusion?"

" 'Course not." His voice was warming. "The bruises were on the sacrum, the backs of the legs, calves and thighs and some definite quite severe post mortem injuries to his occiput. These injuries are more consistent with the body being grabbed by the heels and bumped down the cellar steps than of a body floating face downwards making contact with the walls. Or of a tumble. In that case the injuries would have had different distribution. Forearms, shoulders, etcetera. It isn't only the positioning of the injuries, Martha. It's the severity of them. Besides – even though the cellar was completely flooded we have recovered some hair and blood from the surfaces of the stone steps. The marks match some of the indentations. There was a lot of wear on the actual steps. They were worn with the feet of two centuries. The edge of the steps were rounded rather than sharp."

"And the injuries in relation to the time of death?" she asked delicately.

"Around the time of death or just after. There was a little bruising around some of the lesions, none on others." *He didn't need to spell it out.*

"And what about the circular contusion on his sternum?"

A long sigh. "I haven't worked that one out yet. It was done earlier than the other wounds. I think he was sort of shoved with something small and blunt. Almost poked."

The scene was vivid in front of eyes. The killing had been merciless. A 'shove' in the middle of the chest, an incisive strike to the heart. A dying man's body being bumped down stone steps to a flooding cellar. It was an ugly picture. She squeezed her eyes shut and said her goodbye.

Now she was left contemplating.

It was a week before the inquest, a blustery dry day when the daffodils were forced to kowtow to the fierce winds of March, that at last some progress seemed to be made. Martha had spent an exhausting half hour talking to the widow of a man who had died on the operating table while the surgeons were battling to save him from a ruptured aortic aneurism. It had proved a futile exercise. The surgeons had lost the battle and the widow was left bereft and puzzled. Martha had done her best to explain to the elderly woman and her angry middle-aged son why exactly her husband had died. The son was inclined to blame an incompetent surgeon and no matter how plainly or how simply she explained that this was not the case he had persisted, furiously accusing her of a cover up.

She felt drained after the bereaved relatives had left. Tired and depressed. She may be a doctor but she never would condone negligence or incompetence in any profession, particularly her own. Besides, her role specifically forbade any such opinions. But people these days felt the need to blame someone for death. God no longer fitted the bill so doctors caught it in the neck. They were the scapegoats. Mortality was now their fault, the ultimate failure of a mistrusted profession. And the price was high. The increase in litigation was strangling the Health Service. Obstetricians no longer delivered babies. Surgeons were bordering on dangerous caution, delaying tricky surgery – or not performing operations which might sully their success ratio. Doctors were afraid to speak the truth, to take risks, to allow people to die. The notes of hospital patients were now not only signed by a doctor's name but with his Medical Defence Union number. This, in one swoop, illustrated the depths to which the medical profession was reduced. One day, she mused to herself, cupping her chin in her hands and staring out across the Shropshire plains towards the great lump of the Wrekin, the Health Service would have money to pay for nothing except lawyers to represent their employees against the 'ambulance-chasers' so disliked by Health Service employees.

A phone call from DI Wendy Aitken was a welcome interruption. DI Aitken was brisk and wasted no time on preambles. "Doctor Gunn. You made a suggestion when we last spoke and I took it up. We've interviewed the van driver, Evan Watkins, again, under a light hypnosis. The results were interesting. We've recorded them. I wondered if I might bring them over and discuss them with you?"

"That'd be great." Had she known DI Wendy Aitken better she might have added, "I'll put the kettle on." But it wasn't that type of acquaintance.

The phone call had achieved two things. It had snapped her out of the morass of introspection about litigation. And it had rekindled her interest in the Marine Terrace case. She busied herself with some papers and waited for Wendy Aitken to arrive.

12

Wendy Aitken arrived at half past three, almost quivering with excitement, hovering behind Jericho who ushered her in with his customary deadpan expression. The door had hardly closed behind him when she slapped a small cassette on Martha's desk. "I'm sure you'll be interested in *this*, Doctor Gunn." There was more than a hint of triumph in her voice.

Martha poured them both a cup of coffee and sat down, crossing her legs, comfortable in her short black skirt, low-heeled pumps and a fine grey sweater as soft as moleskin. Her favourite.

DI Aitken hardly paused to sip the coffee. "I've spoken already to Alex Randall and he's on his way over. I hope you don't mind."

"No." If anything Martha was slightly amused. She found the detective's enthusiasm endearing. "That's fine."

"I should explain. After you made your suggestion I discussed the possibility of hypnosis with my Detective Chief Superintendant. He was keen on the idea – provided Watkins was willing to co-operate." Martha nodded. "We had guidance from a clinical psychologist who suggested the route we should take to provide the best chance of finding out something Watkins' subconscious knew but his conscious mind was unaware of. So – under his guidance – we carried out the exercise in three stages. First of all we subjected Watkins to light hypnosis – simply to relax him, chatted about his work, his home and so on. Then we asked him to recount the events of Monday night, February 11th. Finally we asked him, still in a very relaxed state, to look at some photographs."

"And?"

Wendy held her hands out, smiling, her face relaxed and merry. Haddonfield had been missing for a month. She must have unearthed something. "I'm not playing with you, Doctor Gunn, I promise." There was something of the tease about her. "But I think you'll understand that if we work in sequence – as we did when we questioned Watkins – you'll have a better picture. You'll understand it." She suffered a swift bout of anxiety. "Is that all right?"

Martha shrugged. "Whatever."

Aitken slotted the tape into a player and sat back while Martha concentrated.

"Your name is?" *Wendy Aitken's voice first.*

"Evan Watkins." The voice was calm, monotonic. A flat line.

Wendy leaned across the desk to whisper. "We used open-ended questions. Nothing leading, you understand, Coroner? The psychologist told us what we should ask, the correct wording." Obviously an enthusiast of psychology, she settled back in her chair.

Again Martha nodded her comprehension.

"On the night of Monday, February 11th, you were driving?"

"From Shrewsbury . . . (He used the Welsh annunciation of the town to rhyme with shoes) . . . back towards Llangollen."

"Which is where you live?"

"Yes – and work. I got a garage, you see."

"Tell me about the weather that night, Evan?"

"It was a foul night. Pissin' down with rain." There was no apology for the Anglo Saxon. Watkins was too relaxed for that.

"At what time did you leave Shrewsbury?" Wendy Aitken mirroring the way he said it.

"Just before six. I was worried, you see. The river was

rising. I thought the bridges might get cut off or maybe floodin' on the A5 so I didn't stay. Once I'd picked up my stuff I left."

"Did you see anyone on the road?"

"I saw a few people."

"Did you pick anyone up?"

"Yes. There was a hitchhiker standing just after the island. Soaking he was. I pulled up, threw the door open and he climbed in." There was a pause.

"What does this man look like?" She was shifting gear as well as tense.

And now Watkins was mirroring her, matching his answers to the questions. The descent to re-enter the past was complete.

"He's wearing a long raincoat, black, the collar pulled right up to his chin. He's quite tall. Taller than me."

Wendy leaned across to whisper again. "Evan's about five-five."

Watkins was still talking. "He's quite slim. Dark hair, I think. Tidy. Not really the sort to be hitchhiking.

"'Where you going, pal?' He's staring at me. Not very friendly-like. 'Look,' I says. 'Do you want a lift or not?'

'I'd like that very much.' Nice voice. Well spoken. Soft."

Aitken leaned across to speak again. "Remember. Haddonfield was a *window cleaner.*"

"'Where are you heading?'"

It was eerie, hearing the recorded conversation between a missing man and the van driver, the last man to see him before he vanished. With or without a puff of smoke.

"'Oswestry.'

'Right then' I says. 'Hop in. I'll take you there.' He does that – hops in. Holds out his hand. 'Haddonfield', he says. 'Clarke Haddonfield.' I shake it. Soft voice. Soft hand too."

"A window cleaner," Aitken reminded her again.

"'So what are you doing out, walking, on a night so wet?'

'Car got stuck in Shrewsbury. They've closed the bridge, haven't they? Can't get my car out.'" It struck Martha then that the reason the reported conversation had such impact was because when Evan Watkins recounted the words of the hitchhiker he altered his accent subtly from his native North Walean. While his contribution to the conversation was unmistakably Borders, Wales or The Marches, the person he had spoken to had had an English accent.

She glanced across at Wendy Aitken to see what the detective made of this. But of course, she was investigating the disappearance of Clarke Haddonfield. Her perspective was from a local angle. It was only Martha who knew that Bosworth was from Chester.

Aitken's voice cut in on the tape. "Would you describe the man to me?"

"Dark eyes. Can't see much of his mouth. Collar in the way. Heavy eyebrows."

"Go on, Evan," she prompted. "Carry on with your story."

Immediately Watkins' voice changed. "'Whereabouts in Oswestry do you want dropping?' He's vague. 'At the service station.'

'Which one?'

'The one on the A5.'

'Oh – you mean Jarvis's.'

'That's the one. Jarvis's. BP.' I'm quiet for a bit. He's talking on the phone, you see. Sounds like he's telling his wife – or someone – that he's been picked up and is on his way back. I cut in, 'I'll take you home if you like, Mr Haddonfield. The weather's awful. You'll get soaked.'

'No. No,' he's saying part to me, part into the phone. 'Don't you worry about that. You just drop me off at the roundabout services. There's a tree on the verge. I can stand under that. My wife will pick me up.'

'No need,' I says. 'Don't drag her out on a night like this.'

'I'd like to drag her out, so drop me off at the tree.'"

The tape was silent although still whirring. Even though this was reported speech it was as though Haddonfield himself had spoken. A sharp rap of an order hiding behind venom worthy of a superbitch.

Wendy's voice again. "Then what happened, Evan?"

"I'm feeling a bit uncomfortable now. Don't quite know what to say. He starts talking into his mobile phone again. I turn the radio down so he can hear. "

"What is he saying?"

"He's talkin' very low. I can't quite hear him. I keep lookin' at him but he's quiet now. Puts the phone back in his pocket. Ten minutes later I see the tree by the roundabout. He jumps out, pulls his collar right up. 'Thanks,' he says. I drive off, watching him in my mirror. Just standing."

Wendy Aitken leaned forward and flicked the off switch. Martha watched her, puzzled. There was nothing there.

There was a knock on the door. It was Alex Randall, hesitating in the doorway. Wendy bounced up and introduced herself.

"We've been listening to the tape," Martha said, "of Evan Watkins' account of picking up the hitchhiker and taking him from Shrewsbury to Oswestry."

Wendy Aitken still had that same, confident smile. "This will interest you, Inspector Randall," she said, pulling out a cellophane file from her briefcase. She laid a photograph on the table, flicking it down as though she was producing an ace. A man in an England t-shirt, pint of lager in his hand, arm wrapped around a blonde, huge grin. He was toasting the picture-taker.

"I showed this photograph to Watkins," she said. "He couldn't be absolutely positive about it but he doesn't think this is the guy he picked up that night."

Randall and Martha stared.

"Which is very strange," she carried on seamlessly. "Because this is a recent photograph of Clarke Haddonfield."

13

The three of them simply gawped at each other for a few minutes.

Martha spoke first. "This is such a complex case," she said to both of them. "In fact my head's reeling. I'm only glad I'm not investigating it. But if it wasn't Clarke Haddonfield in the cab that night who on earth was it? Where is he and what connection does the man impersonating Haddonfield have with Gerald Bosworth? Or with James Humphreys for that matter." Randall moved forward as though to speak but she interrupted him. "I don't think Humphreys is *quite* out of the picture yet. Well – I suppose you two are simply going to have to work together. And in some ways start all over again."

Alex and DI Aitken both nodded. They were slowly adjusting to new facts, asking themselves other questions. Who had climbed into the cab that night?

"I thought it seemed a bit obvious introducing himself," Aitken said. "I mean – you wouldn't normally when you were picked up hitching, would you?"

A sudden flash of a memory. She and Martin struggling with huge rucksacks into the back of a Mini, holding out their hands. Martin. Martha.

"You might, sometimes." She blinked the memory away.

"So the search for Clarke Haddonfield continues?" DI Aitken nodded. "And you've still found no connection between Bosworth, Haddonfield and Humphreys?"

Randall shook his head.

"There are rules in medicine," Martha said slowly, as much to herself as to the other two, "that discourage coincidence, that lead us to expect that coexisting symptoms have a common connection. Given two emerging pathologies you learn to look for one cause. Strikes me, Alex," she said, smiling at him, "that this case should be governed by the same rules. I don't believe in murders and disappearances from one small town happening in the same night being coincident – particularly when a false name is deliberately strewn across our path. I don't want to interfere but it may well be that our 'Mr Haddonfield' with the nice manners and the mobile phone could well be your killer. And if there was someone on the other end of that mobile phone possibly it was an accomplice and nothing whatsoever to do with Mrs Haddonfield."

He nodded. "I do have some ideas," he said finally to Aitken. "Certainly we should be pooling our work. " He stood up sharply, anxious to be gone.

They had both left in minutes, bristling with long ticklists, leaving Martha with nothing physical to do. Except dig. She rang Mark Sullivan.

"I don't suppose you've got any further with the sternal wound?"

"Martha," a touch of humour in his voice. "Who's investigating all this?"

"Alex and DI Wendy Aitken of Oswestry police."

Sullivan chuckled. "You could have fooled me."

She confessed. "Well – I am *dying* to find out what's going on. I'd love to be investigating, Mark. Instead I'm chained to the confines of my job."

"There's nothing to stop you making a few little tentative enquiries of your own."

She knew he was smiling on the other end of the phone. "Stop inciting me, Mark."

"I'm not. I'm simply suggesting you play a more active part in the case."

"How?"

"I don't know." He was losing interest. "Say you're willing to be present at questioning."

"I can't. It wouldn't be ethical."

"I'm sure you'll find a way."

It was a dismissal. Martha reminded him that the inquest was the following day, said goodbye, put the phone down and straightaway dialled Alex's mobile. He answered tersely, "DI Randall."

"Alex, it's Martha. I just wanted to tell you. If I can be of any help you will call, won't you?"

"Of course. If I think of anything." *He was bound by the same constraints as she.* "We're just heading to Chester, to re-interview Mrs Bosworth. We've rung and warned her we're on our way." He gave a heartfelt sigh. "I don't mind telling you I think in this case we're somehow all missing the point. I haven't even thought what questions I'm going to ask Mrs Bosworth that I haven't already covered. The solicitor is a family friend and is . . . solicitous to say the least. I don't think I'm going to achieve anything by this long and very tedious journey." He paused. "Something tells me the answer is nearer home. Back here in Shropshire."

The next words were spoken so softly that afterwards Martha convinced herself she must have imagined them. But she held on to them all the same and revisited them again later. "I wish you could be here with me. I could do with a bit of direction." *Couldn't we all?*

"Hang on a minute, Coroner." He was giving directions to the driver.

He was back. "I think I've learned that where money is concerned people will do all sorts of things to keep it." It was a cryptic remark. "I'll be in touch, Martha."

"You can always use my . . ." But the line was dead.

And who knows who might have been listening.

Martha sucked in a deep breath, watched the trees outside her window waving in a blasting gale and forced herself to move on. Work was piling up. She should not spend too much time and energy on one case when she had so many to consider. She worked steadily for three hours, barely looking up when Jericho replaced empty mugs of coffee with full ones. By early afternoon her desk was almost empty and she could allow herself to think again.

She recalled Watkins' voice, the slow, ponderous, pedantic words describing picking up the hitchhiker. She half-closed her eyes to picture the scene, to renact it with the remembered words. And saw more, filling in details which had been merely implied. The road glossy with bouncing rain, the threat of the waters flooding, panic of being cut off, the deceitful sheen sweeping the road's surface that could conceal millimetres or inches or even feet of water and kill the internal combustion engine stone dead.

The answer was in the water. It had lapped at the cellar steps, flushed Bosworth's body from its hiding place, somehow hidden Clarke Haddonfield only to vomit up someone else. Some mystery person who had, in turn, vanished back behind stairods of rain.

Water.

So what had been the point of it all? She had always considered murder to be a sequential, logical crime. Even random killings were a result of a killer's personality. He *would* kill at some point. It was written in the darkest corner of his character. The only random, unpredictable factor was who would die, when and where. And planned, clever murders were born out of a collision between circumstance. The usual motives. Greed, fear, love, hate. Sometimes combinations of all four. So what was this? Really? A *crime passionel*? Really? It was possible.

So from motive to mechanics. Where was Clarke Haddonfield? Was he alive or dead – like Bosworth. Is it really possible to hide a body? To destroy flesh and bone completely? Of course. There are ways to do it. But to be effective, suspicion needs to be diverted. The eyes should be deflected so friends and family believe their loved one is still alive. But always somewhere else. Just beyond the horizon, the other side of the hill, there when you are here, always elsewhere. So the hitchhiker's journey had been that – a deflection. A clumsy one but had it not been for Wendy Aitken's persistence, egged on by her, it might have worked. And now she felt restless because she could do so little. She needed to walk off her frustration.

She parked at Gay Meadows, paid her pound and crossed the English Bridge. No red sky tonight or Munch's *Scream*. The wind had subsided. The river today was picture-postcard peaceful, gliding smoothly, graced with swans and one, solitary canoeist ruggedly ignoring the cold weather, sculling along with the grace of all sports – properly executed. She watched him for a moment, thinking of Sam and his football, somehow knowing that at the back of her mind she had reached her decision.

We are given ten talents. It is up to us to use those talents, to take them to the heights written in our minds and in our bodies. Not everyone could possibly be a footballer. Her son had been given that subtle combination of muscles and skill.

She turned left along Marine Terrace to stand in front of number seven.

She too had been given talents – of curiosity, of intrigue, of an insatiable desire to unravel tangled skeins of wool to restore order, peace, ensure justice for the dead and for the living. So she allowed her eyes to feed her brain. All external signs of the drama were gone. There was no police tape. No loitering Press. No curious bystanders. The house looked an innocent, pretty, blue-painted cottage; the one she and Martin had seen all those Christmases

before.

And yet. She peered down between her feet. There was a grille on the floor, a wired window beneath, the well filthy with flood debris, mud, leaves, sodden paper. Beneath must be the cellar. She was tempted to kneel down and look. But it would not do. People were walking past. She looked down again and wondered. She would have thought the police would have cleared this grille.

She left Marine Terrace. It would yield no secrets to her. Instead she turned and on impulse started up the hill. But even Finton Cley's shop was closed this afternoon. She tried the door in frustration. No opening times were displayed. Something told her he would resent such a strait-jacket. She returned to her car and the office. None of the messages were from either Alex or Mark. She picked up her work.

There were other deaths.

14

It was a relief to re-enter the real world, to arrive home and be greeted by Agnetha, Sukey and Sam. The house was lively, full of light and music. Life. Sukey grabbed her hand the moment she walked in through the door. “Come and see, Mum.” Martha followed her into the sitting room. The furniture had been pushed back. Agnetha took up position centre floor, in bell-bottomed trousers and a tank-top.

“Right,” Sukey ordered. Agnetha took two steps, pressed play on the video. And the action began.

Super Trooper filled the air and the pair of them did the dance routine in time with the foursome on the TV screen, arms swinging, back to back, one at right angles to the other, and turn to the front again, Sukey prompting occasional directions. They must have been practising this one for hours. When they had finished, breathless and exhilarated, Martha clapped loudly and enthusiastically.

Sukey tugged her arm again. “Agnetha’s going to make me a stage costume, Mum. What do you think?”

“I think it’s great.” She allowed herself a swift reflection. Had she been a stay-at-home mum would she have spent this amount of time with her daughter? Doing this? Was this, possibly, a recommendation for au pairs? She glanced around. “Where’s Sam gone?”

“Back to his bedroom.” Neither seemed interested. Agnetha pressed play again and they continued their dance routine. Martha climbed the stairs with the familiar heaviness of the burden of guilt. Life was so difficult for Sam. No dad, mum at work most of the time, sister and au pair practically forming their own tribute band.

Martha knocked on his door.

His "come in" sounded glum.

The room was festooned in Liverpool red and white, pictures of Michael Owen, Heskey, Redknapp and Babbel. But mainly Michael Owen. Schoolboy's hero. Action shots rather than line-ups. In most of them he looked as though he was grimacing in pain. Sam was sitting on his bed, leafing through a sports magazine. He hardly looked up. "Hi, Mum."

She sank down on the bed, next to him and he closed the magazine, looked at her, sensing she was about to say it.

She didn't speak for a moment or two but searched his face, loving him terribly, knowing his father would have done too, yet here she was, a lone, perceptive witness to his growing up.

"Anything the matter, Mum?"

She just wanted to hug him. Tell him all these things. And more. Instead she laughed and made what the twins called 'one of her faces'.

"No. I just wanted to have a word about this sports school your teacher's so keen on."

"Mr Grant?" He turned away.

"Mmm. Sam. Do you want to go?"

And Sam was, suddenly, disturbingly, a small boy again, vulnerable. "I don't know, Mum." He stared at his slippers now. Huge, red and white footballs made of foam with the Liverpool logo on. "I don't know if I'm really good enough."

Does anyone ever know the answer to this question. What is this movable goalpost of 'good enough'?

His eyes were wide open. Asking her with an unchildish depth behind the hazel irises. "How can I know if it's the right decision?" Another stare at the slippers accompanied by a gulpy swallow. "What would Dad have wanted, do you think?"

Martha shook her head. She could not know either. It was up to both of them to guess. To leave Shrewsbury and attend a sports school and then fail would be a double whammy. Family, friends, education would all have been sacrificed for The Game. If The Game then let him down the sacrifice would finally have been for nothing. Even to succeed in the luck-and-champagne world of professional sport could be less than the blessing it might seem. Success was fleetingly transient, and even at its peak not always the source of happiness. There was the spectre of injury at any time – in any game – in the fragment of a second. An unwise or unfortunate move could earn them revulsion from their 'adoring' fans. But the counter-balance was worse – not to have tried – to have waived the chance because of fear of failure. And so she helped her son to decide.

"Sam," she said very softly, hesitating before putting her arm around him and drawing him to her. "I love you hugely. You're my only son and I don't have your dad any more. You and Sukey are all I have of him except memories and photographs. And that dreadful video of him taking the pair of you for a walk in the buggy. My temptation is to keep you close to me, to protect you from everything. Life. But that would be unforgivably selfish and I don't think it would necessarily be the best thing for you. I don't even think it's what Dad would have wanted. If you're that good, if Mr Grant thinks you may have a chance of succeeding professionally, I think you should at least try." She was more decisive now she had voiced it. "Maybe you should give it your best shot. I would not be a good mum if I stopped you from fulfilling your potential for selfish reasons. It would be wrong."

"You won't mind my not living at home?"

She nodded. "Yes. I'll mind. I'll mind a lot. But I must-n't be selfish. If it doesn't work out you can always come home. I'll always be here but the opportunities won't. They'll pass you by." She stared deep into his eyes. "If you don't grab the chance now, Sam Gunn, it won't come again. It will pass you by and you may regret it. Maybe for all your life. You'll never know what might have been."

He nodded, eyed one of the pictures of Michael Owen – the one where he looked the youngest – barely fourteen – and smiled at his idol. "When will you see Mr Grant?"

"I'll ring him tomorrow."

Sam jumped off the bed, his load lightened. "Great. What's for tea?"

It was an hour later while they were tucking into salmon and asparagus pasta that Agnetha covered her mouth. "I don't know where Bobby's been digging," she said, laughing, "but he has been bringing home the most extraordinary things."

It was as though a stone had thumped on the table. For some reason Martha felt chilled. "Like what?"

"An old record. In his mouth. He must have found it in some old rubbish dump, or something."

Martha put her knife and fork down. "There isn't a rubbish dump anywhere near here, Agnetha. Anyway – Bobby doesn't go out alone. Hardly."

"Well it's a filthy old thing. I put it in the laundry. It's covered in mud. Absolutely disgusting. I left it in the sink. It's an old forty-five though." She winked at Sukey. "And I wish he wouldn't bring dead little animals and put them on the doorstep too as though they were gifts."

"Oh? I thought he'd stopped doing that."

"Many days something is there. Uugh." She gave a shake of her delicate shoulders. "I told him off. I said he was not to bring horrible, dirty things back to this house or he would no longer be welcome." She gave one of her long peals of laughter and Martha laughed too.

They spent one of their funny treasured evenings, all four of them playing a quiz game, *Who Wants to be a Millionaire,* almost getting their cheque for the valued million but they couldn't decide which team had won the Ashes in 1987. It was ten before both Sam and Sukey had retired to bed and Agnetha left too, saying she wanted to send some emails home, have a bath, shampoo her hair and go to bed. Martha was abruptly alone. Awake and fidgety. She had some wine opened in the laundry and the thought of a glass beckoned her.

But instead she found the record, where Agnetha had put it, in the sink. It was, as she had said, an old forty-five, caked in mud. It must have been buried for a while. She turned the tap on and rinsed it.

The label read, *A Message For Martha.*

This was no coincidence. It felt a mystical threat, a promise, a tease, a lure, a tell, a warning. She held the record in her hand for some minutes. Knowing only one thing. Whatever the meaning was of this object it was personal. She could no longer hide behind her profession, her position, her anonymity or her status. Someone was directing thrusts at her, at her home, at her family.

Like the Mafia say, *"It's all personal, baby."*

15

But there was no time to dwell. Whatever the message was, life must continue. Maybe one day she would understand. Until then she must be patient.

Wednesday, March 13th, was the appointed day for the inquest on Gerald Bosworth. And though it was currently a formality – the inquest would inevitably be opened and adjourned pending police enquiries – Martha took every aspect of her job seriously. To her nothing was a mere formality – or a foregone conclusion.

Usually family and friends of the deceased attended and, in cases like this, the police, the police surgeon, the pathologist, the press, witnesses and members of the public as well as any other interested parties. Inquests were rarely held *in camera* but were open to all and there were no reporting restrictions, which was why many coroners used their courts to broadcast statements and views. So far Martha had resisted the temptation to become a media star and make political comment. But maybe, one day, the temptation would seduce her.

It was her custom to speak to the bereaved family before the inquest opened, to allay their fears and address any concerns, also to tell them what would be expected of them. It was a sort of dress rehearsal. After all – to the police, doctors and other professionals this was an everyday affair. But to the relatives it was likely to be their only ever appearance in a coroner's court. She did wonder how Frederica Bosworth would respond to her but she need not have worried. Mrs Bosworth was demure in manner as well as in dress, in a black suit, the skirt modestly reaching to her knees and black ankle-boots. She was wearing little make-up and looked pale and apprehensive. She was leaning heavily on the arm of a suited man who introduced himself as Patrick Carpenter, family solicitor and close friend. He and Freddie exchanged a lot of eye contact but it was not up to Martha to surmise.

Freddie spoke first, as soon as they were inside the room. "I'm sorry, Doctor Gunn. I was a bit off with you the other day. I was upset."

Martha made a soothing noise, assured Freddie that it was natural – under the circumstances – and Freddie returned a half-smile. "Thanks."

They spoke for a few minutes and Martha led the way into the court. She never entered it without a feeling of both awe and pride. It was formal, 1920's oak pews, a witness box as beautifully carved as a pulpit, a long bench behind which she sat. The jury, when there was one, sat in an enclosed set of oak seats reminiscent of a Welsh chapel and the public in a galleried courtroom. Full, it could seat three hundred people but rarely was called to do so. Today it was almost empty. She spotted a cub reporter from the local paper, a tall blonde woman, and a few familiar faces. In the second row Freddie Bosworth stared straight ahead, as though wishing herself elsewhere. The solicitor-friend looked unmoved and uninterested, picking his nails halfway through. The front row included Alex Randall, Mark Sullivan and Police Constable Gary Coleman who looked as nervous as though he was the accused. Martha smiled inwardly. The first appearance in a coroner's court was very nerve-wracking for a young police officer. At the back of the court, a stocky man in a black puffer-jacket sat with his arms folded.

Jericho opened the proceedings, giving the name of the deceased, the date of the discovery of the body and the place. The rest would be ascertained during the hearing.

Martha gave one of her short, introductory speeches,

explaining the format very gently and simply to the court. Coleman was the first witness to be sworn in.

He used his notebook to prompt him and when he wasn't reading stared at his big black shoes as though he wished he could climb inside them and hide from view.

"It was Tuesday, the 12th of February. The River Severn was bursting its banks and I'd been detailed to make sure everyone was out of the properties along Marine Terrace. About four o'clock, as I approached number seven, I noticed the door wasn't quite closed." He flicked the page over. A fly was climbing up the courthouse window. *Calliphora. "I," said the fly. "With my little eye. I saw him die."*

"I called out. No one answered but I was concerned the property was not secured. I pushed the door open, flashed the torch around. There was a swell in the river so the door opened further and something bumped into me. I saw the body of a man."

"And what did you do then?"

A helpless glance around the courtroom. Martha felt sorry for him. "I touched him. He was cold. I called for help."

Jericho interrupted to address the court. "The emergency call was logged in at 4.05."

Coleman wiped some sweat from his forehead. Martha smiled encouragingly at him. "Thank you, PC Coleman."

He stood stock-still, not understanding that this was a dismissal. Jericho came to the rescue. "You can step down now."

And Martha caught the faintest tinge of disappointment from the young constable. *He would learn.*

Alex was the next to take the solemn oath. Not for the first time. He was well used to it and needed no prompting.

"Detective Inspector Alex Randall, Shrewsbury Police. When the emergency call was put through to me I was about to go off duty but realising this was likely to be a serious and unusual case I decided to attend Marine Terrace in person." He did not need the benefit of notes. "I arrived at four-twenty to find, as Constable Coleman has just said, the body of a man lying face down in shallow water. I ascertained he was dead, informed the coroner's officer and summoned Doctor Delyth Fontaine, the police surgeon. She arrived at five-twenty." He paused, knowing, for now, that would be the sum of his evidence.

Delyth Fontaine was called next. She was a vastly overweight, experienced police surgeon in her fifties who worked part time as a GP in the town. Martha knew her very well. She had long, straggly grey hair, a wide, warm smile and perceptive intelligence. She also had a palpable no-nonsense attitude to her work. Martha had only ever seen her upset when dealing with the death of children. Otherwise she did not allow emotion to get in the way of facts.

"I arrived at Marine Terrace at six pm," she said crisply. "There was a certain amount of turmoil around the place because the Severn was still rising and there was some threat from the river. Attendant were Detective Inspector Alex Randall, Police Constable Gary Coleman and Detective Sergeant Barry Klisco." She paused, glanced down at her notes, tucked a strand of long grey hair behind her ear. "In the corner of the room was the body of a man. He was quite cold and rigor mortis was beginning to wear off which led me to believe he had been dead for more than thirty-six hours. I could see no external wounds and no obvious case of death."

Again she paused, licked her lips, glanced again at her notes but Jericho knew better than to prompt her. "Given the circumstances surrounding the death I asked DI Randall to summon the Home Office Pathologist, Doctor Mark Sullivan." Her clear eyes met those of Martha and again Martha smiled her thanks. Delyth Fontaine sat down heavily.

Now it was Sullivan's turn. He took the oath and also read from notes. Martha knew Mark's need for precision. He left nothing to chance. His evidence concurred with Delyth Fontaine's but he was able to add the results of the post mortem. The stab wound, the injuries, the bleeding into the pericardial sac.

Martha stole a swift glance at Freddie Bosworth. *These were harrowing facts to learn about your husband's death.* The widow was leaning forward in her chair, her lipsticked mouth slightly open. Something more than pain but less than anguish passed across her face. She was frowning, chewing her lip, concentrating. More distressed and anxious than Martha had realised. Jericho handed her a glass of water and Freddie gulped it down gratefully. And to her amusement Martha could have sworn the attention from the deceased's wife had made Jericho blush right to the roots of his hair.

She dismissed Mark and called Freddie Bosworth to the witness stand, watched while she took her oath. Freddie was waxy pale. "Would you like to sit down, Mrs Bosworth?" Jericho was there with a chair and Freddie Bosworth dropped into it gratefully. This was an obvious strain.

"When did you last see your husband?"

"On Thursday, the seventh of February," she almost whispered. "He was setting off for a business trip to Germany, packing his suitcase with a spare suit and other clothes. He often went abroad. I didn't think . . ." Tears welled up in her eyes. "I'd never . . ."

Martha nodded encouragement.

"I didn't think there was anything unusual that morning." Freddie's blue eyes swept around the courtroom to meet a wave of sympathy – except for the stocky man at the back who had now removed his puffer-jacket and was staring at the widow with visible dislike.

The sympathy from the courtroom appeared to have a recuperative effect on Freddie Bosworth. She continued with a stronger voice. "It was the same as lots of other mornings. Gerald was planning to drive himself to the airport. If he was planning to be away a long time he'd normally have taken a taxi or asked me to drive him in. The airport charges. They're really steep. I thought he'd be back in a couple of weeks."

"But you didn't worry when you didn't hear anything from him?"

"No. It was like Gerald not to phone. He forgot everything when he was away. Out of sight . . ." The brave attempt at a joke added pathos to her statement.

"You have no explanation for how he came to be in Shrewsbury instead of Germany?"

Freddie's wide blue eyes stared back at her. "No," she said. "I have absolutely no idea."

"And you were summoned to identify your husband?"

Freddie nodded and threaded a hankie out of her pocket. She sniffed into it loudly, dabbed her eyes carefully to protect her mascara and put it back again.

Although Martha knew the answer to the next question it was a formality.

"You're sure it was your husband?"

"Yes. It was him."

"Thank you, Mrs Bosworth."

Martha next addressed the court. "Police enquiries are ongoing," she said, "and it is the custom to adjourn the inquest until the investigation is complete. If anyone has anything to add I would be grateful if they would contact my office. The date for the final inquest may not be for some time. Today's proceedings mean that Gerald Bosworth can be buried, his business affairs completed and his widow grieve without hindrance. Thank you." She stood up and most of the people in the courtroom stood too. Except the stocky man at the back whose arms were still folded. Her eyes flickered over him curiously and he stared back, insolently.

She watched as Freddie Bosworth and Carpenter made their way towards the exit. The stocky man was pushing towards them, shoving the tall, blonde woman out of the way quite rudely. Martha halted, anticipating an altercation. It wouldn't be the first time in a coroner's court for emotions to erupt. Investigations of death could bring all sorts of old resentments and bitternesses to the surface. She noticed that Alex Randall was watching the scene too. In the end Freddie, the solicitor and the stocky man exchanged words but there was no violence. Only rumblings. Then they filed out with the others leaving Martha staring after them, Alex Randall at her side. "Did you know who he was?"

"No."

"It might be worth you finding out," she suggested and Randall grinned at her. He knew exactly what she was up to.

And suddenly only she and Jericho were left in the empty courtroom. "What did you make of Mrs Bosworth?" she asked him curiously.

"I don't think she'll grieve long," her assistant observed.

16

After the inquest she felt a desperate need to escape Shrewsbury and during the next day, Thursday, she laid her plans.

On Friday she raced home for five, showered and had the car packed up by six. They put Bobby into kennels – London was no place for a dog. She braved the M54 and the Birmingham box, reaching London late and in time for some supper, a few glasses of wine for her and Agnetha and bed for the exhausted twins.

They rose late the next morning, spent the day at the Natural History museum, ate an early supper and headed for the West End. Agnetha and Sukey went into frenzies as they watched the show and even Sam seemed happy. She knew why.

But all through *Mamma Mia*, however gaudy and wonderful the costumes, however loud and explosive the tunes were, the case continually nagged at the back of her mind like toothache, and just as impossible to ignore.

She thought back to the dramatic discovery of Gerald Bosworth's body, the river rising steadily, embracing the town and flushing him from the cellar. Coincidence. It had to be. Even she couldn't believe that a killer could organise a river to flood. And although it was partly predictable what would happen it was never completely so. Even for locals it was still a bit of a shock. Days when the river was expected to peak sometimes passed without incident whereas the unexpected could still happen. That was the point. Rivers were unpredictable. Untameable. Laws unto themselves.

"*Waterloo . . .*" The show pounded on in candy pinks, gold platform-heeled boots and swirls of lycra bell-bottoms. The choreography indistinguishable from Sukey and Agnetha's routine a few nights ago.

What difference would it have made if the river had not misbehaved? What had Bosworth being doing in Shrewsbury – in Marine Terrace? Why had he not gone to Germany? Why had he died? Had it been a random killing? Martha made a face. Difficult to believe. A premeditated murder then? Had to be. So why? How had he been lured there? Why had *no one* seen him arrive? They were all such little questions and so impossible to answer.

Halfway through the show she got restless legs and sat flexing and unflexing her calf muscles until Sam tapped her on the arm. "Are you very bored?" he whispered. She shook her head, laughed, and forced herself to concentrate.

She drove back on the Sunday afternoon after a morning of frenzied shopping in Oxford Street, which Sam had tolerated remarkably well. As soon as they were through the front door Sukey ran to the answerphone to pick up the messages. "Granny," she hissed, then "Granny again" before listening, redialling and finally putting the phone down. "Our mystery caller," she said crossly. "The one who never says anything or leaves a number. He gets on my nerves." She stalked into the kitchen.

Sam was halfway up the stairs. "If the mystery caller never says anything how do you know it's a man?"

Sukey came out of the kitchen to stand at the bottom of the stairs, hands on slim hips. "I can hear him breathing, Sam. Anyway – no *woman* does that sort of thing."

And it suddenly hit Martha. There were a lot of anonymous callers to this number. More than there should be by the law of averages. Odd things did happen. A wreath left when there had been no death? A muddy record. *A Message to Martha. What message?* It was beginning to infuriate her. What message, she was screaming inside her.

And now she believed someone was out there beaming some emotion right into this household. Into her. For what purpose, when it was done so randomly, so ill-directed, so obscurely? What was it achieving? And if it was not malevolent why did they not speak? If there was a message why not bloody well leave it? Why not simply explain what they were trying to say? Was it some nut? Connected with her job? Should she speak again to Alex about it? Request police surveillance? Because of the nature of her job she knew her request would be granted. Provided she made it. And what was it, really? Nothing. There was no threat. She did not feel threatened. More invaded. This was an isolated house. Private. She was a private person. She welcomed the house's isolation rather than seeing it as a problem. She could consider moving but she didn't really want to.

Then she started to understand – a little. The reason she did not feel threatened was because she was not threatened. It was not a threat. It was simply a message – for Martha. The trouble was with her: that she could not read it. One day she would. Not yet.

She glanced at the telephone. Strike while the iron is hot. There had been other telephone calls too. She dialled her mother first then Martin's mother and invited them both to come for the weekend. Both accepted. Husbands too. It would be the weekend of the grandparents and she could tell them about Sam, and Sukey and Agnetha could show them their dance routine. She felt virtuous. Virtue is a pleasant emotion. By Monday mid-morning her emotions were much less pleasant.

How surprising that in this overcrowded age a corpse can remain undiscovered. In a populated area. For more than a month. It had intrigued her before that there were black holes through which a person can disappear for months, weeks, sometimes forever. But in these sophisticated days instinct and observation have been bred out by civilisation. We no longer use our senses properly – our five precious senses: taste, touch, smell, hearing and sight. Unlike Calliphora whose multi-faceted eyes see all and whose instincts lead her unfailingly to find the right source. Dogs have as keen a sense of smell as Calliphora. And both are irresistibly attracted to the scent of rotting flesh.

Martha was at the hairdresser's. As usual Vernon had picked up her unruly red locks and scolded her for leaving it too long between cuts. Vernon Grubb was not the archetypal camp hairdresser but a stocky he-man with the build of a rugby player. Whenever she visited him (too infrequently) she was invariably intrigued as to what had led him along this particular career path and how he had coped with hairdresser college. One day, she vowed, she would ask him.

Not today. He seemed in particularly tetchy mood. His x-ray vision homed in accusingly on her split ends as though she had deliberately nurtured each one. She knew he considered so many of them on a client an affront to his profession. She let him rant for a minute or two, reminded of the restaurateur who had first uncovered her inability to set a table properly (a penalty of being left-handed) when she was a waitress during the university vac. Vernon provoked the same mix of guilt and apprehension. However he finally handed her over to a junior shampooist and she was draped in a black nylon gown, her shoulders padded with towels and her head lowered over the sink before the blissful feeling of warm water and rich, creamy shampoo being massaged into her scalp. She closed her eyes, luxuriated . . .

And was rudely awakened by her mobile phone. She apologised to the shampooist and clamped it to her ear.

"Hello?"

"Martha. It's Detective Inspector Wendy Aitken, Oswestry police. Sorry for . . ."

She sat upright. Water dripped down the towels.

"I'm afraid we've found another body," she said, "almost certainly our missing man. He's in a bit of a state."

The stylist was watching her with round eyes and scarcely concealed curiosity. Martha responded quickly. "I can't talk at the moment. I'll call you back." She glanced at the number display. "On your mobile. I'll be about forty minutes. Don't move the body please." She ended the call and lay back, her hair drowning, Ophelia-like, in the sink, while she pondered. Two bodies. One killer? Or two? Make no assumptions.

"Conditioner?" She glanced up at the shampooist's face. And nodded.

Twenty minutes later she was admiring the back of her hair in the mirror and again running the gauntlet of Vernon's scolding. "Now don't leave it so long next time. Your hair. It needs trimming – once a month. Or else the condition. Mmm." He stood back, pursing his lips, patted a lock into place and appraised again.

Martha agreed with him, took a last glance at the unfamiliarly neat, shining bob, slipped out of her gown, paid her bill, tipped the shampooist and escaped. As soon as she was in the privacy of her car she re-dialled Wendy Aitken's mobile number. The detective answered in a tense voice.

"Whether it's Haddonfield or not his throat's been cut," she said. "Some time ago I would think."

Martha put her hand in front of her eyes to block out the vision. "Has Mark Sullivan seen him yet?"

"He's with him now."

"Which is where?"

The answer surprised even her.

"In the supermarket, Aldi, in the clothing bank."

She was appalled. "And no one realised?"

"Not until the number of flies began to proliferate." She paused, adding quietly. "We're lucky. It was due to be emptied later on this week."

"And then what?" The possibilities were endlessly mind-boggling.

"Don't worry." She could hear a smile in her voice. "They do sort it out before it gets distributed to the refugees."

"I'll be right over."

As she covered the few miles to Oswestry she couldn't help thinking. She put clothes in the ragbank. Lots of people did. She drove into the Aldi carpark, disturbed.

Half of it had been sealed off, police tape strung across, a white canopy shrouding the sensitive area. A couple of police cars blocked the entrance and their lights strobing the dull day gave the growing clumps of voyeurs some drama to focus on.

A young, uniformed police officer tried to stop her until she explained who she was and watched his face turn a dark shade of beetroot in embarrassment.

The clothing bank was a large, square metal container with a huge letterbox in the front which folk generous with last year's fashions posted their offerings through. Behind, the PVC sheeting lights had been erected throwing moving shadows against its sides. She lifted the flap and joined Wendy and Sullivan minutes before they noticed her. They were too intent on two plain-clothes officers removing the back of the container with a oxy-acetylene cutters.

It was a sordid sight: the pile of castoffs, wool, linen, silk, rayon, every conceivable colour of acetate, plain and multicoloured, cheap and expensive, rubbing shoulders and knees with each other lit by two powerful arc lights. Some of the top layer of clothes had already been removed and bagged. The smell was overwhelming, every single jaded adjective moving through Martha's mind to describe it, rotten and stinking, musty, fusty, unwashed and dirty, and even in the cool afternoon the scent attracting marauding flies drawn irresistibly towards their raison d'être: their breeding ground, their fun, their food.

Martha watched only the flies for a moment. *"I," said the fly, "with my little eye. I saw him die."* And wondered. Haddonfield had been hidden in the rags.

Except his hair, thinnish, gold-brown, cut short across a white, unlined forehead, and dark eye sockets in which something writhed. Martha's eyes sorted out anomalies from the tangle of old clothes.

"Rag and Bones, Rag and Bones." Bound hands, white skin, clothes that were not empty, a pair of grubby blue trainers tossed on the top, a rust-stained nest. Yearned after, dreamed for, borrowed or paid for. Treasured clothes become rags. Loved, adored, feared, hated people are all finally bodies.

The smell was overpowering. Martha backed away, towards the flap rattling hysterically in the rising wind.

March – in like a lion; out like a lamb.

Randall arrived. He raised his eyebrows in greeting and otherwise said nothing, addressing his remarks to the pathologist.

"How long has he been dead?"

"Over a month, I think."

Wendy Aitken tried to explain. "There were a lot of clothes on top of him."

"How often do the council change the container?"

"Every month to six weeks." Wendy Aitken again.

Randall looked around. "Is there CCTV here?"

Wendy turned to look at him. "They don't keep the tapes longer than a fortnight or so. So effectively – no."

Martha's turn now. "And is it Haddonfield?"

"We think so. The clothes match the description of what he was wearing."

Martha was busy working it out. "So he did come back to Oswestry that night. Watkins must have been mistaken. He simply didn't recognise him. Maybe not surprising on such a dark, wet night." *Surely the simplest explanation is the likeliest?*

"Is he in a fit state to be identified?"

"That's up to his wife. It isn't a problem, Mark. We can always use dental records."

Alex was staring at her. "Well I hope she's got an iron constitution, Martha. Put it like this. If it was my wife I wouldn't want her last memory of me to be this." Haddonfield's dead, empty face stared back.

Martha moved outside to speak to Randall. "So," she said, "if Mark's reckoning is right the two murders took place within a short time of each other."

He nodded. "DI Aitken and I will work together. We'll try and get some identification and then the post mortem."

She glanced back at the canopy flapping in a rising wind. "Good luck," she said impulsively. "It's a lot to unravel. But this must have made the case much easier."

"Yes." Randall's eyes flickered and he pressed his lips together. "There'll be some story behind this," he said. "Some fraud, some business gone sadly wrong. Money. Greed."

Martha threw her head back. "Why, Alex," she mocked.

"You've got it solved already."

His face softened with a touch of humour. "In my dreams."

"By the way," she said, "who was the guy in the puffer-jacket sitting at the back of Gerald Bosworth's inquest?"

"His brother. Not too fond of his sister-in-law, it seems."

"Oh?"

"He'd offered to do the identification but Freddie was having none of it. And she's the one with all the rights, as next of kin."

"Quite," she said.

Then, "I'll be in touch," he promised.

Wendy Aitken and Sullivan appeared behind him. "I think we'll have the body brought back to Shrewsbury for the post mortem. All right by you, Mark?"

He nodded.

"Wendy?"

"I'm happy at that," she said.

"So – we'll get the body moved now and post mortem in the morning? Nine am?"

All three agreed.

To her surprise when she arrived at the mortuary on a fresh, March morning, a little after nine, (the traffic had been bad), Mark Sullivan was washing his hands in the sink. Haddonfield's body was already laid out on the slab and Peter was using his rotary saw to remove the cranium.

"I thought we were going to get him identified first."

"Too late, Martha." Alex joined them. "Lindy Haddonfield was adamant she wanted to identify him. She was here at eight thirty."

She gave him a swift, puzzled glance. "I'm surprised," she said. "He's . . . Well he isn't my husband but -"

She glanced at the face herself. "Did you warn her what

he looked like?"

"Oh yes." Mark was examining the brain already, taking neat slices for histology. "Nothing here." He looked up. "I did warn her but Peter and I tidied him up. He didn't look too bad. And it is so much easier once you've got positive ID. Easier for all of us."

"Mmm." She was surprised. But then, maybe, nothing in the case should surprise her.

"I don't suppose she could shed any light on his death?"

"You guessed right, Martha."

Half an hour later Mark Sullivan straightened up. "Well," he said. "No surprises here. Cause of death aspiration of blood following single *deep* incised wound to the throat. Not that it helps us but it was left to right."

"Thought that would tell you whether the killer was left- or right-handed."

"In your dreams."

Wendy Aitken sighed. "Homicide or suicide?"

"We-ell." Mark Sullivan's eyes were bright. "If he made the knife vanish into thin air, moved his own body, after death, bound his own hands and laundered a ragbank full of blood-drenched clothes I might swallow the suicide theory."

"So homicide." She allowed herself a tight smile at his levity. "Just checking."

He nodded. "All the hallmarks of homicide are there. No tentative wounds. Bruising under the chin from the restraint. Death would have been very quick."

"And the weapon?" This was Alex, showing interest.

"A very sharp knife. Sorry, Alex. I can't be more specific than that. Something – oh smaller than a carving knife, about the size of a paring knife. Very sharp indeed."

"Thank you, all. So – Clarke Haddonfield, death homicidal. Probably about a month or so ago. And his body was brought to the clothing bank. How did the killer get his body in there?"

"The flap's big enough – just. There are some quite nasty grazes on his chest, arms and lower limbs done post mortem as the killer shoved him through the opening." *It seemed the final lack of respect.*

The file landed on her desk at the end of the week, during a bright, sunny Friday lunchtime. Spring was definitely in the air. Clipped to the front was a typewritten note from Wendy Aitken.

> "Lindy Haddonfield formally identified the body as being that of her husband, Clarke Haddonfield, of 14, Playton Gardens, Oswestry, last seen when he left to travel to Shrewsbury on Monday morning, February 11th, at approximately nine thirty am.
>
> She denies he had any criminal leanings or contacts, describes him as an unambitious, unexciting sort of man whose big love was his hi fi. She says he had no enemies, had not been threatened and had caused upset to no one.
>
> (Here Aitken had inserted an exclamation mark and a handwritten comment. *He seems to have led a blameless life!*)
>
> She coped well with the identification and did not seem unduly upset, only reflective. She declined the company of a WPC, an offer of Victim Support or Trauma Counselling."

She'd signed with a flourishing "W"

Martha read through the post mortem report, noting the damage which had led to Haddonfield's death: destruction of both carotid arteries, the jugular veins, the trachea, the damage almost extending right back to reach the cervical spine. Blood had been found in the airways and bruises underneath the chin. Haddonfield's hands had been bound.

Cause of death had been listed as:

a) asphysxia secondary to
b) inhalation of blood
c) due to a major incisional injury to the neck.

Reading between the lines, someone had bound Clarke Haddonfield, then approached from behind, jerked up his chin and sliced along his neck. It was a completely different assault from the attack on Bosworth. Bosworth's had been one precise and incisive stab to the front. This had been the very opposite, the killer stealing up behind, a clumsy strong swipe to the neck. The killer had dumped the body without caring whether it was found – it was pure chance that it had taken so long. And he might well have been spattered with blood on his sleeve. She couldn't see that the two homicides bore any marks of having been committed by the same person.

Martha returned to the PM report and read under the heading *Comments.* Mark Sullivan had noted that Haddonfield's hands and feet had been tightly bound with nylon yachting rope causing extensive chafing to the wrists and ankles indicating that he had been bound for some time before he had died.

Why? If you're going to kill someone why would you tie him up? To keep him still. Make him more easy to kill. To intimidate him? To imprison him and prevent escape. Where? And what was the connection – if any – between the three men – a philandering car salesman from Slough recently decamped to rented accommodation in Shrewsbury, a businessman from Chester, who was supposed to be on a business trip to Germany and a window cleaner from Oswestry? The little questions continued to buzz around her mind like a huge, noisy bluebottle. *Calliphora.*

The frustrating thing for her was doing nothing . . . Well not exactly *nothing.* She had her in-laws and her parents coming for the weekend.

17

It was always tricky mixing her mother-in-law with her own parents. Martin's father had died suddenly a year before his son had been diagnosed and the double shock had proved too much for the quiet, family-orientated woman. Martin did have a sister but she was an elusive, secretive woman, constantly butterflying from one career to another, never *quite* settling down to either house, husband, family or anything else for that moment. It was as though Martin had inherited all the family stolidness and pedantry, leaving none for his sister. Sneakily Martha quite liked Valentine though she found her unpredictable. Unpredictable to her was exciting.

Martin's mother, heavy with her bereavement, had the unfortunate habit of clinging on to the twins as though she was contacting her dead son through them. She would scrutinize first Sam then Sukey searching for resemblance to their father. With Sam it was easy. He was almost a clone for his father. But when she stared, for long, silent, disapproving minutes, at her granddaughter, she would shake her head, as though disappointed. And this upset the child. Both children. Because twins share each other's disappointment as well as their elation. And twelve-year-olds are more perceptive than folk give them credit for.

A result of Martin's mother having failed to shake off this terrible burden of grief meant that when she came for the day Martha felt guilty for any smile, any outward sign that she was not still grieving herself. She could not explain that she did grieve. But it was a private, permanent scarring grief and she preferred to deal with it alone.

Her own parents were hugely different. Her mother was a quixotic, intuitive and intelligent woman, her father a quiet pipe smoker who would study her for minutes before removing his pipe and making some long, deep comment. Her mother was a busy, practical woman, who always liked to be doing something. Otherwise she fidgeted and fretted. She found some ironing Vera had left, tidied rooms which Martha preferred 'lived-in', baked cakes no one would eat, washed up when there was a perfectly good dishwasher which, truth be told, did the work more efficiently – polished the glasses without smears, removed baked-on food.

Her father sat around, smiling at Sam when he confided his dreams in him, watching Sukey's Abba-antics, talking to her when she dropped into a chair, exhausted at keeping going. She loved her father. He was a tonic. An encourager. A rock. She loved her mother too but found her constant restlessness tiring.

The two mothers may be different. But one thing united them. They deplored her continuing widowhood, finding the *situation* unsatisfactory – a failure on Martha's part. If it was possible they felt the loss of a husband and father even more keenly than she and the children did. And in some perverse way Martha resented this. It was her family's problem. Not theirs. And they made it no easier. In their attitude they reflected that Martha was too young to be a widow and the situation had continued for too long. This was their inward emotion, which they manifested in their different ways. Martha had a suspicion her mother found it easier to bustle than to talk and Martin's mother sighed and asked whether Martha had *any* life. Only her father, banished to smoke his pipe on the bench in the chilly outdoors, brought her real comfort.

They finally left after a Sunday afternoon walk, early dinner and games of Monopoly and Ratrace. Martin's mother's face had cracked into a smile when she had bought her second Porsche and was divorced for the third time and Martha had the briefest of glimpses of how her mother-in-law must once have been – sensitive, intelligent, perceptive and happy. Like her son. Martin had been all those things. And her own mother, useful, kind, with an imagination which stowed other people's sufferings deep into her own heart. She gave them both an extra-special hug because they meant well. It was not their fault that it was her father who achieved what they would have liked to have done – brought her some real solace. They rose to leave at the same time, at nine o'clock exactly, as though each had secretly been clock-watching and had set this exact minute to go. Martha waved the two cars down the drive. Both of them, she knew, looked after her and the twins' welfare and would always do so. They were her family.

She had an appointment with Sam's teacher first thing on Monday morning and agreed that Sam should be trialled for the Liverpool Academy with a view to starting in September – if he was picked. As soon as she had finished speaking she felt a sense of relief that she had finally come to a decision and acted on it.

What the decision had been, whether right or wrong, wise or unwise, was less important than an end to vacillation and uncertainty. She sat in her car, outside the school, transfixed, for a moment, by a brief vision of Sam in Liverpool strip, in front of a roaring crowd, then scolded herself for jumping ahead with her imagination and moving into her castle in the air. So she threw objections in front of her dreams. He may well not be chosen. There were other talented boys around. Other parents shared the same vision. Enough to populate ten Liverpool football teams. She might have to deal not with elation but disappointment.

Yet she smiled, leaned forward and started the car acknowledging that it was no use pointing out that there were other football clubs. Liverpool was the only one for Sam. Anything else would seem like second best. It was his dream. She manoeuvred out of the car park still lecturing herself that even if he was successful there was always the spectre of injury hovering behind the shoulder of every wannabe professional footballer. A knee injury. A torn ligament. Fragile metatarsals to shatter. But even so, all day long, she was aware of a secret sense of elation. An air-thumping, "Ye-e-es." And she felt especially warm when she recalled that when she had served up tomato soup with croutons of white toast last night for supper Sam had stared for a while, reading its significance then flung his arms around her neck. "I'm going to make you so proud of me, Mum," he had said, before sitting down and slurping it so noisily Sukey and Agnetha burst out laughing. It had been the happiest of evenings and she knew she would remember Sam's words all day. Treasure them all her life.

What she could only hope was that they would never return to haunt her.

But her job meant there was always death and formality to deal with. On the Tuesday, at a little after nine, Alex Randall rang her.

"Martha." His voice was cordial but formal. "I thought I'd better give you a ring, let you know how our investigations are proceeding."

He must have sensed her unseemly curiosity in the case. He didn't usually keep her quite so well informed. She tried to keep her voice cool – detached. Suppress the intrigue that was bubbling up. "That's good of you, Alex."

He cleared his throat and she caught the flicker of paper down the phone line. "Haddonfield almost certainly was killed sometime after February the ninth. That's when the skip was last changed. And his body dumped in the clothing bank soon after he died. There's some leakage of blood on the surrounding clothes."

She interrupted him. "The clothes could have been dumped with him."

"There are all sorts, for all ages, all qualities and sizes. Too much of a variety for one person to have dropped them. At least, Martha, that's what we *think.* We haven't had any firm sightings of him in Shrewsbury on Monday, the 11th, but there's no reason to doubt his wife's statement that he rang her mobile from home on Monday morning. The call was logged. And after all – his van was driven here, into Shrewsbury. The most likely explanation is that he drove it in himself. There is some corroboration from the next-door neighbour. He watched Haddonfield backing his car down the drive about ten o'clock on Monday morning. It's a narrow turn and he's on long-term sick and is very possessive about his new Renault Clio. He was worried that Haddonfield might scrape it. Hence the interest."

A pause. "Haddonfield's wife drives a Vauxhall Calibra and was seen driving home on the Monday night coming back from work. She'd been there all day. She's vouched for."

"Convenient." She couldn't keep the sarcasm out of her voice.

"Yes." Neither could he.

"Where does she work?"

"It's a health farm. A posh sort of place just south of Chester. Fanciful name." He laughed. "Lilac Clouds. In fact if I worked for the drugs squad I'd be investigating it for hallucinogenics."

She laughed at the joke, seeing his point. It did sound

very sixties. "Have you found any connection between Humphreys and Bosworth?"

"No." Said shortly. "I mean – we're looking into it but we've come up with nothing so far."

"Have you any ideas why Bosworth was wearing Humphrey's suit rather than his own?"

"Again no."

"Or what he was doing in Marine Terrace in the first place?"

Randall shook his head.

"And I don't suppose Haddonfield connects with either man?"

"No. Nothing there either. Haddonfield's murder may well be quite unconnected. Although . . ."

She waited.

Randall's tone was tense. "Haddonfield was someone who would do anything for a few quid. A sort of minor Steptoe."

"Oh?"

"Some sort of scam would be right up his street."

"This is a bit more than a scam."

"True. But it could be a scam that went wrong."

"We don't actually know that he died on my patch."

A wisp of a smile. "Don't complicate matters, Martha. Haddonfield vanished from sight somewhere, sometime, between Oswestry and Shrewsbury on the Monday and your jurisdiction extends to most of north Shropshire so it's pretty safe to say that he died almost certainly on your territory. There isn't any point involving another coroner at this stage, Martha, particularly as you're already handling the inquest on Bosworth."

"But -"

"I know. We haven't found any connection yet between the two killings but even I'm not sure how far the long arm of coincidence can extend."

She caught a tired smile in his voice and heartily agreed. Without waiting for further comment he hurried on.

"Mrs Haddonfield doesn't seem able or willing to supply us with any answers. She doesn't have a clue about why her husband was abducted, where he was between February the 11th and him turning up inside the clothing bank. She has no idea of who might have killed him. She's never heard of or met James Humphreys or Gerald Bosworth or heard her husband mention them. We've re-interviewed Humphreys and he can't help us either although I think there's something bugging him about all this. He seems badly scared and it isn't just his wife biffing his nose that's getting to him. It's something much much more than that but is he going to tell us anything about it? No. And he and his wife appear to have formed an uneasy truce about his peccadillo. He's back at work and in Marine Terrace again. She's gone back to Slough and Sheelagh Mandershall is still with her husband. So everything's returned to normal. She hasn't been of any help anyway – in spite of us having questioned her a few times. She doesn't seem to know anything and I believe her."

"I see. So what line are you working on?"

"Just between you and me I think this is the work of an organised gang. Some sort of car scam involving Humphreys at the Jaguar garage, Bosworth doing the foreign side of things and Haddonfield – somewhere on the periphery. A sort of runner. They must have trodden on some gangland bosses' toes and got their come-uppance. It would explain why Humphreys is so scared. I have spoken to a forensic psychiatrist who's studied organised crime and he feels the two murders were done by different people which points us in that direction."

He seemed to feel the need to justify his reasoning. "It looks suspiciously like two perfectly ordinary middle-aged men were killed violently within days of each other and their bodies both found in north Shropshire. It has to be more than coincidence."

"Absolutely. I agree."

"See, Martha, I remembered your lecture about coincidence and have looked for one explanation." He was trying to win her round, still sounding like a little boy who expected a pat on the head.

She gave it – verbally. "Good for you. And how about the hitchhiker?"

There was a pause. "That I cannot understand or explain. We've tried everything. Everything to find out who he is. We've stopped traffic on the road to Oswestry, put boards up, re-interviewed Watkins, gone right through his van with the finest of toothcombs." He sounded worried. "I don't know who he was. Maybe our killer. We won't stop hunting for him."

They set a date for Clarke Haddonfield's inquest. She thanked him for his call, put the phone down and continued with her work. But after a few minutes her head jerked up.

She did not fault his reasoning. Only his conclusion. He was looking the wrong way. A bluebottle climbed slowly up the window.

Half an hour later she was still sitting, staring at the fly moving jerkily up the glass, rolling her pen to and fro between her fingers, arguing silently with herself and hardly seeing the dullness of the day outside.

She could justify it. *Oh no she couldn't.* She owed it to herself. *No she didn't.* She could pamper herself. *It was outside her remit.* A beauty treatment was what professionals did when they wanted to chill out or dry out. *She* was a professional, in a high-profile, demanding job. *It was none of her business and, if uncovered, would be viewed as unprofessional, unwarranted interest, which might even prejudice the outcome of the inquest. The court case.* She could always plead ignorance – coincidence. *Lindy Haddonfield might recognise her. They would inevitably meet at the inquest.* That was the point at which reason lost the argument.

Every woman loves the thought that they can wear a disguise, radically change the way they look. She could wear glasses during the inquest, pin her hair up, wear frumpy clothes. People didn't really look at a coroner. It was the office which grabbed the attention. And as Martha Rees . . .

She made a few phone calls quickly, before she could change her mind, told Jericho she would be away all day Wednesday and booked in for a day's Anti Stress treatment at Lilac Clouds, making a special request that her allocated beautician for the entire day would be Lindy Haddonfield. Now Tuesday was simply a day to be got through.

She arrived at 10 am with a full day ahead of her and her heart in her mouth.

She was so nervous she could hardly park her car and ended up noisily reversing in then realising she hadn't left enough room to open her door and spending another five minutes moving the car forwards then backwards and forwards again.

She stepped out. Her white fleece and cut-off black pedal-pushers gave her confidence. A brown hair rinse which promised to wash out in three shampoos, lots and lots of make-up, hair teased out like an eighties soap star, high-heeled strappy shoes. She tottered up to the imposing front door, following the signpost to reception.

Lilac Clouds was an Elizabethan black and white half-timbered house with a huge, modern extension dwarfing it from behind. She slung her bag containing lycra and bikini (she'd been told Lilac Clouds would supply the towels) over her shoulder and felt a sudden rush of apprehension, elation and excitement. She was not only a coroner but emulating her fictional idols. She was Martha Rees, female sleuth.

Lilac Clouds was going to make her Stress Busting Day a smooth run. She was aware of that as soon as she stepped inside, greeted at once by a white-uniformed blonde wearing soft mules and the scent of patchouli and lavender clinging around her, strong enough to act as a major tranquilliser.

The blonde flashed white teeth and lifted heavy, blue-mascara'd eyelashes. "You are?" Her eyes drifted across a white clipboard.

"Martha Rees." Martha spoke with ebullient confidence. It was her maiden name.

"Oh yes – Ms Rees," the blonde echoed in a Barbie-doll voice.

Relief. "Welcome to Lilac Clouds. To our Stress Buster Day. We are so glad to have you chill out with us in these beautiful surroundings. I'm sure you will benefit from the experience." She had the speech learned word perfect. She crinkled her eyes, which Martha translated into a smile. She returned it.

The girl launched into her spiel again. "My name is Lucy. Would you like coffee or a visit to the powder room before I take you across to our salon so you can meet our team?"

The word 'team' threw Martha. "I'd asked for . . ."

The blonde dropped her eyelashes quickly down again towards her clipboard. "That's all right," she said smoothly. "We've made a note that you'd requested Lindy. You've been here before then?"

Martha had her answer ready. "A friend recommended

her."

"Ri-ight." No suspicion.

"I think I'll leave the coffee. I'd really like to start on my treatments, if that's OK, Lucy."

"That's fine. Uum maybe you'd like to sort out the . . ."

Martha handed the girl her money. Cash. All her credit cards would be in the wrong name. She felt ridiculously pleased with herself that she was already thinking like a PI.

The Stress Buster day included full body massage, Deluxe Non-surgical Facelift and seaweed wrap followed by a manicure with a detox lunch, optional pool, sauna and solarium and workout in the gym for the afternoon. And she didn't feel a single tinge of guilt – even at the £250 currently being counted with the deft expertise of a professional gambler.

"Would you like a receipt?"

"Thank you, no." Martha couldn't begin to imagine explaining this as a tax-deductible expense – even to her long-suffering accountant. She followed Lucy down a long hallway, red-carpeted, timber-beamed, scented with lavender and expensive pot pourri, lined with convincing looking oil portraits and leather-look wallpaper, making conversation all the way, tossing back the comments when Martha lagged behind. "Lindy is one of our best and most dedicated beauticians." Martha glanced at her reflection in a rococo gilt mirror and didn't recognise herself.

Women are so lucky, she reflected. No man could ever disguise himself so efficiently. It simply went to prove that what we take note of are the superficial features, what her mother used to call 'window-dressing'. She was almost tempted to wink at herself.

They passed buttoned leather seats clustered around tiny wine tables beneath leaded casement windows, chandeliers blazing above her as she followed Lucy's footsteps, silently sinking into the deep pile. As she passed a mirror she risked another peep at herself and noted her secret, excited smile, her hair dark rich brown, as the packet had promised, and wonderfully unruly despite Vernon's attentions. She pushed it a little more out of place. Her eyes gleamed back at her, green and mischievous, her orange mouth curving. She forced herself to concentrate on Lucy's swaying bottom.

Through two double doors and they were obviously in the modern extension. The smell changed. Beneath the lavender and pot pourri was a vaguely threatening odour of chlorine. They must be near the pool. The sound altered too – from subliminal easy-listening to echoing shouts and strains of gluppy whale-music. Lindy Haddonfield was standing behind a wooden counter, a little plump, the buttons of her white uniform gaping slightly to reveal a lace-covered cleavage and beneath that a roll of fat. She wore a name badge and illustrated 'window dressing' at its nadir – skin sunbed orange, with vivid red lips, sparkling blue eyes neatly outlined in lilac kohl, impressively neat eyebrows and a wonderful complexion framed by enviably neat, straight brown hair sunstreaked with blonde. A woman who would like money, Martha thought, as she greeted her with the warmth of a long-lost-friend and the same Barbie-doll voice as her colleague. She too had learned her lines.

"Miss Rees, I'm sure you'll have a wonderful day. Now we do want you to relax." Even, white teeth a dentist would be proud of. thoughts flashed like stars through Martha's mind. *She didn't look like the wife of a window cleaner.*

Lindy Haddonfield babbled, "We don't call it the Stress Buster for nothing." She had a pleasant Shropshire burr, which blended nicely with the high-pitched tone. "Now then. I suggest we do the facial first and then I can wrap you in seaweed while you have a fruit tea and after that the massage. Later – after lunch – you're free to do as you wish until the manicure at four."

She handed Martha a white towel then discreetly left the room while Martha stripped down to her knickers and wrapped the towel round her, hovering uneasily, waiting for Lindy to return.

She was seized with the sparkly, excited feeling again, looking around. It was clinically clean; the room smelt of antiseptic and Aloe Vera. Trolleys lay neatly side by side – almost surgically laid up on white towels: tweezers, antiseptic, strips of material, bowls of viscous liquids, blue, green, clear. She dipped her finger in the blue bowl and found the substance gelatinous. A thick film stuck to her fingers.

"Now then. It's best if you lie on your back."

She hadn't heard her return. Guiltily Martha climbed up on the couch, clutching her towel around her and lay back to the order. Tilted – as in a dentist's chair. Lindy flicked a switch and she was lying flat, on a couch.

"Close your eyes."

Martha obeyed and surrendered herself to the strange sensation of soft hands massaging her face, using rotary movements to rub in cream then swabbing, still with the same gentle, circular movements, with cotton wool pads. Something clean and fresh, scented like rose-water, was next and Martha relaxed even further under the sensation while Lindy Haddonfield rubbed on tightening masks, astringents, special collagen-containing moisturisers, some tightening, some relaxing, some dream-making. It was like being hypnotised and all the while the Barbie-voice explained what she was doing like the blurb on the back of a make-up bottle.

"This closes the pores."

"You can feel the collagen working."

"This is guaranteed to reduce the bags under your eyes."

If she noticed the dark patches where too much dye had remained on Martha's scalp she made no comment. Probably thought it was simply a clumsy hairdresser. Sorry, Vernon.

Hours later from a distant planet she heard Lindy's Barbie-doll voice say, "There. You're done."

She opened her eyes. The face staring back at her from the mirror was, to put it politely, zonked, eyes unfocusing, relaxed. It didn't look anything like her normal face. Lindy Haddonfield would never recognise her. She didn't even recognise herself.

"Oh."

Lindy pointed out the brightness of her eyes, the soft texture of her skin, the vanished pores, the lack of bags underneath her eyes and all Martha could think was that she had wanted it to go on for ever.

But it was time for the seaweed wrap. "Drawing toxins from the skin."

This time it was evil-smelling mud on strips of cloth which tugged as it dried to a dusty film. Relaxing music played for twenty minutes before Lindy returned, rinsed it off and slapped oil noisily on her palms before kneading her flesh. Starting with her shoulders. She made more encouraging comments as she worked.

"Nasty bit of tension here."

"Don't mind me. Oh – got a tender spot?"

"I can feel your stress going away under my very fingertips."

Martha closed her eyes and drifted again. *Soft hands but strong. She'd never before realised that to massage you needed such muscular, powerful fingers.* She was lying on her stomach, her arms down by her sides, soft music playing. Hump-backed whales this time. Now Lindy was silent, tossing out only the occasional comment. "There's a stiff bit here. Now, Miss Rees. This leg is . . ."

Martha let her mind drift on. Something was bothering her. Oil was slapped on next, a chipping rhythmic action from the sides of her masseuse's hands.

Lindy's talk became more personal. "Got a partner then?"

Instinctively Martha sighed. "Sort of."

"Men – all the same. Waste of space if you ask me. We'd be better off without them. Have more fun."

Martha agreed, aware at the same time that she was taking a significant step. Moving beyond something. Towards something else. But she did not know what.

"OK. Roll over onto your back."

"And of course divorce – lose the lot." A cynical laugh. "And these days the age of chivalry really is dead. However hard a woman works her husband's quite happy to take half."

Again Martha agreed. "Yeah."

She couldn't have said exactly when she first began to feel uneasy, to lose that completely relaxed feeling. Or how. Only that there was something about the competence of these hands, of the precision, the familiarity with anatomy, that made her uncomfortable. Or maybe it was the very softness that reminded her of Watkins' statement. *Soft hands. Soft voice.*

She was lying still, on her back, practically naked except for a towel over her, nipple to thigh. It was hard not to stare up into her face, to read determination, ruthlessness, cruelty? Martha closed her eyes then opened them again. And met those of Lindy Haddonfield. Closed them again, against a coolness of dislike that chilled to something akin to fear.

18

To dislike is a deep instinct but it threw no light on this case. What was she saying anyway? That she did not like Haddonfield's wife. So what did that mean? Nothing. Absolutely nothing. Lindy Haddonfield could not have been implicated in her husband's murder. She had an alibi for the time he had gone missing. She had been at work all day Monday when her husband had driven to Shrewsbury.

What had really happened to Haddonfield? How had he returned from Shrewsbury to Oswestry? When had he made the journey? Dead or alive? Where had he been killed? When had he been killed? When had his body been dumped in the ragbank? And who had been the hitchhiker Watkins had picked up? Not Clarke Haddonfield, according to Watkins.

Martha frowned. Surely, Watkins was mistaken. It must have been Haddonfield. But even in this theory there was another big flaw. Wendy Aitken was no fool. She would have checked out Watkins' story thoroughly as well as Lindy Haddonfield's alibi – and looked for any evidence that she could be connected with her husband's murder – however tenuously. So should she mistrust her instincts? Martha felt her scepticism grow.

Lunch was a paltry affair, a tiny mackerel salad, prettily set out on the plate, with drizzles of *fromage frais* and herbs enough to stock a garden centre and consisting of micro-calories. She shared a table with another of the beauticians and two middle-aged women who were terribly jaunty and suggestive. The rest of the day passed in a hazy sort of nightmare although the contact with Lindy Haddonfield was not so personal during the afternoon session; with her clothes back on Martha felt less vulnerable. The swim in the pool almost restored her to her normal self so while she lay underneath the sunlamp, sat in the sauna and plunged in the jacuzzi, she tried to plan her next move. The trouble was she didn't have a clue what her next move should be. She didn't know anything. She felt an instinct – that most derided of sleuths' intuitions. And dislike alone didn't make a person suspicious.

And again returned full circle to her original thought. Both investigating officers were very capable. And now they were working together. Both would know as well as she did that in 40% of homicide cases the spouse was responsible. They would have considered both Lindy Haddonfield and Freddie Bosworth very carefully before deciding they were innocent. Besides, where did James Humphreys fit in?

Surely, surely she must be wrong. Her instincts were taking her to silly-land.

Her final contact with Lindy Haddonfield was the manicure, which took place in a large, bright room noisy with the chatter of other women having their hair set or their nails done. Lindy Haddonfield was friendly and invited her back but by the time Martha left Lilac Clouds she still felt confused, wondering why she had taken such a strong dislike to a perfectly pleasant woman and why the voice still nagged away behind her. She had looked into Lindy Haddonfield's eyes and read behind them some steeliness. A hardness mixed with ruthless determination which pointed her towards mistrust. She could not believe she had imagined this. Worse she had no idea what bearing it had on the dual murders. She did not know how to proceed except to try and encourage Alex Randall to at least consider that this woman might be connected with her own husband's murder.

At this point she began to understand, that whatever the portrayal in popular fiction, there were some very real shortcomings for the PI. She was powerless. She had no authority. She could not break the law. She had no jurisdiction. She had no access to police records or to their findings other than those that affected her role as coroner and likewise she had no access to witness statements or interviews. She could not tap into the Police National Computer and learn who drove what car or who had criminal records. But what put her into an even weaker position was this: Randall sensed her interest. Interest was OK – as a coroner. Anything beyond that could be construed as prejudicial. In fact, her 'investigation' should stop right here.

She caught sight of her face in the mirror, at the vivid lips and teased-out hair and smiled. Should was not necessarily would. She drove home in reflective and frustrated mood. Until she turned into her own drive when her habitual resolution came to the fore again.

"Stop whingeing, Martha," she scolded herself. "Just stop it. OK – so there are disadvantages in your position. There are also advantages. Use them." Goading herself further she tapped the side of her forehead. "Get smart, woman. You can talk to Alex Randall and he may be less guarded with you than with anyone else. Ask him things – innocently."

She was within sight of the front door. The car roof was down, the weather fine, but cold. She sat quite still for a moment, listening. Heightened senses. Furthered by guilt. A whispering in the trees that did not seem to be simply the wind funnelling through pine needles or evergreen leaves. It whispered words.

"A Message for Martha."

Not whispered. *Breathed.*

"Message for Martha."

It was one of the few times in her life she had ever been really, physically frightened. In the next second the car must have inched forward without her realising. The outside security light suddenly flooded the area. But that only made it worse. It cast a circle of light, like a lit stage, beyond the auditorium of a rim of blackened trees. Her pupils constricted and however hard she peered into those trees she could see nothing and nobody. She could almost have convinced herself she had imagined the episode.

Until she heard the words again. Quite clearly.

"Message for Martha."

"Who's there?"

The silence that came now was even more threatening. Had the wind suddenly dropped that it no longer formed a hundred thousand musical instruments as it blew through the trees? Because now there was no rustling. No whispering. Nothing but an awful silence which told her what she had to know. *It never was the wind.*

She let herself into the house, glad of the light, the locks, the telephone, the twins, Agnetha who made her a coffee with whisky in it and commented how strained she looked. So much for the Stress Buster Day!

After dinner of pasta and bacon, Sam and Sukey seemed to sense she needed to be alone. They said they had some homework and vanished into their bedrooms. She took herself off to the study and sat in the dark.

Years ago, when she had still been practising medicine she had been discussing a complicated case with Martin. She could picture him now, sitting in that very chair, steepling his fingertips as he listened to the bizarre collection of symptoms, her own fuzzy interpretation of them. "Stick to the facts, Martha," he had said. "Never mind all the adjectives that accompany your patient's symptoms.

Just list them." So she did.

Now. Two men dead. The first, Gerald Bosworth, a businessman from Chester, had been stabbed during the evening of Sunday, February 10th. On the very next day, Monday, February 11th, the last sighting of another man, Clarke Haddonfield. Who had also died violently.

Gerald Bosworth had died in the rented cottage of James Humphreys, a car salesman from Slough. No one knew where Clarke Haddonfield had died.

Apparently there had been no connection between the two men, other than the town of Shrewsbury. Bosworth had died in the town, Haddonfield had last been seen heading away from the town. Humphreys temporarily lived in the town. There any similarities ended – except for maybe age. Haddonfield had been in his early forties, Bosworth, 42 Humphreys, 47.

All three had been married men.

So the connection between the three men was, at best, tenuous. Circumstantial. And being realistic, probably nonexistent. She narrowed her eyes and forced her mind to track in a different direction, one which she could not ignore.

What if the river had not flooded? A different scenario. Almost certainly Humphreys would have been the one to discover Bosworth's body while Haddonfield would have driven home in his own vehicle and not been picked up by the lorry driver. What difference would that have made? She could not work it out.

On impulse she dialled Randall's mobile number. And immediately wished she hadn't. He answered, sounding hassled. Preoccupied. Had to explain to someone – she got the impression a female – that he was speaking to the coroner. She felt awkward and intrusive. So instead of opening a discussion on the dual murders she simply asked whether they had investigated Lindy Haddonfield for the disappearance of her husband. He answered her testily. You see another side to people when you burst in unannounced.

"She was at home all night. We've got witnesses. She rang her mother to say she was waiting for Clarke to arrive."

"From a mobile?"

"No. From her landline."

She wanted to ask how he knew this important fact which anchored her in her house. Surely police mistrusted every statement anyone said, tested it for watertight-ness? Particularly when the person questioned should be suspect number one.

He answered her unasked question. "Her mother's got caller ID and we've got the BT printout."

How far do you take simple dislike? As far as an accusation? On no grounds? Would a mother provide an alibi for her daughter? Even if the crime was murder?

It was as though Randall was reading her mind. "Besides – a neighbour's car was blocking hers in. As I said before there's a problem with parking. It's a very tight cul de sac. She could not have gone out later that night, not without the neighbour letting her out. And he didn't." *So he says, she thought*. But even she knew her suspicion was beginning to look foolish.

Lindy Haddonfield was off the hook. She had an alibi for the time that her husband had disappeared. She *couldn't* have picked him up. Ergo she had had nothing to do with his murder. Unless . . . And this wasn't even a worm of an idea. Nothing formed at all. Just another feeling. She didn't like Lindy Haddonfield.

She thanked Randall politely and apologised for having disturbed him. Surprisingly he laughed. "It's all right,

Martha," he said, almost jokingly now. "Any time. And I mean it."

She put the phone down with a feeling of cheated petulance. Had her instincts about Lindy Haddonfield been wrong then? Out of kilter with the facts? Was her prejudice illogical? She sat in the empty room and resolved. Maybe she had better stick to being a good coroner rather than a rotten PI.

19

The inquest on Paul Haddonfield was opened two days later. As she had expected, the press attended in force. It was inevitable. A second murder in North Shropshire was bound to inspire more headlines and give rise to speculation. From their point of view, after the initial flurry of interest, Bosworth's death had been disappointing. *Body flushed out by floods* and *Man stabbed in flooded cottage* had been a promising start, but the subsequent investigation had been arid, supplying few headlines. They had kept the secret of the double mistaken identity and the juicy titbit that the dead man's wife had actually been summoned to the corpse of another man. So even the local papers had drifted on to other stories. However the discovery of Clarke Haddonfield's body in similarly dramatic headline-inspiring circumstances was the opportunity for a second bite at the cherry and Bosworth's murder was dragged out again, like a maiden aunt at a wedding; his case inserted at every opportunity in the discussion surrounding the murder and sad disposal of Clarke Haddonfield's body.

More headlines. From the unimaginatively factual, *Body found in supermarket ragbank*, to the sensational, *Woman discovers window cleaner's corpse with throat cut.* (Someone must have used a thesaurus to find alternatives for a place where you dump unwanted garments.) Never rob the papers of their drama.

Knowing that in court she would be referred to only as Doctor Gunn, the coroner, Martha had deliberately dressed down for the event so heavily as to be disguised. She was wearing her most dowdy suit, not quite black, but not grey or brown either. More the colour of dullness – of oldness. It had a loose-fitting jacket that unflatteringly piled on the pounds, and a skirt to mid-calf, gathered around the middle adding yet more bulk. She had never understood quite why she had bought this suit except that an overbearing shop assistant had combined with a day commemorating the anniversary of Martin's death to bring down a heavy curtain of depression which she had counter-acted with a sugar-lust so strong she had had pockets full of Woolies Pic'n'Mix. The Pic'n'Mix plus the suit had made her miserably guilty even as she had paid for it, knowing she would probably never wear it. So it had hung, like an albatross, not around her neck, but at the back of her wardrobe – to remind her of an indiscretion and an unhappy shopping trip. Still, it had its uses. And today was one of them.

To complete the transformation she had rigorously shampooed the hair dye out and tied her hair back in a floppy ponytail instead of the Lilac Clouds bouffant, or her usual look – *au naturelle.* She wore a pinky shade of foundation two shades paler than her usual tint, absolutely no lipstick, and to complete the disguise she had replaced her contact lenses with gold-rimmed glasses containing smoky-tinted lenses. She smiled at her reflection in the mirror. Maybe she should have been a character actress. Not a coroner. Martha Rees. Character actress.

Unfortunately Agnetha had caught sight of her just as she had been leaving the house that morning and had made a brief gesture of surprise. "Mrs Gunn, are you not very well?"

She had shrugged. "Just trying out a new look."

"Well –" Agnetha had ventured doubtfully before remembering her position, smiling and saying she hoped she'd have a nice day.

So Martha had sneaked out, tossing back the lie that she also had a bit of a headache.

The personal comments dogged her all through the early part of the morning. When she reached the court Mark Sullivan gave her a startled stare as did Alex Randall. It was Sullivan who spoke first. "Are you all right, Martha?" Staring and frowning. "You look . . . different."

Had it not been so vitally important that she *did* look different she might have been either flattered or insulted at the attention. As it was, it was simply a relief. Wendy Aitken gave her a sharp glance but said nothing. Jericho alone appeared to notice nothing and no one else passed comment on her appearance. Randall, however, continued to look puzzled and Martha felt he needed an explanation too. She gave him a tight smile. "Contact lenses irritating and . . ." she tapped the side of her head, "I have a headache."

The policeman managed a grimace of sympathy and she breathed a prayer that Lindy Haddonfield would not recognise her. She needn't have worried. Lindy Haddonfield turned up with just one minute to spare so there was no time for the usual pre-inquest interview, which Martha had been apprehensive about. In fact Lindy Haddonfield hardly looked at her. She kept her eyes on the floor as she stood at the back of the court, Jericho meeting her at the doorway.

Martha's nerves were jangling. While she believed that her 'disguise' was good enough to deceive Lindy Haddonfield, the consequences of her realising that her client last Wednesday had been the coroner responsible for holding her husband's inquest didn't bear thinking about. So Martha watched her approach the front, led by the grizzle-haired Jericho, with a frisson of apprehension.

She had wondered whether the feeling of dislike for Lindy Haddonfield might have evaporated but as the widow drew nearer Martha felt a heightened sense of mistrust, like a waft of a cheap but subtle perfume. Today

Clarke Haddonfield's widow was dressed not in her gaping white overalls but a modest black suit with a knee-length skirt – her only whisper to fashion the split to halfway up a plump thigh – high-heeled, knee-length, black leather boots and a slash of red lipstick. She also, curiously, wore a wide-brimmed black felt hat which hid most of the upper part of her face – less a fashion statement, Martha suspected, than a veil. She hardly glanced at Martha but sat down in the chair Jericho indicated without acknowledgement of the woman who sat, judge-like, on the platform. Maybe the reason she wasn't looking at Martha was because she was leaning heavily on the arm of an expensively-suited Asian man, in his late twenties, who wafted exotic aftershave and was already suffering a weight problem around the middle. He was the one who gave Martha a sharp stare before taking his place in the front of the court, to the left of Lindy.

It is easy to jump to conclusions, easiest to jump to the wrong ones, and appearances can be deceptive. There are plenty of clichés to protect false assumptions but Martha had already formed the impression that the Asian man was more than close to the bereaved widow. Her instinct (still active) whispered they were lovers, in which case it was an audacious move to have him accompany her to her husband's inquest. Particularly when her spouse had been murdered and as yet there had been no arrest. *She must have known the police would be here, antennae quivering. She must be very sure of herself. Or stupid.*

Martha risked a glance at Alex Randall and had her suspicions confirmed. He was actually leaning forward in his seat, his eyes fixed on the square shoulders of Lindy Haddonfield's escort. Wendy Aitken seemed more relaxed, sitting back in her chair, her eyes roving the room. Martha squared her papers up and moved her gaze across to Lindy to try and read her face. It was no good. She was dipping her head so the hat-brim covered all but her lipsticked lower lip. *It was a very useful hat-brim.*

Time to open the inquest. Inquests are formal, legal affairs; although many coroners do their best to put the relatives at ease by assuring them it is an informal proceeding. This is not the case. It is the most important consequence of a death. The verdicts available to her: suicide, homicide, misadventure, accidental, or open (when the exact events leading to a death were not clear), pointed fingers at the innocent, the guilty, the dead and the living alike without respect for status. The verdict is the last chance for a dead man to speak. If a coroner finds a result of accident, misadventure or suicide the police cannot charge anyone with homicide. So it is essential for police, pathologist and coroner to work in harmony towards the truth.

Martha leaned back in her chair, suddenly drawing back from the brink. It is unusual for a coroner to face someone they believe is guilty of a crime and it unnerved her.

She cleared her throat and opened the proceedings, explained to the court the purpose of an inquest – to ascertain, as far as possible, who had died, when they had died, where and how they had met their death. She asked Lindy Haddonfield to take the witness stand, listened to her high heels clacking up the four steps, watched her take the oath and begin her statement. The widow spoke with dignity, in her Barbie-doll voice, of the last time she had seen her husband. It was easy now to peer beneath the hat-brim, watch the heavily mascarared eyelashes quiver with emotion. Grief? Nervousness? She continued speaking and was surprisingly good at sticking to the facts, her gaze fixed on the dark eyes of the guy on the front row, her expression inscrutable – almost deadpan.

And now Martha felt no vibes. No guilt. No innocence. It

was as though the slate had been scrubbed clean. There was no writing on it. She frowned and struggled to concentrate, to extract the juice from Lindy's words.

"Clarke realised he couldn't clean windows that day – because of the rain – so he thought he'd drive into Shrewsbury to pick up a bit for his hi fi what he'd ordered at the shop . . ."

Martha was listening intently. As was the Asian man sitting on the front row. She could almost have thought he was a director checking his actress knew her lines. Acting as prompt. Martha took a better look. He had expressive, rather beautiful dark eyes, slightly greasy, olive skin, very good teeth, the blackest of hair. On closer scrutiny maybe he was thirty years old and quite a contrast to the dead man.

When Lindy reached the end of her evidence Martha directed her to sit down then called Wendy Aitken to relay the circumstances of the discovery of the body. She read out the witness statement, the origin of the *Body found in supermarket ragbank* headline. In fact, as usual, the newspaper facts were a little fable around the truth. The woman who had discovered the body had had a large binbag of old clothes which she had emptied in one by one. While the wide flap was open she had been alerted by the smell, had peered in, seen wispy brown hair and had shakily called the police from a mobile phone.

Martha thought for a moment. If Haddonfield's head had been sticking out above the clothes he had probably not been buried too deep. How many garments were tipped there in an average week? Could Aitken not make a rough guess as to when Haddonfield's body had been placed in the clothing bank? She made a note on her pad and looked up to see Alex Randall eyeing her with a glint of amusement in his eyes. *He knew exactly what she was up to*. She laid her pen back down and sat back again, deliberately avoiding the policeman's eyes.

It was Sullivan's turn next to give the forensic evidence. Preliminaries first. "On Monday, March the 18th, at four pm, I was summoned by Detective Inspector Aitken to Aldi's store in Oswestry. There I observed the body of a middle-aged man, naked but almost covered by clothing discarded by members of the public in their clothing bank. Once I had ascertained that the person was dead I made notes as to his position and contacted the coroner," Martha kept her face impassive, "who allowed the body to be removed to the mortuary for further examination."

She smiled.

"Under the coroner's direction I carried out a post mortem examination on the following day and ascertained that the man, later identified by his wife as Clarke Haddonfield, had been dead for roughly a month and had had his throat cut. The incision had severed major blood vessels causing blood to fill the airways and the lungs. Death would have been through asphyxiation due to aspiration of blood."

Martha glanced across at Lindy Haddonfield to see how this cruel evidence would affect her. But again her head was dipped, her face concealed. She was clutching the Asian guy's hand as though it was her lifeline. Maybe it was. Then she noticed something. *Lindy's fingernails were painted the exact shade as her own, filed in the same, square shape.* She coiled her own fingernails tightly inside her hands and dropped them down onto her lap, out of view and diverted her attention back to Sullivan. His evidence, as always, was clear and concise. She had to acknowledge that he was good at his job. And today he looked sober – bright-eyed, standing tall, reading clearly from his notes held in a steady hand. He was reaching the end of his evidence.

"The injuries were incompatible with life. Death would have been virtually instantaneous."

"Was it your opinion that Clarke Haddonfield had died where he was found?"

Sullivan shook his head. "No, Ma'am. I believe his body was put in the clothing store after death."

She waited.

"There was little blood found on the clothes in the store indicating that he had not died there. Due to the nature of the injuries there would have been considerable blood loss."

Knowing the answer already Martha still had a duty to ask one question. "Is it possible that Clarke Haddonfield inflicted this wound upon himself?"

Sullivan looked straight at her. "Not possible at all."

She directed her next question across to Wendy Aitken, another question to which she already knew the answer. "Are police enquiries still proceeding?"

"They are, Ma'am."

"Then I adjourn this inquest pending police enquiries."

Everyone in the courtroom relaxed. Except her. *Now she must speak to Lindy Haddonfield.*

"Hello, Mrs Haddonfield, I'm Doctor Gunn." She spoke in as different a voice as she could manage. Lower. Slower than Martha Rees.

Lindy shook the proffered hand then lifted her head. "Thank you for all you're doing." Now Martha had caught full sight of her face she had to revise her original impression. Lindy Haddonfield was upset. She was pale and her eyes were full. She certainly wasn't up to studying the coroner's face. The Asian man hovered in the background.

Martha ushered them into a backroom, wondering whether Lindy Haddonfield would introduce her escort –

and if she did, how. “I thought you might want to know what happens next.”

The hat-brim dipped again.

“What will happen now is that when the police finally feel they have all the facts, hopefully after they have made an arrest, we will re-open the inquest and return a verdict of homicide. Opening the inquest means that at least you can make funeral arrangements for your husband, Mrs Haddonfield.”

Lindy gave a watery smile and Martha felt an edge of sympathy for her. “I am sorry,” she said.

Lindy nodded. “It was . . .”

Martha never knew what she had been about to say. The Asian man was tugging at her arm. “Come on, darlin’,” he said. “Time to go.”

20

Alex was hovering at her elbow, giving her that 'knowing' look. She turned to face him and had the horrible feeling that he read something into her plain disguise. Something gleamed, hot, curious and mellow, in the grey eyes. She met whatever it was boldly.

"How are your investigations going, Alex?" A formal question, formally asked.

"They're going," he answered, equally formally.

"In what direction?" He was forcing *her* to ask the questions.

"We've got people checking up on every single piece of clothing in that damned ragbank," he said. "We've made a little map of exactly where and how each article was discarded, tagged with dates, so we can make a little more than a guess when exactly Haddonfield's body was dumped."

"Mmm." She hesitated. "Alex – I've been wondering. How did they get the body into the waste- clothing container without being seen? Haddonfield was slim . . . but not that slim. Certainly not slim enough to have been posted through the mouth of the bin."

"My private opinion is that they kept his body in a large plastic sack, one of those huge bin liners or something. If anyone saw they'd simply assume it was a rather large bag of clothes. People expect the ordinary. I have mentioned this to DI Aitken and she agrees it's a possibility. They wouldn't have risked posting a naked body into the clothing bin at any time of the day or night. There is a limit to what the public will keep their curiosity in check. Sullivan thinks that the way the body was placed suggests he was dropped in rather than placed in which would fit."

"I see." But she didn't really. Something was very wrong here. And she couldn't simply rely on the fact that Randall was too experienced and intelligent not to pick it up. She remained in the courtroom minutes after it was empty, frowning, trying to work out an explanation for why she felt so unhappy with the case and came up with nothing specific. Except . . . She'd tasted the excitement of investigating for herself. She was tempted to pursue the instinct.

She called in to an empty home in the middle of the day, chiefly to return to normal – change clothes, alter her makeup and comb her hair – but Bobby greeted her so delightedly she did not have the heart to turn down his doggy-beg for a walk. So she unhooked the lead and stepped out into the muggiest, foggiest, dampest March day she ever remembered. Too miserable for even Calliphora to fly.

The fog had dropped low to river level and with the Severn encircling the area she knew it would not hastily lift but would sit, immobile, and cling to the marshland. As she closed the door behind her she regretted her capitulation to the dog. It was a *horrible* day for a walk. But Bobby was, as always, oblivious to the weather. He scampered and tugged and she followed. The fog was so thick she could hardly see her hand in front of her face. It was a good job she knew the woods as well as the back of the hand she could not see, but still she stumbled once or twice over fallen branches and invisible logs which Bobby must have leapt over. She kept him on the lead for the first hundred yards but he kept pulling and she finally gave in. He shot off and vanished.

She walked on for twenty minutes or so, wishing the fog would lift. She missed the view and the reassuring landmarks. One path looked very like another; one tree the same as all the rest. It was easy to feel disorientated. She began to feel uncomfortable and called the dog over sharply. Heard his bark a good way off. Knew now why she was uneasy. Because in her ears the words still rang. *Message for Martha*. The phrase haunted her, threatened to saturate her thoughts. Finally she felt Bobby's damp snout pushing into her hand and turned to walk back towards the house. She was unnerved. It would not do for her to start growing paranoid and imagining episodes.

She spent the afternoon working at her desk, dealing with paperwork and telephone calls, ringing and speaking to a few doctors who hesitated about giving causes of death. By five o'clock she was again fiddling with her pencil and she stood up. It was simply an excuse. She needed to walk.

What she would have *liked* to have done was to have rung Alex Randall and tried to push him in the direction of Lindy Haddonfield. Check out her alibi a little more thoroughly, investigate the man who had accompanied her to the inquest. She would have liked to have confided in the policeman about her conviction that Lindy Haddonfield knew plenty more about the murder. She even wondered about ringing Wendy Aitken and finding out how her investigation was going but in the end she didn't.

The only action she did take was to ring Freddie Bosworth to ask whether her husband's funeral had taken place yet. But there was no answer and she declined to leave a message, at the same time knowing that if Mrs Bosworth dialled 1471 her number would be withheld. There was so much she wanted to know but her hands were not only tied, but tied tightly and behind her back. She was powerless – a wolf with no teeth.

So she walked out into the hazy evening, into the town still shrouded with the fog which made the interiors and the shops appear ten times more colourful, clear and alluring. She was tempted to call in at the *Lion & Pheasant*. It looked so pretty viewed through the looped back curtains, a fire blazing in the grate. Instead she walked past, hesitated outside the antiques shop and was spotted by Finton Cley who pushed the door open.

"Hello again," he called. "Am I right in thinking you were contemplating walking straight past?"

She laughed – out of embarrassment.

He took no offence. "Busy day?"

"It has been."

"Mmm." He chewed his lip. An awkward silence dropped between them.

"Well, are you coming in?"

"Of course." She laughed again and heard the shop door jangle behind her.

She browsed round the contents for a moment or two while he watched. "We decided about my son in the end," she offered – more to fill the silence than because she thought he really was interested.

Maybe she had misjudged him. His smile almost divided his face in half. "That's great, Martha," he said. "Just great."

"I mean – it's up to the Club – Liverpool, that is."

"Oh exactly. But I'm glad you came to a decision. It must be hard . . . being on your own."

His eyes flickered with something as he looked at her. Something she could not interpret. He reached into a dusty cupboard and drew out a bottle of port and a couple of tiny green glasses. "Let's," he said and she nodded. Needing the reassurance in the strange shop and the confident, almost arrogant masculinity of Cley.

She sat on the settle while he perched on a duet stool badly in need of reupholstery. His bottom dropped so far through he rested on the front rail. They chinked glasses and sipped. The port was strong and would have been more to her taste with a slice of lemon but it gave her warmth and comfort and after the stresses of the day she felt happy. They both fell silent for a time.

Then her mobile phone rang and broke the spell. She could have left it but mothers always answer their mobiles. They dare not ignore them or switch them off just in case it's the one, vital telephone call that could affect their children's welfare. She didn't even apologise to Cley and he acted as though he hadn't heard the tone, still sipping his port with a slow rhythm. "Hello?"

"Martha – it's Mark Sullivan here."

She was very surprised.

"I wonder if I could call round again this evening. Don't go to any trouble. Please. I just want a quick word."

"You'll catch me at home in an hour."

"Fine."

After that she drained the contents of the glass and handed it back to Cley.

21

Mark was round a little earlier than 'in an hour' and he'd been drinking. She opened the door to see him leaning against the pillar and invited him in. He didn't apologise for the intrusion, neither did he refuse the coffee Agnetha brought in on a tray with a sharp glance at him. Martha could read her mind. Agnetha exited the study, leaving the door ajar. It was a gesture of patent mistrust. Sukey and Sam were out with friends, at the pictures, so the house was quiet. Even Bobby hadn't rushed to the front door to greet the visitor.

Mark began without preamble. "I've been doing some research," he said, passing his hand across his face to brush away some of the sweat.

"What sort of research?" Her voice was sharp. She hated to see him like this. It was such a waste. She didn't know what caused it or she might just have been able to help. As it was she simply felt angry with him. She wanted to tell him that, like all alcoholics, he was destroying himself. To witness a man of such talent, such knowledge and such intelligence pressing his self-destruct button was depressing.

They were in Martin's study and in spite of the half-open door the room seemed close and claustrophobic, their voices strangely muffled. Even from across the room she could smell the alcohol seeping out of every pore of Mark Sullivan's body. He must have been on a bender.

"Putrefaction," he said, slurring the word only very slightly. "It's taken me a while to put the facts together and work out what happened. The thing is that although the weather's been cold Haddonfield's body was well-insulated by the clothes which would have slowed down putrefaction. That means he probably died sooner after his disappearance than I'd previously thought. Maybe even the very night he was last seen. Possibly before." His eyes fixed on her through the thick glasses.

"Wait a minute," she said, holding her hand up like a traffic cop. "That isn't possible. He can't have died *before* the 11th of February. He was seen alive on the Monday by the van driver and more importantly by the next door neighbour who obviously knew him. He rang his wife from home."

Mark stayed silent, looked down at the floor.

"So have you told Randall this?"

"Not yet." A long pause. "I wanted to see -" Eyes lifted "- if it made sense."

"Of course it doesn't make sense," she said. "It doesn't make any sense. None of this does, Mark. And besides. You can't be that sure. Time of death is notoriously difficult to pin down."

"I know that," he said. "But I've really been thinking."

She poured him another coffee – black. Didn't even consider offering him alcohol.

"I don't think his body's been in the clothing store all the time but somewhere else. Somewhere cold."

The image of a cellar flashed through her mind, like a rocket, exploding into brilliant stars. However illogical. He couldn't have been in the cellar. The cellar had been sealed off by the police.

Mark Sullivan ploughed on, gaining in confidence. "So the real question is – where was his body kept?"

She stared at him, speechless, unable to confide in him.

The twins drew up just as Sullivan was leaving. Noise and chatter, music, feet tramping around the house, calls for supper, comments on the film. On the doorstep he gave her an awkward pat on the shoulder. "Must be difficult for you, being on your own."

She answered as truthfully as she could. "Yes and no."

He glanced down. "Well, at least the dog brings you presents." And held up a dead fieldmouse by its tail.

"Oh, he's always doing it," she said. "However much I smack him. I suppose it's his instinct. Throw it away. In the bushes. Please." She shivered. "It upsets me. Poor little thing."

But Sullivan didn't throw the tiny rodent into the bushes. He was studying it with cold, pathologist's interest. "And does your dog always kill his prey by tying a ligature around its neck?"

She gaped at him and watched while his finger stroked the animal's furry back so she could see a shoe-lace or something similar, fine, strong and black, knotted around its neck.

Her mouth was dry. She could not form an answer.

Questions. Mysteries. Things were spinning round her subconscious like a surrealist's dream world. Nonsensical as Alice's Wonderland, illogical and inexplicable. She could not begin to understand it. She only knew these odd occurrences were threats. Not even subtle. They lay, heavy and sticky as uncooked dough, at the back of her mind, to upset her, to frighten, menace her. She ran through all the people she had contact with and came up with not one name. She did not know who was sending occult messages to her. Neither did she know who might lay presents of dead animals on her doormat. Except that in her heart she had always known it was not the dog. Never had been.

The next morning it was the lamb of March which was back in evidence. The brightest of skies shone innocently down on fresh, dewy grass. Buds were everywhere, on trees, on the end of daffodils' long stems, bunches of crocuses, purple, yellow, cream. It was a beautiful day. An early morning mist wafted from the grass.

Martha threw open her bedroom window and drew in a deep lungful of air. The scent of pine was rich and pungent. She flung open her wardrobe doors. Just for once she would wear what she wanted to wear and ignore the restrictions of her post. She wanted to wear something smart, something bright, something pretty. She found a beige suede skirt, brown shoes, a soft, creamy sweater and laid them carefully on the bed then stood underneath the shower for a full ten minutes, gasping and soaping herself vigorously, tilting her head up as though it was a waterfall in Bali, or somewhere equally exotic.

The house was still silent. It was early yet. But she felt restless. Alex Randall was a good policeman. But he was barking up the wrong tree. Likewise Mark Sullivan was a very good pathologist. But he didn't understand what the signs were telling him. She was a good coroner. Not exceptionally good – she had no solution to this puzzling set of events. But she reckoned she was nearer finding out the truth than either Randall or Sullivan.

She slipped her clothes on, brown leather boots completing the ensemble. Sat and brushed her hair until it felt smooth. Not that it would stay like this. Then she applied the token amount of make-up she habitually wore. A smear of brown eyeshadow, mascara, foundation, blusher and lipstick. Now she was ready to face the world. She opened the bedroom door. Sam clomped past her to the bathroom, hardly sparing her a look. He was not a morning person. That was left to Sukey and Agnetha, already bouncing out of their bedrooms. Sam clomped back again and she went downstairs, ready for fruit juice and toast.

Agnetha seemed to know that today was a special day. She eyed Martha's clothes critically, then with approval. "Cool," she said. Sukey shot her a swift, puzzled look.

Mums aren't supposed to be cool. Martha winked at her and gave her a hug. Today she felt confident and happy. Because she had a plan.

She'd asked Agnetha to take Bobby for a walk while she dropped the children off at the school before driving to the Jaguar garage. If Randall and Aitken couldn't winkle out the truth then she, Martha, was going to have a try herself.

She recognised him as he moved towards her. Salesman shark to the kill. He was already assessing her outfit and wondering whether she could afford to buy a new Jag. She gave him a wide, open smile. Let him work for his money.

Humphreys opened with a salesman's, "Hi. Can I help you?"

He didn't recognise her.

"I'm really just looking," she said. Her eyes fell on an impressive red car with a price tag a little in excess of her annual salary. "This is nice."

She could almost sense his palms sweating with anticipation. He rabbited on for a few minutes about the car and its talents while she studied him. *He was nervous, sweating, eyes watchful, smart dark suit, flashy tie, coloured shirt. Twice he wiped his brow with a handkerchief though it wasn't warm in here. When the door opened his head shot round, bullet-fast. Relaxed when he saw it was a young couple in his'n'hers fringed brown cowboy jackets.*

He took a deep breath in. Ready to launch into more spiel. She could read his mind. Couples are always a better bet to buy a car than a single person – especially a woman. He drifted off, murmuring something into the air. Martha watched him move across the room, her eyes half-closing. He had not known her from the encounter on the bridge. She watched him dealing with the couple, the smooth, salesman-act not quite coming off. His movements were jerky. He kept one eye constantly on the door. When a receptionist who could well have been Sheelagh Mandershall brought him a cup of coffee he seemed abstracted. Martha wandered around the cars, pretending to admire the lines of their bodies, their ccs, their complicated dashboards which belonged in a jumbo jet. Finally Humphreys saw the couple off and returned to Martha.

"Would you like me to work out finance?" he offered.

"Just roughly."

They sat opposite each other. Humphreys' fingers skipped over a calculator and he scribbled some figures down on a piece of paper.

Martha took the typical customers' opt-out, "I'll think about it," and left.

But sitting outside in her car she struggled to gather her thoughts. It was time she collected them into some semblance of order. Firstly – she believed Humphreys knew something about Bosworth's murder. It had been no coincidence that the corpse had floated out of his own cellar. Secondly – she believed that there was a connection between Bosworth and Haddonfield whose body had been so unceremoniously dumped. Thirdly – she believed that Lindy Haddonfield had something to do with her husband's murder. Fourthly – the time factor which Randall had touched on was significant.

Then she began drawing lines. If Humphreys knew something about the murder in Marine Terrace there must be a connection between the two men. If Lindy Haddonfield had an alibi for the time her husband was last seen she could not have killed him. Sullivan thought it was possible Haddonfield had died before Monday the 11th but not after. But it was hardly a huge jump of logic to deduce that a man could not have died before he was last seen.

Martha leaned forward and switched on her engine, revved it up a couple of times. Humphreys was watching her through the window, his forehead wrinkled up. Struggling. Maybe he did remember their encounter on the bridge. Oh, fool, Martha said to herself. Humphreys had been crossing the bridge as he had done before.

Some other image was pushing to the fore. Superimposing lightly over Munch's *Scream*. Humphreys crossing the bridge at another time? On the afternoon of Sunday, the tenth of February. Seeing someone else. Not her at all. Marine Terrace was clearly visible from the English Bridge. What if . . . She swallowed. What if he had seen someone emerging from his own house just after he had left it? Who? Someone he knew. So had he known Bosworth?

She rang Alex Randall from her mobile and hardly waited for him to answer. "How sure are you that Gerald Bosworth didn't know James Humphreys?"

"I'm not sure," he answered testily. "What I've said – all along – is that we haven't found any connection. As you well know, Martha, that isn't to say that there isn't one. It simply means that we haven't found one. They come from different parts of the country, have – had – rather different professions. We haven't found a common demoninator and we've looked hard. I think if there was a connection we would have found it." A pause and when he came back his voice was more conciliatory. "Don't suppose you'd fancy lunch, would you?"

"What had you in mind?"

"Nothing special. Pie and a pint at the Boathouse and a walk through the Quarry Park. I don't know whether you've noticed but it's a lovely day out there."

"Sounds OK to me." They arranged to meet at one.

* * *

She was perfectly within her rights to ring Lindy Haddonfield and ask about funeral arrangements, also to speak to Freddie Bosworth – the two bereaved women. She rang Mrs Bosworth first – and this time the phone was picked up straightaway.

"Freddie Bosworth here." Spoken sharply.

"It's the Shrewsbury coroner, Doctor Gunn. I wondered how you were proceeding with plans for your husband's funeral."

Freddie Bosworth breathed in hard. "Already done it," she said. "There wasn't much point delayin' the funeral so we had it last Wednesday. Poor lamb. We got a nice plot in the municipal. I'll get him a headstone sorted out too. Just can't quite decide on the wording. Anyway, the funeral went very nicely, thanks. Apart from his brother making a bit of a scene. Never did get on, me and him."

Martha recalled the stocky man in the black puffer-jacket. "And how are you?"

"Copin', thanks. I'm grateful to you for everythin'. Don't suppose you know when you'll finally be done with the inquest?"

Martha explained that she had to wait for the completion of the police investigation.

"But that could be years." There was a note of panic in the woman's voice.

"I'm sorry but it's normal practice."

"I didn't think things would go on so long." Spoken quietly. "I thought it would be signed, sealed, delivered by now."

Martha sympathised with her but at the same time certain things had struck her during the conversation. As soon as she had put the phone down she dialled Lindy Haddonfield's number – and got a jaunty, almost flirtatious answerphone message. "Hi, Lindy here. Was looking forward to your call. *Unfortunately* I'm otherwise engaged at the moment. When I'm through with that I'll get right back to you, whoever you are." It finished with a breathy, "Bye", that Marilyn Monroe would have been proud of.

Randall was waiting for her outside The Boathouse, a pub which stood on the river, right by the footbridge over the Severn, today deceptively tamed and peaceful, the only movement the V of ripples behind the swans taking their constitutional. They ordered a meal and sat, overlooking the view and making small talk until they'd eaten.

"Did you attend Gerald Bosworth's funeral?"

Alex's sharp eyes met hers. "Still at the Private Investigator stuff?"

She blushed. "Just asking – that's all."

"We did, as it happened." Randall's face relaxed. "I always have this Godfather superstition that anyone who lingers over the coffin is the killer."

"And did you have any such instincts this time round?"

"No-o," he said carefully.

"And how is the Oswestry case progressing?"

"Equally slowly."

"Have they found out anything about the man who accompanied Mrs Haddonfield to her husband's inquest?"

"David Khan, Indian from Leicester, part owner of Lilac Clouds and as far as we can find out perfectly legitimate. She's practically living there with him now. He might be exploiting her but there's nothing illegal in that and Khan doesn't have a criminal record. He's hard-working, ambitious and rich. He also gives Mrs Haddonfield a perfect alibi."

Martha shot Randall a sharp glance but his face was impassive. She paused to give him an opportunity to add something but there was nothing. "Do you know the bit I find surprising?"

"No." He was listening.

"That Lindy Haddonfield was ever married to a window cleaner."

Randall frowned. "I think he was a bit more than that, Martha. He was a bit of a jack the lad. Bit of a Del Boy. Always fancied himself just about to make it big. Maybe she was swept along with his dreams."

"Maybe."

He was grinning at her. "You're not convinced, are you?"

"Tell me about Mrs Humphreys. Cressida Humphreys. What's she like? I never met her, remember."

"Why on earth do you want to know about her?"

"Humour me."

But Randall was regarding her with frank suspicion.

So she tried to explain. "I'm very much on the edge of your investigations," she said. "Sometimes it's where I want to be. At other times it's tantalising. I almost know what's going on but sometimes, as in cases like this, I hardly get to meet the main characters. Cressida Humphreys is one of those."

"OK," he said steadily. "She's a big woman. I should say five-feet-ten – something like that. Well-built too, with a deep, booming voice. She's a strong personality. And when she took a swipe at Humphreys . . . well -" he was sniggering – "she could have really hurt him."

She recalled Humphreys' swollen, blackened nose. "She did."

"Exactly."

She moved on. "So, what's your impression of Frederica Bosworth?"

Randall flushed.

She put a hand on his arm. "Oh, Alex," she said. "Are all men so susceptible?"

"There's something about -"

"So I have my answer. And yet her husband cheated on her."

"We don't *know* that."

"Why else would he lay a trail – that he was off to Germany on a business trip – and turn up in Shropshire?"

Her mind was suddenly busy. Buzzing like a honey bee on a hot day. She could smell nectar. Sweet reward.

"And your conclusions, Alex?" *Different from hers.*

Randall's was the pedantic one-foot-in-front-of-another policeman's answer. "We need a lucky break. It'll turn out all right. Some routine enquiry will unearth some facts and from there we'll move to another one."

Her mind was tracking along a quite different path. He stood up. "Mind if we walk? I'm getting restless legs."

They crossed the Porthill footbridge then turned right to stroll along the river together with half the population of Shrewsbury, it seemed. Lovers and mothers, aged couples and loners, friends and business acquaintances. The spring sunshine had tempted them all out of doors to take the river path, forgiving the Severn its bad behaviour at the beginning of the year. So the people of Shrewsbury ate their sandwiches sitting on the benches that were provided every few yards, licked their ice creams, zipped the ring-pulls on their cans of Coke and Fanta. It looked a peaceful scene, one that smacked of tranquil, beautiful England.

"Excuse me." An octogenarian pushed past them on an invalid scooter, followed by a child on a bike frantically ringing her bell. A couple of teenagers surreptitiously smoked underneath a tree, trying to appear grown up and managing to draw attention to the fact that they were simply kids. The girls had their midriffs bare, tattoos on much of the available skin. The boys had their hair carefully gelled into a casual, windswept style that made them look like shocked cartoon characters. They wore huge jeans while the girls' jeans threatened to slip down their bottoms. Martha took a deep breath in and turned to Randall. "I love spring," she said. "Don't you?"

Even he appeared more relaxed out of doors. He too was looking around with approval. "Fact is, Martha, we keep slogging away at the little facts and hope that one of them will strike us at some point. Then . . ."

"And the alternative? I mean if nothing does strike you?"

"I don't even like to think about it." They walked a few more paces before he answered her question. "Maybe even another murder."

And all she could think was Humphreys, who had looked scared even when he should have been safe – at work.

22

It was an audacious idea but the more Martha really thought about it the more it seemed the obvious answer. The trouble was she couldn't work out the logistics. She didn't know exactly how or when it had happened. Nor exactly what had happened. Or how it had been planned. Much of it was very obscure. Worse – how could she hope to find out the truth?

Not alone. It wasn't possible. She needed allies. But even though her knowledge was patchy she did know her instinct was right because it was like ringing the most perfect crystal glass. It rang true, clear and loud in the purest of tones. It explained everything – all the irritating anomalies and inconsistencies – all the things that *couldn't* have happened, yet they all knew had.

Somehow it must have been like this. The connection ran like a thread of scarlet silk through pure white linen. You couldn't always see it – alternately visible then vanishing behind the cloth – yet you always knew it was there. But to know something is far from being able to prove it. She could prove nothing. And without proof her theory was simply an idea in her head. And ideas in heads had never sent anyone to prison. Not for murder.

She considered confiding in DI Aitken. She was another woman. Maybe she would lend an empathic ear to Martha's feelings and instincts. She rejected that idea. Aitken was not the right person. But she did need to talk to someone. She considered speaking to Alex. Rejected the idea. Thought about Mark Sullivan.

Considered Alex again. And decided on them both.

* * *

It is more difficult arranging a meeting between people who have tight schedules than you would think. Alex was unavailable until the early afternoon by which time Mark would already have started on his afternoon list of two post mortems. One a death on the operating table and the other a drunk who had been knocked down on Saturday night outside one of Shrewsbury's nightclubs. With the result that they finally held the meeting at three thirty in the afternoon in the mortuary, as soon as Mark had finished.

Alex had picked her up and tried to pump her about the reason for the meeting. She put her finger against her lips. "I'd really rather we talk about this when the three of us are present," she said, "if you don't mind."

"OK." He grinned. "Let's change the subject then. How are the twins?"

She told him that Sam was hoping to be spotted by the scouts from Liverpool Youth Academy and Sukey was turning into an Abba clone, at the same time conscious that he never volunteered any information about his own family – partner or children.

When they were almost at the mortuary she plucked up courage.To say, with a smile, "I know so little about you, Alex. Are you married?"

His hands tightened around the wheel. "Yes." His lips were pressed firmly together. To have pursued the questioning would have been intrusive. Unforgivably nosy. So she didn't.

They had arrived. He parked the car, pulled the handbrake up, switched the engine off, turned to her. "I am married, Martha. My wife. . ." Pain twisted his face, passed and left it normal and familiar again. "She isn't very well."

He climbed out of the car, waited for her to do the same and she knew she would never ask him anything about his wife or family again. *In fact, she wished she hadn't.*

Mark had changed back into black jeans and an olive green sweater. He ushered them into the room set aside for grieving relatives. A strangely soulless room, neutral colours, vertical blinds shrouding any view, a watercolour of a flower so bland and indistinct as to be almost abstract, coffee and tea machine as well as a water cooler. He played host, setting them all up with drinks, Martha and Alex watery coffee, himself, a plastic cup of water. Then he closed the door and immediately started apologising to Alex. "I'm really sorry," he said, "for keeping you waiting. It must be a busy time."

Alex smiled. "It's OK, Mark." There was an obvious bond between the two men. They sat down, both looked for their cue to Martha. "Well then? Fire away."

And she didn't know where to start. Mark's glasses were glinting in her direction and Randall was regarding her with an almost patronising expression. If she was to retain her credibility she would have to produce something better than this.

Mark spoke, she thought to ease her doubt and tension. "I know you wouldn't have summoned us unless you had something definite to say. So – fire away," he finished encouragingly, folded his arms and sat right back in his chair.

"I wanted to ask some questions."

"OK." It came from both of them.

She turned to Alex. "Is there, in the police opinion, a connection between the two murders?"

Alex frowned. "We've got an open mind on that, Martha." The line of his mouth was straight. "I thought you realised that." *What he was saying was, in essence, please don't tell me you've called this meeting simply to ask questions you've already asked many times before.*

"Did the two men know each other?"

Again Alex answered very carefully. "Not that we can discover, no. They did different jobs. Lived in different areas of the country, moved in different circles . . ."

"What about their wives?" Martha interrupted and held her breath.

If Randall was surprised he didn't show it. "We haven't discovered anything – yet."

"But you think there could be one," she persisted.

"What do you know that we don't?" This came from Mark who had been quietly appraising her.

Martha almost hiccupped in a nervous breath.

"I was looking at the case from the other side."

Both men looked at her enquiringly.

"We have three women," she ploughed on. "All less than happy with their marriages."

"We don't know that."

She ignored him. "Lindy Haddonfield who was discontented with her husband – a small-time probable crook and window cleaner when she could have the glamorous and wealthy Mr Khan instead."

Neither man commented.

"Then we have Cressida Humphreys whose husband leaves her for another job, quickly finds himself another woman – and gets found out. Don't tell me *she's* in a blissful relationship?"

Still silence from Randall and Sullivan.

"And lastly we have Freddie Bosworth, Babe, who could probably hook-up with any man she liked. She's every man's fantasy." She glanced from one to the other. Alex's dark eyes blinking quickly, Sullivan's eyes very bright blue behind his glasses. "So why does her husband cheat on her?"

"We don't know that he did."

"Then why was he in Shrewsbury instead of Germany?"

Alex again. "It could have been some sort of shady business deal that diverted him."

"And have you found one?" she asked sweetly.

Alex shook his head slowly.

"OK, so let's stick to what we know. Bosworth told his wife he'd be out of the country – but he wasn't. Neither did he contact her after the Friday he was supposed to be leaving."

"Can I mention something else?"

"Bosworth was found wearing another man's suit whereas Haddonfield's body was naked." She looked from one to the other. "Does that seem significant to you?"

Both men looked blank.

"OK then, Mark." She was not letting the pathologist off the hook yet. "Bosworth had a small, circular contusion in the middle of his chest."

He nodded.

"Do you have an explanation for this?"

He simply stared back at her without making any attempt to answer.

She didn't even mention Lilac Clouds at this point although she knew she should have. It was possibly the common denominator. But she salved her conscience with the argument that the police would surely have explored the beauty salon. It was such an obvious focal point. If she mentioned it they would wonder what her interest was. And she didn't want to lead them down that particular path. After all, she reasoned, it didn't take much deduction to realise that Freddie Bosworth was exactly the sort of woman who would use such a place. She wouldn't be surprised if Cressida Humphreys was too. And Lindy Haddonfield worked there. The problem was how exactly had this then translated into a double murder and the complicated morass of facts which surrounded the cases? All she knew was that the three women were bound as tightly by evil as witches in a coven. The problem was conveying this fantastic idea to pathologist and policeman.

She tried to inch them forward. "What I'm suggesting," she said slowly, "more to Alex than to Sullivan, is that you focus on the *women* of the case."

"But they don't know each other. There is no connection." Randall spoke for both of them.

She fidgeted. Sullivan was eyeing her carefully.

"Do you think the two murders were done by the same person?"

He was shaking his head dubiously. "I don't really think so."

Randall gave a heartfelt sigh as though he was very very tired. She must try another tack.

"Do you think Freddie Bosworth murdered her husband?"

"Not possible. She was staying with friends from Saturday morning, in the west country, and left there on Monday morning."

"And you're sure Gerald Bosworth died on Sunday night or in the early hours of the Monday morning?"

He nodded, not even bothering to answer.

"And Lindy Haddonfield? Do you think she killed her husband?"

"The same. She was elsewhere when her husband was murdered."

She challenged the statement. "But you don't know *when* he was murdered."

Alex looked uncomfortable. "We know when he disappeared from view, Martha. It doesn't take a huge deduction to believe the two events were within a short time of each other."

"And Cressida Humphreys?"

Alex looked at her as though she was mad. "She doesn't need an alibi. Her husband is well and truly alive and kicking."

"Of course – that's true. I think -" She looked from one to the other. They were not impressed. "- it might be an idea if you interviewed the women again?" She left it at that. It would have to be enough. *A word to the wise.* She had pointed them in what she believed to be the right direction. She could do no more.

As she drove home she went over and over the facts in her mind, tried to extend them into some reasonable solution. And failed. As Randall had said, it was not possible that any of the three women had murdered their husbands. All had been miles away at the time when they had died. That much was proven.

Randall was right. Lindy Haddonfield had been in full view of the staff at Lilac Clouds during the time when her husband had last been seen. And how did all that business of the hitchhiker fit in? What had been the point of the entire silly charade – if charade it was? She pressed the button to wind her window down and sucked in a deep breath of air. Whatever her instinct told her, it was not possible that Lindy Haddonfield had murdered or kidnapped or whatever. Without an accomplice.

And what had James Humphreys to do with the whole thing? What had he seen from the English Bridge that had made him look as though the world was screaming into his ears? Who had been on the mobile phone when he had glanced across the river and seen the pretty blue door of Marine Terrace open?

There was nothing for it but to follow her own nose. She had made the acquaintance of Lindy Haddonfield and of James Humphreys (briefly). Freddie Bosworth was, presumably, back in Chester, while Cressida Humphreys was, again presumably, in Slough. Three women. Continuing with their own lives. Two recently widowed. But there was nothing to stop her from taking the river walk that led past Marine Cottage. She stood on the bridge, for a while, looking. It was such an idyllic scene. The spring light had changed the row back to being pretty fisherman's cottages. She descended the steps and strolled past the blue door, the river Severn sparkling to her left. No sign of life. She would have loved to have pushed her way in to the house, to have refreshed her memory of that dank cellar, of the body, of that initial, morbid scene. She thought. The body. The beginning of it all, the body where a bluebottle had laid its thousand eggs. That had been the start of it all. The fly had given Freddie Bosworth an alibi, the pathologist a time of death. In a way it had been the beginning of it all. She was reminded of the old nursery rhyme, Who killed Cock Robin? *I said the fly, with my little eye.*

The door to number seven opened. Martha froze. It wasn't Humphreys who stood there but a tall, blonde woman. Cressida? Martha pretended to be studying the English Bridge, admiring the view of the peaceful river. The woman was speaking to someone inside the cottage. *Words travel across water.*

"Your hands are tied, James."

Martha could not hear what he replied. But there was no mistaking the threat in the woman's voice. She also sounded very confident. She flung back one final remark. "I don't really think you have any choice, my dear husband."

Martha caught a momentary glimpse of a white face. Humphreys. And then the door was slammed shut and the woman hurried back towards the English Bridge.

Martha walked in the opposite direction for a few minutes then looped back. The door to number seven was closed now. A light was on inside. There was no sign of the blonde woman. Or Humphreys. She hurried back to her own car and drove home.

23

Surprisingly it was Sullivan who made the next move. She could still make no sense of the entire business. Every time she thought she had a solution she realised it could not have been like that. Something was wrong but it took the pathologist's brain to light her way.

He rang her three days later, moving through the official channel of Jericho. In fact at first he discussed another case and she believed that had been her reason for telephoning but just as she finished giving her comments on the case of an old man found dead in his bath he paused. "Actually, Martha, I had another reason for wanting to speak to you."

"Oh?" She knew instantly that it was the Marine Terrace murder.

And he confirmed it. "It's Haddonfield – and Bosworth," he said. "It's the problem of identity."

She was surprised. "I don't understand you, Mark. What do you mean? Haddonfield's wife identified him and so did Freddie Bosworth. There is no doubt about identity. That's the one thing in this case we are sure about."

"Let's just look at Haddonfield," he said patiently. "It's the point that the wife did identify him that makes me unhappy."

"Explain."

"OK," he said. "Why did she insist on identifying him? He had an awful injury. We'd told her that. The front of his neck was virtually destroyed and he'd been dead for weeks by then. He was enough to turn the strongest of stomachs and I'm a pathologist. I've seen every variation of the degradation of the human body. So why did Mrs

Haddonfield insist on identifying her husband?"

She had her answer ready. "Oh – come on, Mark. You know the answer to that as well as I do. People want to identify their loved ones for a variety of reasons. To be sure they really are dead, that there hasn't been some awful mistake. As you well know in cases of sudden, violent death the next of kin often has trouble believing they really are dead. It's like a still-birth. At the back of the mind sits the question, *What if they were wrong? What if it is someone else's baby who is dead and mine is in a crib somewhere, crying?*"

Even though she did not quite believe herself what she was saying she was aware of what she was doing – playing devil's advocate – because this was an aspect she had not considered. She continued. "Maybe Lindy Haddonfield thought the same – what if it was someone else's husband who died and mine is still alive? Particularly with the confusing evidence of the van driver who seems to have dropped him off into a void. She must wonder what on earth happened to him. Maybe she thought if she saw his body it might help her to accept his death. It can be part of the grief process. Sometimes it's important to say goodbye – physically – just to assure yourself your loved one is at peace."

There was a brief, respectful pause before Mark Randall spoke again. "Who are you trying to kid? We heard what you said the other day. You can't have it both ways, Martha."

He was right.

"Well, she may still have wanted to reassure herself that he really was dead, at peace."

"At peace? Loved one," he scoffed. "You saw her at the inquest, Martha. I wouldn't say she was exactly prostrated with grief, would you?"

"Mark – what are you getting at?"

He wasn't going to tell her – not straight out – not yet. "How many post mortems, inquests, enquiries have we been involved in together?"

He must know the answer as well as she did. "Hundreds."

"So you'd agree we should have a good instinct for what is right?"

"I would think so, yes."

"And for a while now you've been trying to get Alex and me to see that something about this case is not right."

She had to admit it. "Yes."

"I don't want to sound fanciful, Martha. And I don't know what it is but something is screaming at me."

After she had put the phone down the word bumped around her head. How strange that he should use that word. *Screaming. Like Munch's painting.* She knew now that she had convinced Mark Sullivan.

Screaming. The word troubled her for days. Sometimes she believed she could understand what had happened. Bits appeared then vanished, or appeared not to fit. Like pieces in a rogue jigsaw puzzle.

It was almost the First of May before she had any idea what was going on. It was two jigsaw puzzles – or maybe three. Deliberately shaken out into the same box so the picture would make no sense. Never would. Clever. And piece by piece she began to understand.

At first she thought the three women, Mesdames Bosworth, Humphreys and Haddonfield, must have met. A day later she corrected herself. There was absolutely no need for the three women ever to have met. They had only needed a catalyst. Lindy Haddonfield. A beautician who pumped her clients for complaints about their husbands. That bit was easy. So, somehow Freddie Bosworth and

Cressida Humphreys had, probably separately, made the acquaintance of Lindy who had sensed some great dislike – hatred, even – of their husbands. Enough hatred for her to knead. Then came the dangerous bit, translating hatred into murder. Proving the dough. Complicated murder which would leave the women free. But it had all gone wrong because the river Severn had flooded its banks.

First of all Cressida Humphreys had lured Gerald Bosworth to Seven Marine Terrace. To kill him. The idea had been to leave the body in the cellar, leaving her husband with some explaining to do. She would have enjoyed that. Seeing him squirm. Perhaps trying to dispose of the body himself – Humphreys was a bungler. He would mess that up and maybe go down for murder. Or possibly conceal the body – leave it there. And one day even Martha could see the dark humour behind this.

Haddonfield must have driven to Shrewsbury that day, hitchhiked back to Oswestry and . . . Martha could not quite follow this. It still seemed unclear, the waters muddied. She did not understand it all but she thought she did know why Humphreys had looked so struck on the bridge when she had seen him that day, a week or so after the murder. It had been an action replay of a previous event. *What if, standing on the bridge on the Sunday afternoon, he had seen his own wife come out of his front door?*

He would have had a guilty conscience about his infidelity – only that. But what if later he had begun to mull over exactly *what* he had seen, tried to work out the full significance of his wife being in such a place at such a time, maybe even started to construct some explanation of his own – possibly even confronted her?

Martha recalled the bloody nose. So why hadn't he told the police? Cressida must have given him some explanation and Humphreys must have gone along with it. No wonder he had looked stunned as he crossed the bridge again and looked again across the waters. She wondered what explanation Humphreys' wife had given him for Bosworth being there.

Oh, clever women, because while the women were keen on getting rid of their husbands and collecting their 100% widow's share they had *no intention of going down for the crime* for a life sentence. Ergo they swapped murders, gave each other alibis. Made their cases watertight. Martha managed a thin smile at the word. Watertight it had not been. Thanks to the River Severn.

She was sitting in Martin's study, where she could think, ponder very carefully, structure events into some sort of order.

So Cressida who had never needed an alibi because her husband had not been murdered had entered number seven, Marine Terrace, and stabbed Gerald Bosworth, a man she had probably never met before. Martha gripped the arms of her chair. Bosworth had been wearing Humphreys' suit. When he already had plenty of his own? She hadn't arrived yet.

In fact, the case was wonderfully logical. Apart from this. And in her experience if an aspect of a case doesn't fit then you have not yet solved it. Near she might be. But not spot on.

How had Bosworth been lured to Marine Terrace? Lindy? Cressida? Even Humphreys with some sort of business deal? Pretend Humphreys. That would be the plump favourite. But there should have been a role for all the women. Otherwise they were not bound by the blood spill. The lovely Frederica must have had her role to play. She was wasted had she not been the honey trap. She should have been the silver lure dangling in bright, clear waters.

Something else was not quite explained. The hitchhiker. The hiker who had kept his collar up, talked into a mobile phone to whom? Hidden his face from Watkins – Watkins, the fall guy, the innocent driver. Had it been Haddonfield? Or could it have been Cressida Humphreys who, having killed Bosworth, had walked across the Welsh Bridge, stuck her thumb out and claimed to be Clarke Haddonfield?

Soft hands. Soft voice. The more Martha thought the more she liked this second option. So when had Haddonfield died? How could he or his body have been transported back from Shrewsbury to Oswestry? Had he ever been in Shrewsbury on that day? They only had the word of his wife – and the neighbour who had seen him through the window. But it had been raining. People huddle into their clothes in the rain. Mistaken identity was possible. When we see someone leave a house who resembles its owner and drives his car we make assumptions. And besides – even if the neighbour had seen Haddonfield he couldn't have known where he was going – only that he was going somewhere.

Maybe Lindy had told him later that her husband had been driving to Shrewsbury that day and the neighbour had transplanted the information from person to person and in time. Because in the police statements it did not say that words had been exchanged between the two men.

How necessary had it been that Haddonfield's body was not found straightaway? Had the delay had been important – vital even? Who knew? Cressida Humphreys could so easily have left her car somewhere in Oswestry – maybe even in the service station – and driven Haddonfield's van into Shrewsbury. There to commit the murder before hitchhiking back (masquerading as Haddonfield) to collect her car. Leaving Lindy Haddonfield plenty of time to kill her husband and dump his body in the clothing store. *This was not right either. Haddonfield had vanished from view on the Monday – not before.*

As she moved the facts around in her mind like Scrabble letters they were still not making a sensible word. It had not been like this. Something was still wrong. The suit. And not only that. Mark Sullivan had noted a centimetre-wide circular contusion over the mid-line of the sternum. What was the explanation for that? And why had Bosworth not been wearing his own clothes? Where had his personal possessions been? Had they been removed merely to delay identification of the body? But this had implicated the other two women. Had this been a necessary part of the plan?

Then gradually, over the next few days, she combined Mark Sullivan's telephone call with her own anomalies and came up with something even more audacious.

Again she sat alone, in Martin's study. When would she stop calling it that?

Lindy Haddonfield had an alibi for the Sunday night/Monday when her husband had vanished. She had been working in Lilac Clouds, in full view of plenty of witnesses. Not only her younger boyfriend. She had had no time to return to Oswestry, kill her husband, dump his body and return to work. She had even shared a room. And this fact fitted like a handmade glove. She had shared a room with David Khan. But she had no such alibi for the earlier part of the weekend because she did not need one. Likewise, Freddie Bosworth had an excellent alibi for the Sunday night when Gerald had been stabbed but she had been out of the picture on the Monday and no one had checked up on her movements on that day. And Cressida Humphreys – all she had had to do in this set-up fiasco was to play the injured wife, turning up at the mortuary and her payoff was that had Shrewsbury not been flooded her husband would have been implicated. At the very worst, squirming on the end of a fishhook. Nice touch, Cressida. And as Alex Randall had pointed out, she had not needed an alibi at all.

Motive? Murder is a big risk. OK – less so when you have an alibi for the crime which would have benefited you but no motive for the murder which you may yet be accused of. But it still takes a strong stomach and a certain amount of hatred. No one wants to be convicted of cold-blooded murder. Prisons are not nice places. But then most murderers believe they will get off scot free. No one thinks they will be caught or they would probably not commit the crime in the first place. So Martha worked around the question, worrying at it like a terrier.

But she could go no further without the police. And she had still not arrived at an answer. She needed to speak to Alex face to face so she rang him and asked him to call round to her office – at his convenience.

He was round two hours later and listened without comment, only raising his eyebrows periodically. When she had finished he took in a deep breath. "I think my best move would be to call the three women in for questioning," he said.

"At the same time."

He nodded. "Though it'll really put the cat among the pigeons and the press will have a field day if you're wrong. Possibly even worse if you're right. I can already imagine the headlines. 'Witches of Eastwick'."

"Please," she pleaded, "Don't drag witchcraft into it too." "I'm already spooked by thinking I saw *The Scream* on the Bridge and Dafydd ap Griffith hanged, drawn and quartered by the High Cross. Oh, and someone's stalking me with a 196's record."

His features twisted in concern. "Are you still being bothered?"

"I don't know," she said reluctantly. "I haven't been threatened or approached. Yet there is some subtle warning – a message. I don't know, Alex. Maybe I never will."

"Well – " He smiled, a warm, friendly grin. "Let's get to the bottom of this one first and then we'll tackle your little problem. Now, when shall I set up the meeting?"

"Tomorrow? And is there any possibility that I could observe from behind a two-way mirror?"

"I don't see why not."

24

She dressed in brown – her least favourite colour – but she wanted to blend in with the background. Alex had warned her to arrive early, well before the three women. She parked her car around the back of the police station. He settled her down in the small viewing room. "We'll be ushering the three of them in here," he said, "leave them to stew for half an hour or so then see what transpires."

"What excuse have you made for bringing them in?"

"Further clarification," he said, humour warming his face. He'd lost weight during the investigation. His cheekbones looked more angular and he looked tired.

"And have the press caught on?"

"Not yet."

"Good." She settled back in her chair.

"You'll have to keep still and quiet," he said. "The setup isn't a hundred per cent soundproof."

She nodded and smiled, sat down in the dark and fixed her gaze on the small, bright room. It was like sitting in a darkened auditorium, looking at a lit stage-set. Four chairs grouped around a small coffee table littered with magazines. The door opened.

Cressida Humphreys was the first to arrive. The big, powerful, beautiful woman Martha had spotted emerging from Marine Terrace, a woman with a commanding presence, an almost regal bearing. The woman she had recognised at Gerald Bosworth's inquest. Easy to see that she could impersonate a man without too much difficulty. She had broad shoulders, a wide stride. Her blonde hair was pinned up in a chignon making her appear taller than the roughly 5'9" Martha guessed her to be. She was not fat, not thin but of a muscular build and was wearing a fiercely flame-coloured Prada suit, affected ragged detail on an

A-line skirt, black, patent high-heeled shoes. Martha grimaced and felt dowdy, watched as Cressida sat down in the chair on the left, heard her thank the police officer. The door closed behind her and Cressida pulled out a make-up bag, checked her lipstick and patted her hair. Martha had asked Alex to group the three chairs so all would be facing her but he'd objected. "Too stagy," he'd said. "They'd smell a rat – I'm sure. Better this way." So there were four chairs.

"But I might not be able to see Cressida's face when the door opens and . . ."

"Take note of her body language, Martha," he'd advised. "If you're right I don't want to bungle this or compromise the investigation."

Her own door opened. Wendy Aitken stepped in as quietly as a cat and sat down right next to her. Said nothing but stared straight ahead, hardly blinking.

It was almost ten minutes later when the door opened again. Martha had spent the time watching Cressida with a tinge of respect. She had a talent for sitting still and doing nothing. Not fidgeting. She hadn't picked up a magazine or hardly moved at all but had sat bolt upright in the chair, her profile to Martha, as still as a statue apart from when, periodically, her hand would stray up to her hair, to check it.

The door opened. Martha stiffened, Aitken tensed up. Freddie Bosworth walked in warily. Tight jeans tucked into cowboy boots. Fringed brown, suede jacket. She gave Cressida a vague smile, thanked the police officer and sat down, cross-legged, picked up a magazine, pretended to read. Leg swinging. Martha glanced across at Wendy Aitken. The police officer didn't move.

Now, she noticed, Cressida did pick up a magazine. Whereas she had previously been content simply to sit and relax, the presence of the other woman made her uncomfortable. Even through the mirrored glass Martha sensed this. The women exchanged not one word, not one look – yet they were uncomfortable in each other's company. It struck her as significant.

Freddie put the magazine down, crossed and re-crossed her legs, picked another glossy up. Eyes scanned across down the pictures, peeped over the top to sneak a glance at Mrs Humphreys. There was no response. The other woman was sitting back in her chair, eyes cast down.

Minutes later the door opened again and Lindy Haddonfield walked in, also in tight jeans and a lime green sleeveless beaded top. In the darkened room they could hear the faint jangle of the beads, the squeak of the vinyl cushion as she dropped into the chair right opposite the mirror. To the watchers it seemed a calculated, challenging action. Lindy glanced at both woman in turn and Martha sensed it all. Lindy *had* been the instigator, the organiser. The other two women had never even met. Yet they were aware of each other. They knew about the other's existence.

It was as though someone had stage-directed them, as though the three women had deliberately grouped themselves to face the mirror. Cressida to the left, Freddie to the right, Lindy square on. Lindy gave both women a smile which could have been interpreted two ways – woman greeting two strangers or woman tightly reining in a potentially dangerous situation. Martha studied their entire demeanour and couldn't work out which. Then Lindy appeared to drop something on the floor and simultaneously muttered something and Martha knew, beyond doubt, that her hunch had been right. The door opened and Alex Randall walked in. All three women turned towards him.

He handled it well. Performing introductions. "I don't think you've met each other, have you?" At her side Wendy Aitken stiffened. Martha could read her mind.

"What is he doing?"

Even Martha felt nervous.

He began, wisely, with Lindy Haddonfield. "This is Mrs Haddonfield. She was unfortunate enough to lose her husband, violently, at round about the same time as your husband died, Mrs Bosworth." The women gave each other a watered-down smile and polite hello, before both turning across to look at Cressida Humphreys. "It was in Mr Humphreys' house that your husband's body was found, Mrs Bosworth."

Cressida found her tongue. "And I'm wondering what possible reason you could have for summoning me to the police station."

"Not summoning," Alex said with all the charm he could muster. "Only asking. Inviting."

For the first time a flash of temper crossed Cressida's face. She contented herself with a hostile stare at the policeman.

"We'll be with you ladies very shortly," he said. "If you'll just bear with us."

He left the room and seconds later was in with Martha. "Well," he said softly. "I've got them here. Now what do I ask them?"

"Ask Freddie Bosworth why she identified the wrong man as her husband," Martha said calmly. "Ask Lindy Haddonfield likewise. Before you ask Cressida Humphreys what she was doing in Marine Terrace at around four thirty on Sunday afternoon, the 10th of February and on Monday, the 11th of February, hitchhiking from Shrewsbury to Oswestry, impersonating a man who was already dead before you charge her with his murder."

25

"What?" She could tell Randall was stunned but at last she was sure of her facts. She'd worked them out. Right from the beginning. Only now could she see the triptych of pictures, separately and as a whole. Each one was now complete, each piece in its place. Now she understood everything, each injury, the timing, the reason the investigations had been so distorted.

"That's why identification, face to face, was so important even though Sullivan was right. It was inappropriate," she said. "Misleading us – setting us all on the wrong trail. The sequence of events was, I think, this. Bosworth was lured to Oswestry by Lindy Haddonfield. His car was here so possibly she picked him up from Shrewsbury, moving the car sometime later. She killed him, probably on the Friday, soon after he'd left home and left his body somewhere – probably in her garage. As to how she managed to cut his throat, I suspect bondage was involved. His hands were tied.

"Haddonfield, in the meantime, drove to Shrewsbury on the Sunday night, probably thinking he was in for a night of passion with Freddie Bosworth while his wife was conveniently working. But Cressida Humphreys was waiting for him. She stabbed him, shoved him down the cellar steps with her foot – I think the round mark which puzzled us so much on his chest was the imprint of a heel. She then left him to die there, thinking, probably, that her husband would be back at some point and would then be linked to the crime. Cressida Humphreys put his coat on, drove the van back to Oswestry, made sure the next door neighbour saw her on Monday morning, made a call to Lindy Haddonfield's mobile, knowing the home number would register and drove into Shrewsbury. She then left the van in the car park and hitchhiked back to Oswestry and her car. That's why Haddonfield, the window cleaner, had to be dressed in Humphreys' suit while Bosworth was dumped, naked, in the clothing bank. It was no good him being found in designer clothes when he was supposed to be a window cleaner. All that was left was for the women to identify the wrong men."

"How did the three women meet?"

"Who knows – some chance meeting, almost certainly at Lilac Clouds." She treated Randall to one of her warmest smiles. "I don't know everything, Alex. You'll have to fill in the gaps. All I know is that it was *Bosworth's* body which was dumped in the ragbank and later identified by Lindy as *her* husband while *Haddonfield's* body was flushed out of the cellar of Marine Terrace by the Severn. Maybe we never will know everything. Certainly we don't know how the women would have acted had circumstances not intervened and led to the discovery of the body by a policeman." She risked another smile. "Poor old Coleman. But put it to them and they'll confess. Out of shock. They thought they were being so clever. So beyond detection."

"So if the other two are our killers what role did Freddie Bosworth play?"

"I think," she said, "that when Haddonfield went to Marine Terrace he thought it was Freddie he was meeting. She's so perfect for a honey-trap. She set Haddonfield up at some point. Probably his wife organised some sort of 'chance' meeting between them. Freddie's a fairly irresistible woman. And I would lay a fifty pound bet that the Humphreys' had a weekend at Lilac Clouds and while they were there James, the philanderer, made a pass at Lindy. It's probably what gave her the idea. Everything's right here, Alex. The contusion in the middle of not

Bosworth's chest but Clarke Haddonfield's. Quite a bit of hatred there. Look on the steel tip of some of her high heels. There'll be forensic evidence aplenty – once you know where to look and what to look for."

Alex was still wearing that dubious look she knew so well. Wendy Aitken, on the other hand, looked impassive. But she was listening. Hard. Again Martha visualised Munch's painting, *The Scream*. It had been screaming at her; screaming the truth. James Humphreys seeing his own wife coming out of his house. Wondering what she was doing there. Then hearing about the body. No wonder he'd gone to ground.

Alex drew in a long breath. "We'll have a job proving it all," he said.

"Not when you know how to proceed," she said calmly.

Wendy Aitken understood what she was saying.

"Exhumation," she breathed.

Martha nodded.

"We'll have to apply to the Home Office."

Again Martha nodded.

Randall crossed his legs and opened his mouth.

Martha spoke for him. "There won't be any problem there," she said dryly. "Once you explain the circumstances of the identification."

"They're not going to like it," Wendy said.

"Then break them in gently. Start with telling them you think there's been some mistake," she suggested. "Confusion. If you use that word it won't rattle them too much. They'll think you still don't know what went on and will drop their guard. Tell them you have to use dental records and DNA evidence to confirm identity of both men for legal reasons, Life Insurance. Something. Give them the chance to say they might have been mistaken. Tell them you intend applying to the Home Office for an exhumation – of both corpses. See what happens then. Then look at the guest resister for Lilac Clouds during the months of January and February – about a year ago. I think it will have taken some time to set the whole thing up. Look for an entry in the name of Humphreys. Or Bosworth. Check Lindy Haddonfield's house for forensic evidence of Bosworth ever having been there. Or even Cressida Humphreys, particularly on the telephone. Combine a picture of Haddonfield and Mrs Bosworth and ask around if anyone ever saw them together. She's a fairly memorable woman, especially when she's driving her Porsche. People will remember. Think of it the other way round, if you like." She grinned. "And don't get confused. Remember these three women don't know each other that well. They simply provided one another with a service. I don't think each will trust the others not to talk. Not with so much at stake."

Alex stood up abruptly, Wendy Aitken too. So did Martha. She drew in a long, deep breath and spoke to both of them. "I know that what I'm about to suggest is unorthodox," she said, "but two men have died. And if I'm right they've been buried in the wrong graves. This is my jurisdiction. I wonder if you'd allow me to speak to the three women."

The two police exchanged glances. Then Wendy Aitken nodded. "I have no objection," she said. "Alex?"

Randall met her eyes, finally nodded too. "I'll need to be present." It was all he said.

"Then I'll speak to Freddie Bosworth first."

She almost felt a tinge of sympathy for Freddie, Babe Bosworth, timidly entering the room. The stiff lashes fluttered and dropped as though too heavy to lift.

"Mrs Bosworth," Martha said, "I'm sure you remember me?"

Freddie nodded.

And Martha followed her own advice. "We believe that there may have been some confusion over your husband's identity. We need to confirm through dental records and DNA."

The eyes held a flash of panic, a desperation.

"I think you'd better tell us what you can," Martha said gently. "It'll be easier for you in the long run. Would you like your solicitor with you?"

A slow shake of the head.

Then she took the big risk. "The man you identified as your husband was, in reality, Clarke Haddonfield, wasn't he?"

Freddie's mouth gaped, gasping for air like a fish.

"Although Detective Inspector Randall is here this is an informal chat, Mrs Bosworth," Martha reminded her gently. "We'll be able to confirm quite a lot of what I'm saying when we exhume both graves."

"Resurrection Woman," Freddie hissed, a bit of fight in her. "How can you . . .?"

A brief vision of Martin and Martha felt suddenly angry. "How can you bear to let your husband lie under another name?"

Freddie's face tightened with hatred. "You don't know anything."

"Correction, Mrs Bosworth. We don't know *everything*. But we do know more than you think, I can assure you."

Silence.

"You'd met Clarke Haddonfield?"

Panic again in the eyes. Frozen hesitation. Then a brief nod. "Over the Internet. I scanned myself in. Lindy had told me he used a site for S&M. I just played up to it. I met him once. Just once. But I didn't kill him. I swear I didn't kill him. We just . . . chatted. I wouldn't have . . . I couldn't have . . . done anything."

Martha nodded, feigning sympathy when inside she felt cold anger.

"So all you had to do was to lure him to Marine Terrace on the Sunday."

"I wouldn't have done anything more. But I had to get rid."

"Of your husband?"

Another hesitating nod. "It was the only way."

"Why not divorce?"

"You don't – didn't – know Gerald. Divorce? Deprive him of half his precious money?" She leaned forward, her face pale under the make up. "*He* would have killed me. It was survival of the fittest. Or the cleverest. And lucky for me I had friends."

"Cressida Humphreys and Lindy." Alex spoke for the first time.

Freddie addressed her next remark to him and him alone. "You wouldn't know anything about this," she said. "But women stick together when they have problems."

Martha resumed her questioning. "I suppose you'd met Lindy at Lilac Clouds?"

"More than a year ago but we gelled. We kept in touch. Very empathic, Lindy is. She understands."

Martha nodded. "So all you had to do was stay at home, wait for the police to put two and two together, contact you and identify the wrong man."

Freddie crossed and uncrossed her legs. "That's about it."

It was patently the truth.

Cressida Humphreys was next. This time it was Wendy Aitken who was behind the mirror, Martha in front of it with Alex Randall. She performed the introductions all over again.

Cressida looked boldly at her. "I don't understand what a coroner has to do with me," she said haughtily. "No one connected with me is dead – as far as I know."

"My remit, " Martha explained again, quite patiently, "is to speak to anyone I believe can throw light on cases which have been referred to me."

Cressida drew in a deep sigh. Her anger wasn't quite spent. "I don't even know why I've been brought in," she said. "Apart from the fact that some unfortunate man was murdered in the house my husband rented – while he was not there, I hasten to add – I have nothing whatsoever to do with this case."

"Where were you on the Sunday that Clarke Haddonfield died?"

Cressida looked instantly wary. "Excuse me," she said. "I understood . . ."

It was as though the trap had sprung shut, teeth biting.

"Maybe I should explain," Martha said. "We believe the man who died at Marine Terrace was Clarke Haddonfield, the window cleaner from Oswestry. Now where were you on Sunday afternoon, the 10th of February?"

"At home."

Martha shook her head, almost regretfully. "Your husband saw you, didn't he, coming out of his house? At first he must have thought you were just checking up on him." She looked the woman full in the face. "What story did you spin?"

Cressida recovered some of her composure. "I don't understand exactly what you're . . ."

"We only have to speak to your husband," Martha said. "I don't know why he hasn't come forward."

"To say what?"

Martha said nothing. Let Cressida work it out for herself.

She did – slowly.

"You're saying I was there on the Sunday afternoon when -?"

Martha didn't answer.

"Are you accusing me? Whoever he was, the man was a complete stranger."

"Exactly. That's what so clever about it."

"And then what?"

"You were there on the Sunday. Stayed the night in Oswestry, drove Haddonfield's van into Shrewsbury on the Monday morning to the car park and left it there, hitchhiked back to Oswestry to lay a false trail."

"There's a bit of a flaw in your argument." Mrs Humphreys still had plenty of fight left in her. "Why the hell should I go to all that trouble lying and – " A sudden moment of panic. "You're not suggesting I actually . . .?"

Martha still said precisely nothing. Cressida Humphreys was smart enough to work the whole thing out – just how much the coroner really knew.

"You don't think I committed the -" She couldn't quite say it. "You don't think I killed him?"

No one in the room breathed – not even Wendy Aitken behind the mirror.

Then the penny must have finally dropped for Cressida Humphreys. She must have realised. Her husband would testify. And her face crumpled. Like Freddie before her she gasped at the air like a fish, her face pale, then red, then deathly pale again. "Have you ever – ?" She swallowed, still gasping. "Have you? Do you know what it's like when your husband is a serial womaniser?"

She scrutinised Martha. "No," she decided. "No. You wouldn't. You're not the sort of woman who would be married to the sort of man I was. No," she finished firmly. "But Gerald – and other men." Her face tightened furiously. "They get what they deserve."

She dropped her head into her hands. "We all – some women – we start at the marriage altar." She gave a wry smile. "Appropriate expression, don't you think?"

Martha grimaced, as did Randall.

"Well, we all start off thinking it'll be such a fairytale. And they do this to us. Destroy us. But some of us can fight back when the crown slips and we see them for what they are, balding, fattening middle-aged men who preserve their image of being so sexy by rutting with anything that comes along. And when men have money something always does come along." A suspicion of a smile softened her features. "You've met Sheelagh? Typical of the species."

Then she looked careworn again. "They had it coming. All of them. I would have enjoyed watching James being questioned, squirming inside a police cell. He is a born liar. He would have lied and you police," she shot Randall a quick, almost flirtatious stare, "would have been convinced he was the killer. There's something undeniably shifty about myhusband."

"How did you explain to him your presence at the cottage on the Sunday?"

Cressida smiled calmly. "Simply told him Sheelagh's husband had turned up and there had been an ugly scene, that her husband had assumed Haddonfield was him and attacked him. By the time he knew the truth it was too late. He'd left it too long, already deceived the police."

"Why did you switch clothes?"

"In what Clarke Haddonfield was wearing," she said primly, "you would have known instantly that he was not Gerald Bosworth."

Martha nodded. It all fitted. It was now up to Randall to wring the complete confession out of her. She knew all she wanted to. Cressida Humphreys left the room straight into custody and a caution.

"I suppose we'd better see Lindy."

"In a minute."

It was a phrase Cressida Humphreys had used that struck a chord within her. Sukey and Agnetha singing lustily. "The King has lost his crown". At the time the phrase had provoked some feeling, some sympathy.

This was what happened when the crown slips. This was what it was all about, three women seeing their husbands for what they were and rejecting them cruelly, bonded not to their husbands but to a sisterhood of similarly maligned women.

But in some ways Lindy's story was different yet the same. Haddonfield had not been like the other two men, not a wealthy successful businessman but a loser. A man who had tried schemes only to fail in them all while his wife had been the one to want to move to pastures new. Added to that Haddonfield had succumbed to temptation and perversion. Surfing the S&M websites.

Lindy sauntered in with confidence. She smiled at both of them, smiled again at Martha. Martha shifted in her seat, unsure whether Haddonfield's wife had recognised her as her client or merely the coroner. Something in the direct stare, the double-take. And the ambiguous words, 'Hello again.'

Martha started with the same story, the same justification of her interest and the need to confirm identity. Lindy Haddonfield faked incredulity. But not well. "You're saying that I was wrong? That my husband died in Shrewsbury? That I looked at that body not knowing it was my husband and then a couple of weeks later identified the wrong man?" Her eyes opened wide and innocent.

Which made Martha feel like shouting. "Enough.

Enough." Instead she continued quietly. "Obviously we can prove this either way."

Lindy's face became hard and mean. The murderess surfaced, the woman who had manipulated two other women in her scheme. "Dig them up, you mean." Somehow she was trying the shift the crime to Martha. "And even if I had been wrong – what would that prove? Just that I was upset. It doesn't *prove* anything." She thought quickly and efficiently. "Are you saying that my husband was killed on the Sunday? I was at work all day. There's no way – "

Randall stepped in. "Come on, Mrs Haddonfield. Now. Tell me about the times you met Cressida Humphreys and Freddie Bosworth. They were clients of yours – weren't they?"

"Nothing wrong in that." She was spitting like a cat. Hands clenched.

Randall leaned forward. "Where did you kill Bosworth?"

No response.

"OK then." He moved in closer – for the kill. "Where did you keep his body before you dropped it into the clothing bank?"

That was when Lindy Haddonfield first began to panic and their treatment subtly altered.

They were admitted to the custody suite, their possessions taken from them. They were advised to contact solicitors. Martha left.

Randall ploughed ahead and immediately applied for a dual exhumation.

Certain procedures have to be followed with an exhumation. Safeguards have to be observed to make sure of the grave and the coffin. The graveplot is identified by the cemetery authorities with reference to plans and records. An official must personally point out the grave to be opened. On the previous day a mechanical digger digs down to a level just above the coffin so that the following morning the police, the coroner, the pathologist and others can arrive in time to see the final exposure of the coffin. The coffin nameplate must be cleaned and read to confirm the identity (mistaken in this case) and if possible the funeral director who carried out the original burial should be present to identify the coffin and the plate. A metal cassion is lowered to protect the grave sides.

The coffin is lifted.

The lid is loosened by slackening the holding screws or prising the lid loose. This allows gases to escape into the open air rather than in the mortuary.

The coffin is ready then to be transported back to the mortuary. It is a sort of reverse funeral.

Martha's eyes rested on each person for a while. Impassive faces, grim but all with one strong purpose – to make sure that justice was finally done.

Why are exhumations invariably carried out at dawn? Because you need light and there are fewer people around. But in the first light of day a natural drama exists in spite of the flattened colours. Maybe because of this draining of colour in the same way that a sepia photograph has more atmosphere than a colour snap. The exhumations were carried out on subsequent days, one in Chester, the other in Oswestry. Both corpses were returned to Shrewsbury mortuary, neatly tagged. The funeral directors who originally conducted both funerals identified the coffin lid, confirmed the coffin plate. The lids were removed. The funeral directors next studied the internal coffin fittings – the fabrics and the shroud. And finally the faces themselves.

There was no need for a second post mortem. Sullivan's had been thorough and accurate enough. But they used dental records and DNA evidence. Two days later the tests were conclusive and the tags were switched. Haddonfield became Bosworth and Bosworth was, once again, Haddonfield. Clarke Haddonfield had been stabbed through the heart and his body found at Marine Terrace, while Gerald Bosworth had somehow arrived at the ignominious temporary grave of Aldi's clothing bank after having his throat cut.

It was going to be a long and complicated police investigation. Forensic evidence was difficult to unearth and the burden of proof lay across the shoulders of the police force. Alex Randall kept Martha up to date. Although they confiscated Cressida's entire designer wardrobe they failed to find any trace of Haddonfield's blood on either her clothes or shoes. She'd had ample time to dispose of her murder ensemble. And that traditional giveaway, the lethal weapons, proved equally elusive. In fact they never did find them.

Two weeks later evidence was still a bit thin. The guest book at Lilac Clouds was not as helpful as it might have been. There were a few couples of the name of Humphreys but none of them appeared to have the same address. And there was no record of Freddie Bosworth having been there at all. However, as Martha pointed out, she lived near enough to attend for a day – as she, herself, had done.

Fake names are so simple when you use cash and don't need to prove your identity. When you plan a smart crime more than a year in advance, it gives you ample time to anticipate investigation and baffle it.

Martha found herself shuddering when Randall told her all this over a morning coffee. *Women, she reflected, were so much more thorough than men. When women committed as many crimes as men she feared the police may have difficulty proving their cases. Women are so good at cleaning up messes. At being tidy. Physically and mentally.*

So the focus turned back to Bosworth. And at first the police were hopeful they could construct their case from this point. There was absolutely no reason for Gerald Bosworth to have ever been anywhere near Lindy Haddonfield. There had been no apparent contact. But when his body was discovered he had been naked, his clothes destroyed or lost which reduced the chances of forensic evidence, and they still didn't know where he had died or where his body had been kept. In the end it was Sullivan who came up with the solution. "I think it's possible," he said awkwardly, "that the body had been kept in a deep freeze, wrapped in a bin liner which could easily then have been burnt on a garden bonfire."

It was the beginning of the break the police had been waiting for. The chest freezer stood at the back of Lindy Haddonfield's garage. Although sixteen cubic feet large it was empty. Not even a bag of oven chips. Then the investigation hit the doldrums. The police stripped Lilac Clouds and came up with nothing. They questioned the three women extensively and hit a brick wall. They charged the women anyway and all three were admitted on remand. It was three weeks later that they made their second breakthrough.

They found a hair belonging to Cressida Humphreys in Haddonfield's van, behind the seat. A fingerprint belonging to her on the underside of the table the telephone stood on in his house. She had been bright enough to use gloves. But it is so hard to remember *everything. All the time.* And they needed to connect all three women not only with each other but with their crime. Watkins was dragged back to an identity parade again and wavered when he faced Cressida Humphreys. But he couldn't be sure – until he heard her speak. Then he frowned, closed his eyes tightly and nodded.

And the final breakthrough – staff at a small, smart country hotel in Beeston, a town a few miles from Chester and not too far from Oswestry, recalled the pink Porsche – the woman who had climbed out of it and the man she had been with who had driven up in a white van. They recalled fragments of the number. They matched Haddonfield's Hyundai. Randall charged them with obstruction. It was a start.

In the end Martha was proved right. It was the fact that the three women were virtual strangers that made them unable to trust their partners in crime. And the story was coloured with yet more hard forensic evidence. The identification of the hotel staff was enough to put Freddie Bosworth in the dock. And she knew it. When Alex Randall told Martha this she sighed, thinking of that beautiful pink Porsche Boxster which had concealed evidence which would put Freddie behind bars for a long, long time. She wouldn't come out of prison still a babe. Although a clever lawyer might just get her off the charge of false identification and wasting police time on the grounds of distress, even a babe has to face the music when there is such irrefutable evidence to connect her with the very worst of crimes. In the end it was her very notability which would convict her.

But while Freddie was making her sobbing, heart-rending confession, accusing her husband of infidelity, cruelty and blatant meanness, Lindy and Cressida proved much more difficult nuts to crack. Both were strong women with powerful characters. Both killers had no intention of ending up in prison and they knew that the burden of proof lay on the police. So, they still argued, Lindy had made a mistake identifying the wrong man as her husband and Mrs Bosworth had met Haddonfield. It didn't prove anything but the knot was tightening. Hindered a little when, eight hours later, David Khan arrived at Monkmoor police station and started creating havoc, claiming harassment – even alleging racial discrimination – which was funny because Lindy Haddonfield was pure Caucasian. It was a measure of how desperate the case had become.

And in Martha's mind the song still played, "The king has lost his crown!"

26

It was almost three months later, when summer was in full swing, that Martha re-opened the two inquests. The confusion had caused Jericho no end of trouble. Following the exhumations there had been extensive tests to prove without a shadow of a doubt which man was which.

Without a precedent Martha opened the new inquests in an unusual way: "Fortunately murder in this part of the country is rare. A double murder rarer still. This is the inquest on the body found at Marine Terrace on Wednesday 13th of February, initially identified as Gerald Bosworth but subsequently proved by dental records and DNA analysis as being Clarke Haddonfield from Oswestry."

She was forced to recall Mark Sullivan and Alex Randall as expert witnesses. But this time no wives were present. The press were full of questions.

On the following morning she repeated the procedure, re-opening the inquest on the body found in the clothing bank of Aldi's store in Oswestry, again relying on expert witnesses and dental and DNA records.

No wife. But the stocky man in the puffer-jacket sat at the back with his arms folded, nodding as she spoke.

At the end of the second inquest it was her job to sum up. She put the cap back on her fountain pen, leaned back and addressed the court, studying her polished nails with a faint interest, almost curiosity.

"The identity of a corpse is a hugely important thing. Deliberately misled we may, as in both these cases we were, lose a person beneath the wrong headstone. Mourners will focus their emotions in the wrong spot."

The man in the puffer-jacket wiped his eyes.

"In this case identity was concealed. I can only comment that in cases of homicide it is often identity which leads the police to the killer." Her eyes slid across the front row, across Mark Sullivan, Alex Randall, Wendy Aitken. "It was only through persistent police investigation that the truth was unearthed and the misinformation corrected. I feel that it was terribly important that it was."

Alex's eyes flickered and warmed. His mouth moved slightly, curving into the suspicion of a grin.

She knew when the inquest was over that he would speak to her, make some comment about the part she had played.

He did. But life is neither easy, tidy or simple. Loose ends draggle, waiting to be snipped or threaded back into the complicated tapestry that is a human life. In her own life mysteries may not so easily be solved. She may never be able to read the future, the destiny that had been hinted at.

The hidden, tantalising Message for Martha.

27

Gathering evidence, bringing cases to court, the case itself. It was complicated enough to ensure months went by before the skeins were finally untangled, the cases finally tried and sentences passed.

Martha had kept her eye on the *Shropshire Star* and read what she could but long months of silence had inevitably followed as the facts were protected by the *Sub Judice* ruling. It was only when Alex called in late one spring morning in the following year that she could finally close her files.

It was another bright day when the trees were just turning green and her room was filled with the fresh, clean air of spring. She'd picked some daffodils from the garden and stuck them in a jar on her desk. They cheered her – as this time of year never failed to delight. Early in the afternoon there was a knock on the door and Jericho flung it open. "You have a visitor," he announced ceremoniously.

Alex's huge grin appeared behind Jericho and she beamed at him, unable to hide how glad she was to see him. She shifted moved some papers from the chair to the floor as an invitation for him to sit down.

She'd followed the court case closely. Yesterday had been the day of reckoning for the three women. She knew from the evening news that all three had been found guilty. Sentencing had been this morning.

"Well?"

"We've got the result we wanted," he said, tilting back in the chair, his hands folded behind his head. "Guilty verdicts for all three on dual charges of conspiracy and murder."

"So what did they get?"

"Cressida Humphreys, for the murder of Clarke Haddonfield at Marine Terrace on or around the 10th of February", he quoted. "She got life with a recommendation that she serve not less than fifteen years."

Martha nodded, unsurprised.

"Lindy Haddonfield was found guilty of the murder of Gerald Bosworth and got life too." He smiled to himself. "Nice little bit of summing up from the judge, that the three women had conspired together in a plot reminiscent of the Hitchock film, *Strangers on a Train*, with the intent of committing the murders for each other, thus providing alibis and ridding them of two cumbrous husbands and implicating the third, James Humphreys. He called it a cold-blooded and heartless action, master-minded by Lindy Haddonfield but entered into enthusiastically by the other two women."

She nodded again. "I do read the newspapers."

Randall hesitated then gave a long sigh. And sensing the reason she prompted him. "Freddie Bosworth, Alex?"

"He said that she was morally implicated in the death of both Clarke Haddonfield and Gerald Bosworth, that she was, therefore, an accessory to the double murder and as such he held her equally responsible." He paused before adding, "She got life too, Martha."

She read a ripple of sympathy in his face, heard the same in his voice.

"You don't think it's fair, Alex?"

"She didn't actually commit any crime."

"Oh come on," she protested.

"She broke down completely in court," he said. "Sobbed like a baby."

Men, she thought, with affection and exasperation. Unwitting, willing victims always happy to be dragged in by sirens. There was no hope for them. And, woman-like, she could not find it in her heart to feel any sympathy towards Freddie Bosworth however vulnerable she might appear. She had lured Haddonfield to a cruel death. And yet, like Alex Randall she was transfixed by the vision of the pink Porsche and the tiny, child-woman tripping towards the mortuary in her spiky heels. She had not looked like a killer. And that had been her forte. Haddonfield would not have been lured by anything less when he had Lindy at home.

So the three women were now just beginning the next stage of their lives. Prison.

Randall stayed a while longer, drinking coffee and chatting and she felt restless when he had gone.

She watched Jericho tidy away the files with a huge elastic band and put the computer discs in the filing cabinet with a feeling satisfaction tinged with regret. She would never have described herself as a romantic but to watch marriages crumble, relationships sour and love turn into homicidal hatred made her sad – particularly when she could only wonder how exactly her own marriage would have turned out had it only had the chance.

Besides . . . She glanced across at the pile of new files waiting to be completed. She had enjoyed her brief spell as a private eye. Her fingers rippled down the spines as she read the names. Steven Bowler. Solomon Blizzard. Fortuna Kriss.

Maybe another time. It was all in the future.